Cruelty of Thirst

SPRINGS OF ETERNAL LIFE

J. Suthern Hicks

Inquiries can be made by contacting the author at HumbleEntertainment@yahoo.com

Editor: Shauna Hill
Cover Design and illustrations: Tatiana Minina
A Shophar So Good Book: www.shopharsogood.com

ISBN 978-1966231004 (pbk.)

"The modern State exists not to protect our rights but to do us good or make us good — anyway, to do something to us or to make us something. Hence the new name 'leaders' for those who were once 'rulers'. We are less their subjects than their wards, pupils, or domestic animals. There is nothing left of which we can say to them, 'Mind your own business.' Our whole lives are their business."

—C.S. Lewis, God in the Dock, 1970

Cruelty of Thirst

CONTENTS

CONTENTS

Prologue

Stories are what unite us, no matter the realms in which they are told. Think not for a moment that what happens here does not affect what happens there, for here and there are separated only by the thinness of a page. It is rather hard for me, Beely Rembree-Wren, to describe my realm to those who have never been here, because I have never been to any realm other than my own. How could I know what is so unique that it would require a detailed description? Worse, perhaps, is the unnecessary drivel I might use to explain that which is common to all realms. The wisest perspective might be to describe only that which stands out as special, whether or not it is unique.

The Five Realms of Here make up my world, and I reside in the most elegant of all: the Realm of Pixanese. If you follow along with me and the others, you will find that although the scenery is unlike anything you have ever imagined, you will discover that the events which make up the stories within to be hauntingly familiar.

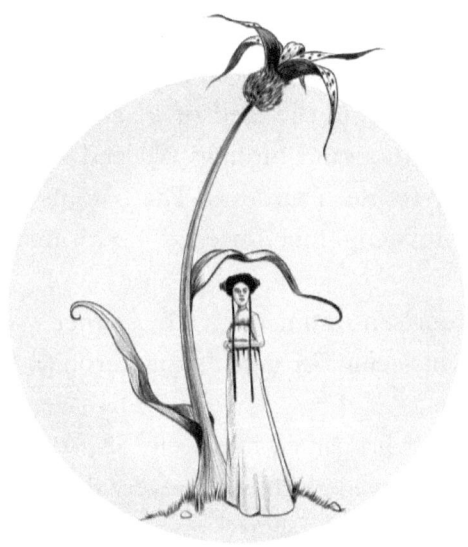

Chapter 1

BEELY

A tall, slender woman caressed the thick flower stalk with her palm. Tiny, hair-like strands softly sprang up, almost dancing, from the warmth of the stranger's touch. She gripped the stalk tighter as she stopped to look behind her. Not too far in the distance, someone—or something—was following.

It was the seventh in a forest of giant flowers to be used as cover by the worrisome traveler. She stopped often to listen for footsteps, or perhaps a whisper. Beely, as she was known to those closest to her, had never before entered the cemetery. She had thought it would be a safe place to meet, but alas, it seemed that no place was safe anymore.

She and her fellow conspirator were having to look over their shoulders ever more frequently. All communications were kept as confidential as possible. Even her own husband was not fully aware of how involved Beely had become with the ancient prophecies regarding *wormwood* and *pharmakeia*.

She traversed the worn paths very carefully, not wanting to disrespect those buried to the left or to the right. Each grave was marked by a turonian flower. A seed is planted at the time of burial for every departed soul in the land of Pixanese. The largest of the flowers are several thousand turnings old and as tall as trees. They bloom once every fourteen turnings. The blooms open for one day and then fall, providing much-needed nourishment to the roots below.

It had been fourteen turnings since her father's seed was planted. The anticipation of seeing her father's first turonian flower grew with each step she took.

He was the one who named her Beely. She was less than fond of the name. She had vowed to change it every day since beginning her formal education. She had favored the name Glyzaria—it sounded like the light of the moons and commanded the respect of a philosopher. But it was not until her father died that she changed her mind instead of her name.

Still, she disliked the moniker, but she loved her father. She would forever be known as Beely. Beely would always strive to make sure she carried her name, and his, with honor. Maliko Rembree, her father, was a beloved scientist and philosopher. He was even more loved as a father. She could still see his face, always reassuring and confident. Her father was the one person who made her feel safe. It was his passion for learning new things that gave his daughter her entrepreneurial spirit.

Maliko's mainstream theories and writings were renowned in nearly all the kingdoms of the Five Realms of Here. However, as it had been rumored, there was an influential contingent of doubters that wanted to completely erase all of his works from public consciousness. His more conspiratorial theories were not appreciated by everyone.

This is why Beely snuck around in hidden places. She was her father's daughter, and she would see to it that his work would always remain available to help conquer the evil she felt was beginning to infiltrate the Realms.

Beely could not help but stare up at the turonians that were in bloom. The magnificent colors filtered down in varying shades of purple, red, and the rare orange. The blooms were perfect five-point stars. She wondered what color her father's flower would be.

Many believed the color of the flower was determined by the character of the one buried beneath it. Purple was thought to be for the most noble of family members. Red hues bloomed over artists, writers, and those who were passionate and bold. Yellow was for innocents who died far too young. Her father's flower had a strong likelihood of being orange—a blend of yellow and red.

The older the plant, the larger the bloom. Those of the tallest stalks, high above the canopy, spread out like giant parachutes, filtering out most of the light. Nothing grew on the ground of a turonian cemetery but the turonian itself.

Today, as she soon discovered, was not the day of her father's bloom. She had prayed for better timing, but it was not to be. Apparently, someone in the distance had been more fortunate, as revealed by an excited gasp. Beely sighed, leaned against her father's unadorned turonian, and slid down until she was almost seated on the ground.

Beely suddenly got a faint whiff of peanuts. "Hello, Propo," she said without turning around to see his face.

"How did you know it was me?" he whispered from behind the thick flower stalk. Beely knew of Propo's unquenchable fondness for peanuts. He mostly ate them creamed and spread on flat dough, but he was not above eating the thick, buttery stuff off of his fingers.

Propo walked around to meet Beely face to face. He looked down disappointedly and said, "I'm so sorry." He was old enough to be her father, but he thought of Beely more as a younger sister.

"Yes. It would have been nice. Perhaps the bud will open in another day or so," replied Beely as she stood to greet Propo properly.

"Will you come back?"

"Doubtful," she replied. "If only there were time for such things." She embraced him and gave him a quick once-over. Although he had always been in good shape, he looked thinner. His face was paler than she remembered.

"Did you bring it?" he asked.

She shook her head no. "But it is safe."

The truth was that she had nothing to bring him. Beely did not like lying to Propo, but she had yet to find any evidence to support her theory that the Five Realms were in danger. She knew she would find evidence soon, but she did not want to risk that her one and only ally might lose confidence in their mission to prove her father's theories correct and to save the Five Realms of Here from certain ruin.

Propo was of average height, but when he walked within arm's reach of Beely, he looked quite small in stature at just under six feet tall. They were of the same clan and had similar features: high cheekbones, medium bronze complexions, and long, thick braided hair. He did not share her family's propensity for great height, however.

"It's hard to believe fourteen turnings have passed," he said.

"And nothing to show for it," she quipped.

"Don't be so bleak. We have to believe the signs and that more signs are forthcoming."

Beely froze after hearing yet another noise. She put one finger to her lips, a signal for silence. They both listened intently. After a few seconds, a petite, round, furry empachic softly bounced around Beely's sandal-clad feet.

Beely sighed. "Reverie, I am so disappointed in you." She reached down to pick up the soft ball of fur.

Reverie was the name of Beely's oldest and most special empachic. At just under six pounds, she was one of the smallest of her species. The average empachic weighed around twenty pounds. Her long fur was mostly white with a few gray spots. Like all empachic fur, it covered her entire body, hiding almost every feature—ears, mouth, and nose.

Occasionally one could glimpse a view of her right eye due to the loss of hair directly above it. Her stubby legs were also buried in fur, which was all solid gray, except for the fur on her right front paw, which was a dull red. Beely loved Reverie dearly—too much to risk having her overexert herself by venturing out during a hot day on such a long journey.

"I told you, very candidly, to stay home, guard the door, and wait for your medicine."

The door needed no guarding, but empachics, particularly Reverie, did not do well by themselves with nothing to do. It was crucial, however, that Reverie get her afternoon shot of Andrene, a potent narcotic for pain. It was delivered daily by the roofah, a bird gifted with caretaking abilities and an instinctual proclivity to help those in need.

Reverie simply squeaked a short reply and rolled around in Beely's arms.

"Forgive the interruption, Propo," said Beely.

"She's a dear wee one, isn't she?"

"Always has been, but what she lacks in stature she makes up in might."

"We mustn't stay much longer. There are spies everywhere. Has your husband decided whether or not he will join us?"

"He has made no indication to me. I have not told him everything. I hope he will come around when he is better informed. The winds do not lie. At some point soon, he won't be able to ignore the signs."

"Signs—how many more signs do people need to see?"

"People have been saying that for too many moons to count. We have time."

"I hope you're right, but either way, you must convince him to join us. It will be impossible to accomplish our tasks without him."

Beely's husband was well-liked in Pixanese and most in the realm would trust him in the event of a crisis.

"Impossible? No. Harder, most likely. He will come around; I'm sure of it. When and where shall we meet again?"

"I will send a message by the oarsman on the first night of the two moons. You will find him at the regular spot." Propo absentmindedly tugged on his beard as he looked around to make sure no one was watching or listening in on their conversation. "I must go."

Pixanese, the home of both Beely and Propo, was small enough for rumors to spread quickly. Some in the village were already openly discussing the preposterous—as the villagers called them—ideas of Beely and Propo. Propo had stopped openly sharing his theories long ago, but Beely had only recently learned that rumors bring unwanted consequences.

Beely always knew Propo to be a bit nervous, but on this day, he seemed more twitchy than normal. He was undoubtedly one of the smartest people she had ever known. He was her father's apprentice in the time leading up to his death. Her father spoke of him often.

Beely thought it was because he was like the son her father never had, but the more she got to know Propo, the more she understood. Propo was a man of integrity and loyalty. He was not only brilliant with the conceptualization of the unseen dimensions and Biblical theology, but he was also loving, kind, and gentle. Beely often wondered why he was unmarried, as he would have made a wonderful husband and father.

"I will watch for the oarsman on the first night of the two moons." Beely reached into the pocket of her dress and pulled out a small brass kaleidoscope. "This was my father's. He said whenever he became stuck on a problem that gave him a feeling of hopelessness, he would look through this and remember that God doesn't see things the way we do. There are infinite possibilities."

Propo raised his brow. "Do you think I've lost faith?"

Beely gave a reassuring smile. "Not at all. I know how much my father thought of you. He would want you to have this."

She reached out her hand, holding the tiny ornate cylinder. Propo lowered his head to hide the raw emotion behind his tired eyes. He did not want her to see what might be considered weakness. Propo was a solitary person, with few friends and no immediate family. Such a kind gesture brought strong feelings.

Propo clasped Beely's hand with both of his. He slowly removed the kaleidoscope, and without ever looking up, he turned and quickly walked away.

ΛNKUR

Peace and harmony had reigned across the Five Realms for untold ages; the oldest mountains were but hills when the tranquility first began. Kingdoms were spread far and wide and were relatively self-sufficient with plentiful resources. Cultures were unique and peoples were distinct. Winds rarely blew from one realm into the next.

There was one thing common to all realms: the Word. The Word was the divine communication between the Creator and His creation. Historically, almost everyone had taken the Word as truth and lived by its tenets. It was not until one of the Realms elected a leader that the winds of change began to blow fiercely. This leader's name was Ankur, and he was from the realm of Okrad. There had never been leaders before Ankur. There was no need. The book of law and grace was the only necessary authority.

Ankur hoped that bringing the Realms together would hasten even more prosperity in an already prosperous world. He also reasoned that having unified realms would ensure lasting peace—or at least, that was what he promoted.

Ankur stood before the assembled group with a casualness that belied his true urgency. He held his most loyal companion by a leather strap close to his side. A leash was not necessary. The dog was happily obedient and certifiably unenterprising.

The beast had two worthy attributes: loyalty and strength, the latter of which was rarely utilized. These naturally protective animals had suffered from inbreeding for hundreds of turnings, causing them to develop compressed faces, floppy ears, and fat, wrinkled, pudgy legs. Much of the population thought the dogs—known as mastadonians—were a reflection of their breeders: complacent, overindulgent consumers of all things superfluous.

"Why are we here?" asked one of Ankur's less patient guests.

Ankur stood at the top of a raised, five-tiered fountain that sat prominently in the center of the small village. Water spiraled up several feet into the air before cascading back down, forming glistening arches in the bright sunlight all around Ankur as he looked down at the village before him.

He did not just speak; he projected a honeyed warmth that seemed to anchor every gaze in the square. When his deep-set green eyes met a stranger's, they did not just look—they acknowledged, making the poorest traveler feel like the most important guest. The village was quaint, with several three-to-five-story buildings made from ruddy bricks and black iron pillars. Smaller structures filled the spaces in between the taller buildings, forming a proper town square. There were flower merchants, cafes, and other shops that one would see in any typical small village.

"Yes, why have you summoned us here?" asked another guest.

There were at least forty in attendance. While some worlds might favor a singular form, the Five Realms were a tapestry of existence. Beings with the iridescent scales of deep-cave dwellers stood beside those with the lithe, furred grace of forest inhabitants; others possessed the long, elegant necks of cranes, yet all held the same spark of reason and the ability to function in their own communities.

However, the crowd had become restless; they were not accustomed to being around strangers from other realms, and they did not like mystery.

Ankur combed his fingers through his thick, wavy hair. He smiled warmly as he looked out over the crowd. Every attendee felt as though they were being personally acknowledged. This was an important moment for Ankur. He knew there was only one chance to make a good first impression.

The crowd settled and relaxed as he began to speak. "First of all, thank you for being here today. I promise, you will all be greatly rewarded for your time and efforts in making the journey. I say we should do this more often."

The crowd murmured, and some even moaned in disapproval. Ankur knew his good looks and melodic voice alone would not win over all those assembled. They were the most respected citizens in their communities—the wisest and most educated.

With time and the right favors, however, he was convinced they would come to understand and join his promising new alliance.

"Just be frank with us," said a four-legged, humpback grassland beast named Chandra. She lowered her head and pawed the ground with her rear hoof, showing subtle signs of frustration. "I traveled here because we humpbacks heard you were an honorable man. It is no secret that you have done much good for the Realm of Okrad."

Ankur's face lit up with enthusiasm as he responded. "Thank you, Madam Chandra. I did not ask you here to give a speech. Rather, I wanted you to see for yourselves how our beautiful Realm of Okrad is flourishing."

Ankur was particularly pleased that the majestic and proud humpbacks had chosen to send a representative to meet with him. He was determined to gain her support and, in turn, that of all of the humpbacks.

As Ankur spoke, his charisma seemed to ripple through the air like a physical heat. Standing over six feet tall with golden-brown hair, he possessed a presence that was infectiously charismatic. Many from the other realms came just to see him up close and to share with their contemporaries how they had "rubbed shoulders" with the new and noble leader of Okrad.

As Ankur was speaking, there were hundreds of tasmangulars scurrying about. Although the furry tasmangulars often walked on all fours, their two front legs were webbed and wing-like. No one had ever seen them fly, but their awkward wing-like arms did not seem to slow them down on land.

They quickly assembled a fine assortment of delectables available nowhere else but Okrad. They placed unique fruits, local vegetables, and the most beautiful glass ornaments—hand-blown using the sacred sands of Okrad—into small crates for their guests.

A guest in the crowd picked out an object from the crate next to him, held it up into the air, and shouted to Ankur, "We know how wonderful your realm is. Have you coaxed us here to boast?"

The guest laughed wryly as a few others joined him. Despite their mocking laughter, Ankur knew that no matter how self-sufficient, prosperous, or happy they were in their own kingdoms, with their own delicacies, they were giddy with delight at the thought of receiving such unique and splendid gifts from Okrad.

"Of course not, my fair friend. Consider these gifts the beginning of a lifetime of beautiful trade amongst our friendly realms. We here in Okrad simply want to be your friends—your allies."

There were immediate murmurs: what use were allies in a world where there were no enemies?

****

Just outside a curiously curated shop, not far from the fountain, stood a woman named Lira. She watched and listened from afar as the unprecedented proceedings progressed.

The shop was colorful, with flowering plants of many different shapes and sizes trailing from a rounded roof down to the walkway below. Lira, the owner, sold elaborate silk head coverings. The silk—a very rare silk—was produced by the elusive Okrad caterpillars. Ankur had asked if Lira would include some of her fine wares for the visiting strangers, but she declined his request. This bold rebuff was in part because she secretly disliked Ankur, but also because the silk strands took much time to form and required ancient skills to weave into unique, individual creations.

The intricate head pieces, known as komas, were worn as a cultural tradition by most women in Okrad. Lira knew that the traditional headwear of her kindred could never be fully appreciated by those in the other realms. She would not have her ancestors disgraced by turning something so rare and meaningful into nothing more than a trivial accessory.

Lira was concentrating so hard on Ankur's rhetoric echoing in the square that she was startled by the sound of a masculine voice behind her.

"I've never seen anything like these before. How do you get such fine, soft material woven into these beautiful shapes?" The man gently ran his fingers down the side of a dark coral koma that was prominently displayed by the entrance to Lira's boutique.

"My apologies. I didn't see you standing there." Lira knew immediately that the stranger was from another realm—not because she had never seen him before, but because he was unfamiliar with the silk koma.

"The silk of the Okrad caterpillar is so thick that it needs no additive or reinforcement to hold the most intricate forms. Yet, as you can feel, it remains exquisitely soft to the touch."

"It's amazing. I've never seen or felt anything like it."

"Well, if Ankur has his way, perhaps it will be available in a shop near you soon."

"You think the others will agree to follow Ankur?" he asked.

"Yes, they will follow. He is, after all, a very eloquent speaker. He has many gifts, but the most obvious is the incredible timbre of his voice. It goes quite well with his perfectly chosen words."

"Do I hear a bit of cynicism?" he asked, smiling.

"Not at all. I've witnessed his rise in Okrad over many moons. Ankur is very persuasive. It was only a matter of time before it happened."

"Before what happened?" He stopped examining the komas and listened carefully, as if she were about to reveal a secret.

"Whatever is happening here."

"Which is?"

"You tell me. You're the one who has traveled from a foreign land to hear him speak." Although she was slight in stature, Lira exuded an underlying strength and fortitude.

"Just look, what do you see?" asked the visiting stranger.

Lira faced the fountain in the square. Ankur was still speaking. If those who had gathered to hear him had any reservations before, they were now fully under his spell.

There was a joyous atmosphere among the visitors. It looked like Ankur was succeeding at whatever he was attempting to do. "Unity, harmony, agreement," she finally answered.

The tall man standing next to Lira wore his own special copper-colored metal headpiece which formed a band around his forehead. Strands of copper trailed off into hair-thin wires that intertwined with his natural dark braids. His skin was caramel in color with random splotches of creamy white patches. He had large, round, trustworthy eyes.

Lira noticed his hands were smooth and soft, contradicting his large muscular frame. It was obvious he was not a laborer. She thought he must be an artist of some sort.

"That's nothing new. There has always been harmony and agreement in the Realms," he said.

"Perhaps. But unity?"

"Unity as well. Realms and kingdoms don't need to become one to be unified. We are unified in our peace and willingness to live and let live."

"So, what is your point?" she asked, becoming slightly impatient with his philosophical line of questioning.

"No point." The man paused as he looked around the town square, possibly admiring the quaintness of it all. "I just appreciated your beautiful creations here. You struck me as a woman with a perspective—a point of view."

Lira abruptly asked, "Who are you?"

"My name is Maximilian. I'm a Nectarion from Pixanese."

"You've made a very long journey."

"Fortunately, travel is easy with our broraydings."

Broraydings resembled earthly stingrays. They were large, gray, flat creatures with featherless wings. Each brorayding had a long horn on the top of its sleek, slender body which provided its rider a place to hold onto during flight.

Because of this, there was usually no need for saddles or reins, although some riders preferred to use them for added stability. The connection between a brorayding and its rider was more intimate than the connection between a rider and the average beast of burden.

"I've never seen one. Where is it?"

"He's off exploring. He will come when I need him to return," answered Maximilian.

"I have heard of such creatures. Very rare, they say." Lira began placing coverings over her komas, preparing them to be stored for the night.

"What do *you* see out there, in the town square?" she asked.

"Greed," he replied flatly.

"Really? That's interesting. I wouldn't have thought of that. Now that you mention it, it makes sense."

"Maybe my wife has made me jaded." He laughed before continuing. "What do people who have everything want?"

"I have no idea," she answered.

"More."

Lira chuckled. She was beginning to like the stranger, although she was not convinced that conversation was all he was after.

"My mom taught me about the sacred silk worms and how to master the art of head wrappings. Her grandmother taught her the same. It is an art and a profession that has been passed down for thousands of turnings."

"Did you always know you would do this?" Maximilian sat down on the windowsill next to the door as Lira continued to carefully wrap her wares.

"I haven't always continued in my ancestral traditions. I moved to a nearby village, still in Okrad, and lived there for many moons until recently returning here. I missed home. I

14

tried my hand at many other things, but it did nothing but show me how much I love what my ancestors taught me. This land, this place—it's in my blood."

"I understand. I feel the same way about Pixanese."

She lifted a rich, gold-colored koma and held it up next to Maximilian. "It's your color."

He smiled. "So beautiful. I would purchase this for my wife. She loves artistic things, but I'm afraid it would only be displayed privately, as no one in Pixanese would understand the historical and cultural significance."

She took a moment to appreciate his like-mindedness before responding, "Your wife is a blessed woman."

"Thank you, but it's me who's blessed. You would like her. She has your entrepreneurial spirit. She also has a deep love for tradition."

"If Ankur has his way, maybe we will meet one day soon. If kingdoms indeed unite and begin to trade."

"It would be a long time before that happens, if it were to happen at all." Lira continued to listen as she carried an armload of komas into her shop. Maximilian followed her inside as he continued, "A lot of changes would need to take place for such a major shift to occur."

Lira knelt down and gently placed the komas in a deep chest. She slowly rose to her feet and paused as if contemplating what to say next. The truth was, she was ascertaining if they were alone and if it was safe to speak candidly to someone she had just met.

"What is it?" he asked.

Lira brushed against him as she looked both ways. She eased the small wooden front door closed until it clicked. She placed a sign on the door. Maximilian could not make out the symbol, but he assumed it read "closed".

"Don't be so sure," she finally answered.

"About what?"

"Ankur has always gotten what he wants, and it never takes him long to get it."

"But he hasn't convinced you?"

"I didn't say that."

He hesitated. "Okay."

There was an awkward silence which Lira ignored by attending to her shop duties. Maximilian looked out of the front window. A few locals passed by, seemingly oblivious to the day's unusual activities. Ankur had finished his speech and was mingling with the crowd. The visitors seemed oddly happy— euphoric almost—as if they had just discovered the secret to eternal life.

"Why are you here, Max?" asked Lira from the back of the shop.

"Because of my wife. Her name is Beely. She is curious. Me, not so much. But I promised her I would try."

"Try what?"

"Try to understand what's happening. Be open to the possibilities."

Lira joined him back at the front of the shop. She watched him watching the people in the town center. They stood silently, taking it all in.

Lira gently touched him on the shoulder. He turned to find her holding the golden koma from earlier. "I want you to take this to your wife. Something tells me it was meant to be hers."

"I brought nothing with me to trade—"

Lira cut him off. "It's a gift."

"Thank you, but this is far too expensive—"

"Take it to your wife, and don't take away my blessing." She carefully packed the koma in a small, sturdy strongbox.

There was another awkward silence before Max spoke again. "I guess I had better be going. It looks like they are all finished up out there."

"It was nice meeting you, Maximilian."

"You as well." He placed his free hand on the front door while holding the gift from Lira in the other.

Before he stepped outside, Lira called out, "Wait." She quickly walked to the back of the store. She walked back toward him nervously and handed him what appeared to be a fruit of some sort. It completely filled his large palm.

"Take it back with you. Don't eat it, and never tell anyone I gave it to you, please."

"What is it?"

Maximilian looked down at the glouscenshire. It was unusually heavy for its size, with a translucent, bruised-purple skin that felt like warm, polished marble. Even through its thick rind, a sickly-sweet scent—like fermented honey and old copper—wafted from it.

"Have someone in your kingdom analyze it. It's a glouscenshire, a fruit from a tree. Ankur has included it as a gift, but the ones he gave his guests are different than this one."

"How so?"

"I can't say anything more. If you tell anyone where you got it, I will deny it. You must go. Keep it safe and tell no one. And whatever you do, do not eat that fruit. Use the information you glean as you will. I'm sure your wife will be very interested in the results of a thorough analysis."

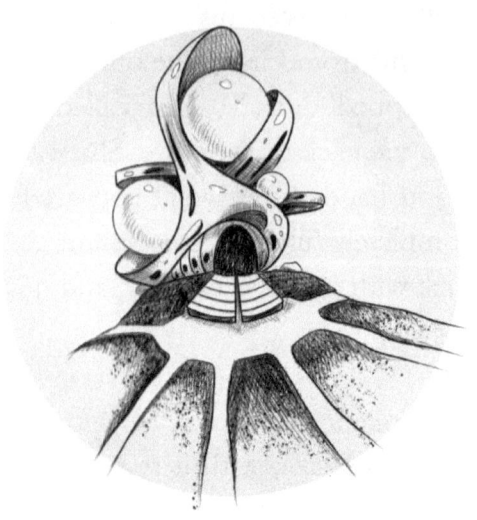

C h a p t e r 3

THE LIBRARY OF TRUTH

Numerous pathways paved in white ivory, veined with shimmering pearl, led to a most unusual structure. Panels of glass, etched with gentle, frozen ripples, stretched high enough to make even the tallest guest feel small. There were no wooden or stone beams to join the glass walls together. Blurred hues of forest green, cedar red, and cobalt blue seeped through the thick, curved, semitransparent walls. The colors emanated from the bindings holding together the pages of sacred books. This building was known to all in the Five Realms as the Library of Truth.

As Beely walked along one of several ivory walkways, she felt a smile pushing her cheeks upward. She was filled with joy. Moments such as this had become rare of late.

Her father was the first to teach her the significance of the library. Within this very special place, the Word was treasured, cared for, and disseminated to anyone who desired to increase their knowledge of higher things.

She stepped through the large archway into an entrance hall lined with sleek wooden shelves supporting hundreds of books. The long rows of custom-made shelves followed the curve of the glass walls. Each bookcase was hand-carved by the giant beavers who inhabited the local creeks and rivers of the surrounding lands. They were the masters of woodcraft and among the finest artisans in all the Realms. They took particular pride in the library, as it held the truth of the Creator God.

There was only one primary caretaker of the entire Library of Truth. His name was Duly. He dedicated his life to caring for all of the books and worked tirelessly to ensure that all things concerning the library were always in order. His task was made easier by the fact that everyone who entered took extraordinary care in their use of the facility.

There were sections of books that could be borrowed, and there was one room inside the library into which no books could be taken, only studied on-site. There was also a room where books were available for free and never had to be returned.

The point of the library was to make sure that all citizens, in any realm, could have access to the Word. The library existed in all realms and in no realm at the same time. It was the only place where sentient beings from differing cultures congregated under the same roof, although they rarely intermingled.

Ironically, Duly was chosen as caretaker because he was not a believer in the Word. He was born into a clan of thieves known as Braewickers. Braewickers were very short, childlike people with pig-like snouts for noses, spiky hair, and ears resembling cauliflower. Those who knew the clan well nicknamed them sniblets. The reason was unknown, but it was thought that they looked and acted more like something that would be called a sniblet than a Braewicker. This particular sniblet was orphaned as a nursling. The only thing he knew about his own clan was what he was told by others. He did not remember his parents or the land from which he came. He had been raised by a friend of Beely's who could not have children of her own.

Beely walked through the corridors until she heard the one she had come to see. He was talking to himself—as was not uncommon—or perhaps to the books themselves. He stood on one of the many rolling ladders with a feather duster in one hand, a polishing cloth over his shoulder, and his thumb and forefinger on the spine of a book.

After coughing into the cloth over his shoulder, Duly spoke sincerely to the book before him. "You must rest no more than a quarter of an inch from the end. I'm sure I have instructed you on this before...right here." He let go of the book and almost fell off the ladder as he waved his hands demonstratively. Fortunately, Beely was there to steady him. She was so tall that even with her standing on the floor and him perched on a ladder, they met eye to eye. "What do you want?" he demanded, appreciating neither the interruption nor the help.

"You do know they can't hear you," she said, referring to the books.

"What do you know? If you spent as much time with these books as I have, you would've learned that they not only speak, but they also listen." Duly awkwardly climbed down the ladder; indeed, almost everything a Braewicker did appeared clumsy. He scuttled out of the room into a long hallway. Beely followed, taking one step for every ten of his. There were more shelves and more books, even in the hall. Not one of them was out of place. They were all lined up perfectly and pristinely, with not a speck of dust to be found.

"I must say, you have been doing an impeccable job of taking care of the library."

"It is not a job; it is a calling. You are the one who told me that. Don't you remember? Furthermore, I don't take care of a library; I attend to the books."

"Fair enough. How have you been? You don't get lonely?" Beely could have kicked herself for asking the question, but it was too late. She was going to get an answer.

"Lonely! How many friends do you have? Three, five, ten? *You* and your kind should be lonely. Look around you. I have thousands of friends and plenty more to get to know. Lonely indeed!"

Before Beely could respond, Duly noticed something on the floor a few feet behind her. He dropped to his knees, crawled faster than a ten-legged ghost crab, and picked up a speck that Beely, even with her perfect vision, could not see. "Did you wipe your feet off before coming in?" He lifted his palm to show Beely the smallest grain of sand.

"I do apologize. I will don the sandal-booties on my next visit. I promise."

"Oh, never mind. It's my *job*, isn't it?!" he exclaimed in the foulest of tones.

"Must you be so contrary?"

He sneezed into his cloth and reconsidered his manner. "Come, I'll fix you a hot cup of ognatia." Ognatia was a type of naturally sweet tea. It was always a bright cobalt blue when steeped to the perfect temperature.

Beely continued to follow Duly until they were in the caretaker's quarters. It was obvious that Duly had inherited the Braewicker lack of housekeeping skills. It was a mystery to everyone how he managed to take such good care of the library when it simply was not in his nature to do so. Consequently, Beely found only one lone chair without any clutter. She sat as

Duly steeped the ognatia. The water was already hot, and it took no time at all.

Duly handed Beely her cup and asked her to hold his while he pushed a few things off of another chair, moving it closer to her. "What brings you here, my friend?"

Once he was settled, Beely handed him his cup. "Do you trust me, Duly?"

He squinched his nose and sucked in a whiff of air, causing him to grunt. All this was in the attempt to keep from sneezing. The effort did not work as his eyes closed tightly, his stomach contracted, and a burst of air loudly escaped from his exorbitantly large nostrils. "Should I not?"

"As in all things, you should use the wisdom you have gleaned from these books to be your guide."

"I read them. I don't believe them."

"Then why do you continue to read them? Why take such special care of them? You even talk to them!"

"What if I'm wrong?"

"What do you mean?"

"What if the words written in these books are true? What if there is a God and a Savior? I could be wrong. What then? My people are said to take better care of lies than the truth. Maybe that's why you thought I would be good here." Braewickers were known as the most notorious of liars and thieves. They were trusted by no one of sound mind. Duly was the exception.

"You are not like your people. You are your own person. If I've told you that once, I've told you a thousand times."

"Perhaps you are correct. Perhaps you are wrong. Nature versus nurture. Who knows?"

"Back to the question—do you trust me?"

"I do. More than anyone, I put my confidence in you. You did not have to ask."

Beely replied, "My father taught me that none of these things—the events written in these books—happened here in

22

the Five Realms because it was not our story. That revelation left me feeling lonely, as if we did not matter as much as those in the world where the Christ will walk on the created Earth."

Duly stirred his tea with his longest finger and after sucking it dry, responded. "I will speak now as if I believed the Word that is held within the sacred books. It is true that the saints and the future disciples, as well as the very Savior Himself, exist in the other world, but that does not mean our story is any less significant. He is your Savior too. He has a plan for you as well. Our lives echo and reinforce that His truth is universal, and one day our story will carry meaning to those who come here seeking wisdom."

"It is true, I know. I think your studying has done you justice. You are very wise," she said with a smile. She reached over to a nearby table and picked up a book. "What is this?" she asked as she read the title to herself.

"The Web and the Crow. The author, like me, is dubious of religion, but he loves the world and the Creation. Great respect, he says, comes not from command but from observation and interaction."

"What's it about?"

"Take it. Discover for yourself."

She placed the book in her satchel.

Duly blew a cooling breath on his ognatia and took a long sip. "What is it you want me to trust you about?"

"I need you to keep everything I say here in the strictest of confidence."

"You have my word." Once again, he squinched his face and tried ever so valiantly to keep from sneezing. At the very least his efforts gave Beely time to protect herself from any flying mucus.

"They are coming for the books," she said while holding a hand in front of her face.

He took another sip of tea after sneezing, of course, and slowly set his cup down on the table. "You've become one of them?"

"One of whom?"

"One of those—the Plotists. You think evil is about to overtake our world."

"I did not realize there was a name for it. Plotist? It sounds like a worthy name. Although, it could be construed as duplicitous."

"I give it no connotation. It's just a word used to categorize those who are—shall we say—overly suspicious."

Beely took a moment to consider what was being discussed. "There are going to be great changes in the Five Realms. These changes will not be good for you and me—or those we love."

"Says who?" He involuntarily raised one of his huge, bushy brows, but quickly placed his hand over it as if he had an itch. He did not want Beely to feel as though he was minimizing her concerns.

Beely set her cup down and walked over to Duly's personal collection of books. These were the ones he held most dear. Their covers were worn from all the readings they had undergone over many moons. "They will take these, too."

Duly joined her in front of his life's carefully curated trove of stories and adventures. "What would you have me do?"

"I don't know."

"Then why are you here?" he asked.

"You were created for a time such as this. You will figure out a way to save them. Maybe not all of them—but enough of them."

"They're not even our stories. You said it yourself. Would it really matter?"

"It is becoming our story, Duly. We are part of it now, just as sure as I am speaking these words. We have a part to play. You have an important role here. Read Esther—Esther chapter four. 'Such a time as this'. Figure out what you want your role to be here in the Realms."

She knelt down beside him and lowered her face in complete humility.

When she looked back up into his eyes, she simply said, "Please."

Chapter 4

THE LAKE OF PROSPERITY

(several turnings earlier)

The River of Providence flowed directly into the middle of a mature orchard. It was more a leisurely flowing creek than a well-carved, rapidly flowing river, but it provided the resident trees, plants, and accompanying insects and animals with the perfect amount of fresh, pristine water. The River of Providence emptied into the Lake of Prosperity. A large lake it was not, but like the creek that filled it, it provided the perfect amount of water for the surrounding life.

The lake water was so clear and clean that creatures from the entire Realm of Okrad visited to drink and frolic. Most of the larger, older trees in the orchard had at least one opportunistic root that drank directly from the lake. The water made them strong and had sustained them for untold ages—

thousands of harvests, in fact. The lake had never gone dry, and as prophecy had foretold, it never would.

Upon the banks of the Lake of Prosperity was an abundant and diverse array of beautiful flora. What caught the attention of most visitors were the stunning rocks that lined the shoreline. They differed slightly in size, from that of small peas to the size of a Braewicker's nose. Shapes varied from oval to round and from slightly angular to fairly flat. They glistened in the sun when dry and sparkled like stars when wet. They mostly radiated differing hues of brown—never a dirty, dull brown, but rather a color as vibrant as the eyes of a beautiful princess, reflecting bits of red, amber, and dark green. It was rumored that the rocks could sing and make music, but their musical prowess had yet to be witnessed by anyone of note. Although they were captivating rocks, to be sure, their musical abilities remained a mystery.

The rocks were indeed the first thing that Athaliah noticed. She was mesmerized by their presence, so much so that she did not wish to step foot on any one of them. Athaliah gazed out at the lake and wondered why she was there. She was eager to be of service to Ankur, as she very much believed in him. Nonetheless, she could not help but think that this was a fool's errand.

As she contemplated the tasks ahead of her, she spotted the two beavers she had come to meet. They were named Saint Elmo and Francis. Although they were young, by Realm standards, they had been married for many moons and were as big as bears. They had long, droopy, purplish-brown ears that nearly dragged the ground. Their ears were attached to heads that looked far too small for such large bodies. The rest of their furry appendages were mostly the color of a rusty orange, aside from their long, furless, rubbery tails, which matched their dark purplish ears.

Francis was the first to rise up out of the water to greet Athaliah. She absentmindedly shook the water from her fur, causing Athaliah to cover her face with her hands and arms. "Hi, dear. I'm Francis, and slow-poke there is my husband, Saint Elmo. A saint, he is not." She leaned in toward Athaliah, extending her nose to within rubbing distance.

"She's not a beaver, and she's not even from this realm, Francis," said Saint Elmo as he climbed up the embankment.

"It's customary to bump noses with those you greet, dear, beaver or not," said Francis.

Athaliah was taken aback but obliged. She leaned over and rubbed noses with the eager beaver.

"Now that wasn't so hard, was it?" said Francis as she gave a cold stare in Saint Elmo's direction.

"Not at all. I'm very glad to make your acquaintance. My name is Athaliah."

Elmo stepped up next to his wife. "Well, you sure are a pretty thing," he said.

Athaliah awkwardly bent forward to rub his nose, but Elmo, unlike his wife, was not accustomed to rubbing noses with creatures of different species. By the time he lowered his head, Athaliah had already moved away. When she noticed, she again bent forward, but by then, Elmo had already lifted his head. This series repeated itself no less than three times before the two finally made the formal beaver greeting. Elmo gave his wife a most unsatisfactory look when it was all over.

Athaliah was Ankur's cousin. She, like him, was also blessed with good looks and a charismatic persona. She was proud of her beauty and secretly cherished her reflection. She had long black hair and large round eyes that could appear blue or green, depending on how the light struck them. She was of average height for an Okradian and had an athletic yet feminine build. Her voice was perhaps her most striking attribute. She spoke softly, but clearly, in a tone that almost hypnotized its audience.

She did nothing to intentionally draw people in; it was simply a natural part of her personality. She immediately put anyone who met her at ease. This was certainly true for the beavers, who warmed up to her quickly.

"I must admit," began Francis, "when I first heard the proposal to make the lake larger, I was a bit skeptical. The lake has never run dry, and the creek supplies plenty of water to the orchard on its way down to the inlet."

Saint Elmo added, "But hey, what's a beaver to do? You ask me to build a bigger dam, I'm going to build a bigger dam. Who better than us to make this the most spectacular lake in all the Realms?"

"Yes, yes. My husband is correct. And now, having met you in person, I can see that you are an honorable young lady. There must be a good reason for all the plans to enrich the Land of Mana."

"Thank you so much for understanding, and your willingness to help is definitely a blessing. I know Ankur will be most pleased, as am I."

"Will you be staying to oversee our progress?" asked Saint Elmo.

"No, there is no need. I just wanted to meet you and confirm that it could actually happen according to Ankur's timeline," answered Athaliah.

"Of course. All is well. You just leave it to our teeth and hands, little lady," said Saint Elmo. He opened his mouth wide and chomped down so his teeth made a sharp clack.

"Thank you both so much. I'm sure you will do a splendid job with the new dams. I wish I could stay longer and get to know you both better, but I have one more important meeting. Do you happen to know where I could find the clonal tree? The orchard is much larger than I had anticipated."

Francis quickly raised both of her hands and motioned for Athaliah to stop talking. "You mustn't call him that. He answers to no name other than Ekrad Oren."

"That's two names, dear," said Saint Elmo.

******

Athaliah could still hear the beavers arguing as she cleared the first hill toward Ekrad Oren. Francis had said the notorious tree resided in the middle of the ancient orchard as she pointed her in the right direction.

Although known as an orchard, the Land of Mana was more of a garden, it seemed to Athaliah—a perfect garden. She passed plant after plant with the most robust and aromatic fruits. There did not seem to be any insects, fungi, or other pests affecting the delicious offerings.

She instinctively knelt down to smell a scarlet, triangular-shaped berry. She had no intention of eating it, but it was in her mouth before she knew it. The soft, sweet-smelling delight was devoured in one bite. She wiped her mouth and looked around, slightly embarrassed, to see if anyone was looking.

She was the only sentient being around, other than the trees. Yes, all of the trees could feel, see, and communicate. In the Five Realms, the trees were the oldest souls. The trees were as wise as they were tall. They were only limited by how far their roots could spread and by how high their limbs could reach. That was not much of a limitation at all, because given enough ages, roots and limbs went farther than any ground walker could see. The trees were more powerful at knowing and being than even the most itinerant spirit.

Athaliah used the inside of her cape to wipe away the evidence that she had eaten from the garden. It was not polite to take without asking, and she was an invited guest. Her family was very proud, and she was very disappointed in her momentary weakness. What if Ekrad Oren suspected her of thievery? It was not illegal to eat from the garden or to share in the prosperity of others, but it was unbecoming of a representative of the new leader of Okrad to give in to gluttonous cravings.

She continued on toward the center of the orchard, passing more aromatic offerings than the one she had previously devoured. She refused to give in to temptation a second time. She stared at her feet as she walked, avoiding the beautiful, tantalizing fruits of the vines, trees, and shrubs all around her. There were so many temptations. She could not avoid the smells. Nothing in her homeland smelled nearly as divine. Her mouth watered.

She needed to focus on something other than the growls crawling out of her stubborn stomach. She ruminated over the scarlet stain on the inside of her white cape. She hoped that it would come out with a little scrubbing. She prayed that no one else would notice it on the rest of her journey, especially Ekrad Oren.

As she walked deeper into the garden, she heard only the crunching of dirt beneath her feet. It was a bright, clear day. The air was temperate. The breeze was refreshing as it filled the pores on Athaliah's fair skin. It was too perfect. Athaliah felt a haunting, ominous dread. Something deep within her did not feel right. It was a feeling that had crept upon her ever since she left Okrad.

She reminded herself that feelings were notoriously unreliable, and she must continue on with her mission—the mission that Ankur had persuaded her to pursue. There was a compelling desire deep within her to please her cousin. Perhaps she wanted to solidify her place within her extended family line, or perhaps she simply needed affirmation, something her father never gave.

"He's just over the next ridge."

The voice stopped Athaliah in her tracks. "Who is that?"

"I overheard you speaking to the beavers."

Athaliah slowly pivoted, searching for where the voice came from. She saw no one.

"It's me. I'm the willow. The only willow in the garden. Won't you come visit me under my branches?"

Athaliah turned until she faced the willow tree, with its branches dangling only a few inches from her face. The leaves brushed against one another, creating a soft, rhythmic dance with the gentle breeze. She moved the branches back as if she were going behind a curtain. Light trickled down through the many leaves, illuminating a path under the willow tree's beautiful, arching canopy. The trail was lined with mushrooms, which were animated with bruised blue faces. They were chatting amongst themselves. There were thick, protruding roots and loamy-smelling soil marking the way. Athaliah followed the path to the willow's trunk. It was a much larger tree than she could have ever imagined, looking at it from the outside.

"Thank you for joining us. There is privacy under my darling little leaves. They will make sure no one else hears us."

"Who else would be listening, and why would they care?" asked Athaliah.

"Don't be so naive, dear one. Your beauty will not sustain you forever. You must become wise to the ways of the Realms," said the willow.

"I don't understand. Why are you interested in me, and who exactly are you?"

"I am one of the most mature of my kind in the Five Realms, certainly the oldest living here in the garden."

"Even older than Ekrad Oren?"

"I don't compare myself to *that* one in any way or form. I know you are here to seek a deal with him."

"A deal? How could you possibly know any such thing?" asked Athaliah, nervously.

"My roots go far, and my branches provide respite for friends who can soar through the air. There is no place in the Five Realms I have not been, in one sense or another."

"You've been spying on me?"

"Spying? On you? Perhaps...not. There is no secret among the knowing as to what plans have been put into place—designs already in motion—that not only affect me, but all those in the Five Realms and beyond."

"And what of those plans? The only ones I know about are well-intentioned efforts to unite all citizens together as one unified empire."

"If the plans are as good as you say, why are you shaking so? Why are your hormones emitting such an odor?"

Athaliah walked around the trunk of the willow. She looked up into her branches and all around, but she saw no one. She knew it was the tree speaking to her, but how was it speaking? She had never before conversed with such a being. The tree, sensing Athaliah's discomfort, formed a face of sorts by manipulating her branches and leaves.

"Is this some kind of wizardry?" asked Athaliah, looking at the image.

"There is no wizardry in the Five Realms. Faith, miracles, and possibilities are all that you see here. I am simply presenting myself in a form that you can more easily relate. Do you find it helpful?"

"It's interesting. I will admit that. You seem to know a lot about me and why I'm here. I know nothing about you or what you want."

"I want you to think about the choices you are making. If you go through with this, you are choosing a side. Make sure it's the side that you want to be on."

"I'm just here to ask for a piece of fruit from the old tree—I mean, Ekrad Oren. What could be so wrong about that?"

"I don't know what Ankur wants with the fruit. Not yet, anyway. Nothing good, I'm sure," said Willow.

"So, what is this about?" asked Athaliah.

"Close your eyes. I want to show you what will become of the Realms because of what you have already done here today."

"I've done nothing here today."

"Close your eyes," whispered Willow.

Athaliah did as requested and closed her eyes. Willow's branches slowly moved around Athaliah's body. She felt them lightly brush against her neck and ankles, wherever her skin was exposed. Goosebumps leapt along her forearms. Apprehension slowly gave way to excitement and then peace. She felt no harm would come to her. She gave in to the ethereal experience. No more than a few seconds passed before Athaliah began dreaming. She knew it was a dream, even though the vision seemed very real.

Bat-like wings were attached to her body, allowing her to fly. Athaliah soared over the orchard she had just been walking through. It was the same garden, but there was something oddly different.

The small lake into which the creek flowed was now a much larger body of water, so large, in fact, that there were waves crashing on the shore. The creek, on the other hand, was completely dry.

She soared along the dry creek until she came to the canyon. She recognized the area, as it was famous and known by all. The canyon should have had a river flowing through it.

She looked around, past the deeply carved walls, and everything was dry, desolate, and dead.

In no time at all, she was over the High Forest. There was no green thing to be found. Every tree was dead. Not one leaf or live plant could be seen.

No flying creatures were perched on limbs. No creatures crawled on the barren soil. There was no life to speak of in a woodland that should have been teeming with all sorts of living, colorful things.

Finally, she was over a land she knew well: Okrad, her beautiful homeland. She saw people, but they were frail and poor. There was no vegetation where the usually bountiful crops had been. There was nothing but dust.

Even though it was only a vision, her heart sank. Athaliah had never felt such remorse and sadness. She fell to her knees, and the vision ended.

She looked up with a tear in her eye. A moment passed before she was able to speak. "How do I know there is any truth to this?"

Willow's leaves cascaded down like a waterfall before forming an illusion of the face of a beautiful woman with long hair of billowing willow branches.

"Ankur will completely dry up the River of Life and divert any remaining tributaries to the Lake of Prosperity here in the Land of Mana," said Willow. "I can only assume he made a deal with Ekrad Oren. For what, exactly, I am not sure. When he is finished, there will be little, if any, water for the rest of the Five Realms. He will control everything."

Athaliah stood and faced the image created by the willow branches head-on, "My cousin is not a bad man. If he is doing anything with the water, it is because he believes it will help every citizen in every kingdom."

"The River of Life is for all. It was never intended to be controlled by any man or any kingdom. If this happens, there will be death and destruction throughout the Five Realms."

"If you believe this, why don't you stop it? If you have the power to see the future, you must have the power to change it."

"I cannot see the future. I can only verify what is currently happening and apply that to the prophetic wisdom of our elders. This was prophesied."

"If it has been prophesied, assuming one believes in prophecy, what can be done about it?"

"It's not the prophecy I am worried about. I never waste too much time on what may or may not happen. I am concerned with those helping to make the prophecy come true—those like you."

"What would you have me do?"

"Make the right choice. Turn around, and become a blessing, not a curse."

Athaliah brushed the hair from her face and softly scratched behind her ear. She had no reason to doubt the sincerity of the willow tree. She also knew her cousin to be a reasonable man. If he knew about what might happen, he would stop it. He would not want to bring harm to so many people, she was sure of it.

"I will go back to Okrad and talk to Ankur. Until I understand what all of this means, I will not meet or make any deal with Ekrad Oren. I cannot promise what will be the outcome of any delay, but I will earnestly strive to do the right thing." Athaliah paused and made a slight bow in front of the willow.

"Please, there is only One worthy of such bowing, and He is not of this world. I trust, Athaliah, that you will make the right choice—the good choice. It is not only written in your heart—the truth—but it is also written in the Word. Persuade your cousin to change his plans. Become a blessing to others, not a curse."

"What if you are right? What could I possibly do to persuade Ankur? He is a powerful and well-liked man. I am nothing compared to him."

"Young girl, I cannot pretend to know what it is like to trod from place to place on feet such as yours, but no matter what we are made of on the outside, it is what we are made of on the inside that dictates our course."

All of the willow leaves fluttered, and the image of the face faded as the many branches hung and swayed as nature intended. Willow continued to speak, even though her image had faded.

"The fibers of a tree only strengthen after many moons of bending to the wind. The wind, with its constant ebb and flow, sometimes blowing hard, tearing leaves from limbs, thinks it has won. In time, the tree stands tall against the fiercest squall, only bending when it must, but always returning to stand forthright. You too may bend, but if you endure, in time, you will be able to stand tall against the strongest of foes."

"Why do you seem to have so much confidence in me?" Athaliah asked.

"I have no confidence in you whatsoever. I have faith in who you *can* be because I have faith in the One who created you."

Athaliah stood under the giant willow tree long after the last words were spoken. She felt safe under the branches. Truth be told, she felt hidden from the realms around her. She did not want to leave to begin the daunting journey before her. Ankur would be dismayed, at the very least, that Athaliah had not completed what he had asked of her. It was a special assignment, he had said, a task that he had only entrusted to her.

She might have stayed longer, hidden safely away under the willow, had several of the many mushrooms not started taunting her. She did not like the bruised blue faces of the mushrooms very much, as they puckered and pulsed, whispering in sharp, clicking voices. It was obvious they did not care for her either.

The bickering funguses had little confidence that the woman wearing white would ever be good.

Chapter 5

PIXANESE

Unlike the earthly world, there was no rain in the Five Realms of Here. All of the inhabitants and vegetation received water from underground springs, creeks, rivers, and wells. The River of Life was the primary aboveground tributary, dispersing water into ponds and lakes—dammed when and where needed— eventually flowing into kingdoms that did not have springs through smaller creeks and streams. Communities only existed where the water flowed naturally or where water channels had been constructed.

Pixanese was most unusual, as it had an abundance of water. The River of Life emanated from an underground spring that lay directly underneath the kingdom. Because of this, Pixanese was a lush paradise with many diverse plants and creatures.

The bulk of Pixanese lay below a huge cliff on one side, with the River of Life pressing up against a lower canyon wall, forming a natural border on the other side. Most of the inhabitants resided in the middle of Pixanese in an area no larger than a person could traverse on foot in twenty minutes. This small communal area provided a harmonious place for the many residents to happily commune. Dwellings were built as far up as the tallest tree and deep inside caves behind the canyon walls. The people, animals, and other creatures were as diverse as the dwellings they lived in.

The empachics were among the most diverse creatures of Pixanese. They were known as the friendliest residents, which is saying a lot, as almost everyone was friendly. "Chics," as they were often called, were native to the land, and they lived wherever and with whomever they pleased. An outsider might have considered them to be pets, kept and trained, but an empachic needed no training, and it was an honor to be chosen by one.

Beely and her husband, Maximilian, lived just outside of the village, partially because they needed a larger ground dwelling than what was available within the village center. More empachics chose to live with them than a small home could comfortably accommodate. The townsfolk could not keep count of how many chics actually lived with them, but it was rumored to be upward of fifteen.

The short, round, furry creatures were cherished for their abilities to soothe, comfort, and heal. They were pure joy to be around and exemplified everything living beings should strive to be—thoughtful, empathetic, and, most of all, loving. The only thing that could be seen of a healthy empachic was its fur, which came in a multitude of colors and patterns. Once in a while, their small, pudgy paws could be spotted if they were in just the right position. If a chic were very old or ill—which was rare—its fur might become thin enough for an ear or an eye to poke through.

The other reason they lived outside of the village was because of Beely's love of gardening. She absolutely relished watching things grow from infancy. Her gardens were perfectly manicured and painstakingly structured. Maximilian sometimes complained about all of the attention she paid to her plots; they lived amid the most beautiful and naturally occurring gardens in the kingdom. He could not understand her need to recreate that which existed in abundance all around them. Nonetheless, he loved his wife, and he gallantly tried not to speak ill of her passions.

Beely was just finishing pruning the vines of her elderflower when she heard the brorayding's loud snort. The large flying creatures were capable of carrying a single rider over great distances. Her husband had just returned from his trip to Okrad. Beely loosened the ties in her hair, which she often wore up while working in the gardens. She rarely allowed anyone to see her long, silky hair in such an unflattering state. She walked down the path to the nearest clearing big enough for the brorayding to comfortably land.

Maximilian was thanking his flying companion with a few light scratches on its smooth, leathery back when his wife tapped him on the shoulder from behind. They had been married for a few turnings, but until recently, they rarely missed the opportunity to show their affection for one another.

They embraced for a long moment before Maximilian interrupted, "I haven't been gone that long."

"I just don't like us being apart these days," she said, taking his hand in hers.

"Are you still feeling uneasy? Worse than before?"

"I'm having those strange dreams more often. The empachics are all over me. They've been following me everywhere. I had to sneak away to avoid them."

"You should let them do what they do best. It's not showing weakness to let them soothe you."

"I want to feel every frayed nerve, Max, until we figure out exactly what's happening. I don't want to let my guard down, not for a moment."

In an attempt to distract his wife from her usual worries of late, Max retrieved the fruit that Lira had given him from his pack. He handed it to Beely. "This is from a woman who owns a peculiar Okrad shop. Very interesting lady. She thought we might be able to discover something unusual about it."

Beely squinted her eyes, intently studying the palm-sized red fruit. "What is it?"

"It's a fruit of some sort. It was one of the gifts Ankur gave to those who accepted his invitation to visit Okrad."

As they began walking to the house, Beely turned toward the brorayding and said, "He's eating my prized rubbios again. Do you know how long it takes to grow a rubbio?"

Max wrapped an arm around his wife's waist. "Let him eat, dear. He worked hard, and it was a long trip."

Beely sighed but knew he was right. The rubbios would grow back, and the brorayding was a loyal and worthy beast of burden. "Well, I'm not long for this world anyway. Those rubbios will surely outlive me. He may as well eat them all."

Max refused to indulge his wife's predilection for worrying about death. She had always thought she would die young, and there was no convincing her otherwise. He simply ignored all references to her self-prophesied demise. "You should have seen how those people clamored to get close to Ankur. They were enamored with him!"

"Really?" asked Beely.

"It was sickening, if you ask me."

"Do I detect a bit of jealousy?"

"You might. Should I be?" asked Max with a chuckle.

Beely laughed and kissed him on the cheek. They chatted about the most unimportant of things as they walked past Beely's beautiful gardens to the house. He might have questioned the amount of time and effort she put into her other love, but he could not argue with the result. Everything Beely put her hands to turned into something amazing, especially her gardens.

Once settled inside, Beely poured Max his favorite drink, a mix of berries and elderflower tea. It was not easy maneuvering around all the empachics, but once the chics knew that she was feeling more at ease, with Max back home, all but Reverie left her side. Beely picked up her most sensitive chic and sat next to her husband.

Max studied the red fruit given to him by Lira. He gently rubbed his index finger around the top and gently tugged at the stem. "I wonder how she knew?"

"Knew what?" asked Beely.

"That you are a geneticist."

"I'm not."

"Even more curious was how she knew that you enjoy reading about genetics and botany," said Max.

Beely set her tea down on the small table in front of her and picked up the strange red fruit. "How could she have possibly known that? She didn't even know that you would be there. Now who sounds suspicious?" She turned the fruit upside down and felt the stem. "Get me a small knife, would you, dear?"

While he was retrieving the knife as requested, Beely placed a small towel on a side table. She took the knife and began slicing the specimen, careful not to damage the middle part of the fruit. With the tip of the knife, she pointed to the white, fleshy pulp running down the center. "Do you see that? It's the outer wall of the ovary."

"I see it. It looks exactly like the bitter part I like to avoid."

Beely leaned over the table, getting as close a view of the open flesh as she could. Reverie let out a small chirp in protest to getting squeezed by Beely's leaning body. "I'm sorry, Reverie. Perhaps you should sit on Max for a while."

Reverie took no objection and quickly changed laps. "Look at that." Beely pointed to a very small anomaly within the white, fleshy vein.

"What is it?"

"I don't know, but what I do know is that it should not be moving!"

Reverie scowled—although no one could see it through all of her fur—and snarled loudly as she jumped off of Max's lap away from the infected fruit.

"Moving?" He looked more closely, and his eyes followed a black dot, no larger than the point of a pen, moving from one end of the vein and back down again. "And fast. That's not normal, is it?"

"It's like nothing I've ever seen." She walked out of the room, wiping her hands and knife with the towel. She returned with a container, in which she placed the now split fruit. "I'll need to study this more. I might even need to get another pair of eyes on it."

"One thing. I promised Lira that we would not divulge where it came from. She trusted me to keep her secret."

"Wow, you really made quite the impression on that young lady."

When Beely picked up the container of fruit, she accidentally tipped her glass over. Max instinctively reached for the towel but was stopped by Beely's hand on his arm. They watched as the liquid split into three separate lines. The fluid raced toward the edge of the table, and just before spilling over onto the ground below, all three lines froze in place.

Max looked at his wife. His left eye was closed more tightly than his right. "That's odd."

Perhaps it would not have been so odd if the table had a raised edge. The three-legged furniture piece was very old. It had been a favorite of her late father's and a piece her mother had tried, in vain, to banish. Not only was this particular tabletop smooth, with no lip whatsoever, it also had one leg slightly shorter than the other two. The liquid should have quickly run off onto the floor below.

"Ankur's going to stop the water!" Beely exclaimed.

"I have to admit that is weird," Max said, raising both palms toward the gravity-defying phenomenon. "There must be an explanation."

He bent down and removed a small shim from under the shorter leg. He looked up expecting to see the liquid roll off of the edge onto the floor, but to his dismay, it remained in place. He stood up and looked at Beely. She shrugged her shoulders. He took his finger and cleared the dust just in front of the fluid, possibly touching the lines of water with his finger in the process. They watched as Beely's drink finally spilled onto the floor.

"You touched the tea. You were the catalyst. I'm telling you, as sure as I know my own name, I know that Ankur has a plan to keep the water from flowing into the Five Realms. I don't know how, but that's what is going to happen."

Max looked at his wife reassuringly and said, "She wasn't all that young."

Chapter 6

TWO MOONS

She was followed. She was always being followed.

The two moons seemed brighter than they had ever been since the first time Beely remembered laying eyes on them. She remembered the moment as if it were yesterday. She was five turnings old and sitting on her father's knee. The masculine scent of spice on his tunic, his firm but gentle hands, and the glorious moons—two of them, reflecting in her daddy's big brown eyes—would forever be etched in her memory. She would never see such glorious moons again, not even on this most important night.

Both moons were full, a rarity to see under the forest trees in the Realm of Pixanese. They were fully illuminated but not so bright that they gave away the interloper who had been following her. The spy, wearing a black cloak and hood, blended seamlessly with the night. Even if the ill-intentioned figure had been spotted, Beely would never have been able to identify who it was. The stranger's identity would not be known to Beely until it was much too late to matter.

Beely made her way to where the oarsman was waiting with the message from Propo. The fact that Propo had used an oarsman to facilitate the delivery emphasized the importance of discretion. There was not a more reclusive being than an oarsman. They were skilled aquatic creatures, able to traverse the waterways in complete anonymity while escorting passengers and cargo.

When Beely spotted the flat-bottomed boat from afar, she could not help but step lightly in hopes of getting a look at its captain. She, like almost everyone else, had never seen one and was curious about the elusive guides. Unfortunately for Beely, it was not to be. By the time she made it all the way down to the water's edge, the oarsman was already under the boat, hidden beneath the dark surface of the river.

The boat drifted with an eerie, silent grace, leaving no wake, as if it were being pulled by the current of a ghost. Beely stepped aboard the small craft, having no idea what would be waiting for her. She looked the boat over and saw nothing out of the ordinary. Before she had the chance to get her bearings, the boat began moving downstream. When it arrived at the middle of the river, it held steady.

Beely remained seated at the front end, waiting. There was nothing left for her to do at this point but wait. She ran her hand along one of the curved planks next to where she sat. The wood was smooth and richly colored where passengers had moved about. Other areas were a dull, washed-out gray and rough to the touch. Beely wondered where oarsmen got their boats, as no two were exactly the same. She assumed they had been commandeered after being abandoned by their original owners.

Beely stared at the moons. The quiet stillness of the surroundings allowed her mind to drift to the losses she had faced in her life. The mysterious and untimely death of her father had occurred fourteen turnings ago, although the pain that still filled her heart made it seem more recent. At times, she had almost come to terms with his passing, but the current political changes in Okrad led her to reconsider the circumstances surrounding his death.

She was convinced a more recent tragedy would haunt her for the rest of her life. Her one and only pregnancy had ended in a miscarriage, and the loss continued to weigh heavily on her heart. She was sad. Anyone close to her could feel her brokenness, especially the empachics. It was an unbearable loss.

Seeing the moons reminded her of the times with her father, a time she would never get to spend with her own child. She struggled to find meaning in life. At her age, with a home, a husband she loved, and no financial worries, a family was the next logical step. Yet, it was not to be. Every specialist she spoke with confirmed that the miscarriage was the result of a genetic trait passed down from her father's side.

The last time she was in the village, she had broken down in tears upon seeing a mother hold a door open for three small children. One by one, they marched through, brushing against their mother's dress and giggling as they spilled out onto the sidewalk. Everything involving children made her heart ache. Maximilian used her pain as the reason he could not believe her current suspicions and conspiracy theories. He said she was too emotionally unstable to reason objectively. His words stung worse than the grief; she was being told that her intuition was merely a symptom of her broken heart.

Tonight was the night she would finally know if she was irrational or if her concerns were warranted. Propo said he would send irrefutable evidence of Ankur's evil intentions. It was not enough to suspect. Beely, like her husband, needed proof before presenting official accusations against a man whom almost everyone seemed to admire.

She sat and took in her surroundings, listening and watching. The faster moon was already sinking just below the high canyon wall. The slower moon was still directly above, as if joining Beely for a moment in time that would change the course of history. Bathed in the light of the sole remaining moon, two witnesses joined as one, confirming the changing of the winds. Ironically, there was no wind at all on this night. The air was calm and warm. The night sky was clear.

After a while of ruminating in melancholic memories, she looked up to see a most surprising sight. There it was—the unmistakable silhouette of the fabled tiny salafus.

The fact that she knew what she was looking at—as the tiny salafus slowly descended, fairy-like, toward her in the rays of the moon—pleased Beely. She had only read about the elusive creatures because of her father's own curious written ruminations. He had given her drawings and books by those who had claimed to have seen or interacted with the fantastical fliers. Although similar, no two renditions of the fabled salafus were exactly the same, leading to doubts that they even existed at all.

There was no doubt now. As best as Beely could ascertain, they were only called tiny because of their small, disproportionate wings. The salafus was actually quite plump, with short, sturdy legs and a long, wrinkly snout. It had no hands, using its nimble nose when dexterity was necessary. One thing she had never read about was the flower-like bugs accompanying the salafus. There were too many of them to count. She wondered if all salafuses traveled with such a strange and colorful entourage.

Before she had time to ask it any questions, the plump salafus, with wings so small they should have been of no use, landed at the top of the boat with a most un-fairy-like thud. The flying flower bugs landed on Beely's head and shoulders, with one last little straggler buzzing around until it found an ear peeking through Beely's hair.

The thought of shooing them away never occurred to her. The bugs not only looked like delicate petals, but they smelled like an exotic perfume. Beely wondered what she looked like, adorned with living flowers all about her head.

The salafus was indeed a strange-looking creature. It was no taller than Beely's longest finger, but what it lacked in height, it made up for in volume. The flying phenom had to weigh more than Reverie on her heaviest day. Beely was quite dumbfounded to see the salafus rise up into the air before her, with its tiny wings buzzing so loud that they made music.

As if that were not enough, the salafus raised its long snout and blew it like a trumpet. The flower bugs responded to the trumpeting salafus in unison as they, too, flew up into the air. They scattered silver dust so thickly that Beely could no longer see the salafus. The silver particles danced in the rays of the moonlight. As the dust touched her skin, it felt like tiny pricks of frost, chilling her despite the warm night air.

Beely watched in awe as the dust fell like a waterfall, forming a stream that circled around her. Beely could not see the flower bugs, but the silver waterfall kept flowing as the flowers buzzed in joyful harmony.

Then, all of a sudden, the splendid buzzing stopped, and the stream of dust evaporated. The flower bugs, one by one, dropped to the ground as if dead, legs straight up into the air.

Before Beely could reach down to touch one of the fallen flowers, the salafus made another trumpet sound. The flowers flew up into the air, scattering their mystical silver dust, which quickly formed into a beautiful tree. Within seconds, the leaves of the tree turned as black as coal and fell from the silver tree before the tree itself turned black and disintegrated right before Beely's eyes. The unmistakable scent of ash replaced the sweet perfume of the bugs, leaving a bitter taste in her mouth.

What would have probably been seen as nothing more than a momentary cloudy mist by an onlooker, was actually several minutes of a profoundly heart-wrenching prophetic announcement to Beely. She had no doubt what it meant.

It was the second affirmation of what was going to happen to the Five Realms. Death and darkness were upon them. Beely shuddered at the thought of all that could happen in such times. She felt a surge of panic—how could she tell Maximilian about this? If she described a tiny creature blowing a trumpet of doom, he would surely believe her mind had finally snapped under the weight of her grief.

When she looked up, her eyes wide open, she saw that the salafus and its musical flowers were gone. While Beely was rightly concerned, she allowed herself to appreciate such a profound moment. For some reason, unknown to her, she had been chosen for a revelatory intervention by the most mysterious of creatures. In mere moments, the creature had led her from feelings of amazement and joy to a dark realization of approaching doom.

Beely rapped her knuckles on the bottom of the boat to signal the oarsman that she was ready to return to shore. Even though she was convinced of what was happening and what had been revealed to her, she was still unsure of how to persuade the one who should have been her most trusting ally—her husband. How would he interpret what had just transpired? Would he believe her?

Beely needed someone to believe her. Propo was a good and loyal friend. She could trust him with anything, but she needed to convince others of the truth, and if she could not convince her own husband, how could she expect to have influence over anyone else?

There was another who was convinced. The interloper, though still on the shore, had eyes like a bird of prey. She had been fortunate enough to witness the salafus in action. Though convincing was not what the interloper sought. Draped in black, from the land of Okrad, she simply needed to know if Beely had discovered the truth. She was absolutely certain that Beely had received the message; but how could she be sure Beely believed it as she herself did? It was an impossible mission—to know the mind of another.

The spy's time in Pixanese was not over. She would need to see what Beely did next. Her belief would only be revealed by her actions. In time, Athaliah, the interloper, would know if Beely was managing to convince anyone else. Until then, she would continue to follow the only one who might be able to save the Realms from a darkness that could consume them all.

Chapter 7

THE STUDIO

She had an overwhelming sensation of needing to relieve her bladder. The false warning was from a surge of excitement and nervousness. Beely had not been inside her father's studio since he passed away. A thick layer of dust lay quietly on every surface, telling a story of forgotten dreams and hazy memories. In Pixanese, it was not uncommon for homes to sit abandoned long after someone's death. Yet, fourteen turnings was extreme.

Beely could never bring herself to make any changes to the place her father treasured most. Maximilian had often expressed that she should close this chapter of her life and sell her father's belongings, but she had always refused.

The memories of spending time with her father in his place of sanctuary were priceless. The studio had been far enough from Beely's childhood home that her mother rarely interrupted his work, but it was close enough for him to be an involved and loving father. Her mother never knew how much time Beely spent with her father in his favorite place. When she was older,

Beely understood how patient he had been in allowing his young, curious daughter to be such a close part of his creative and philosophical world. She had developed an abiding respect for her father's work and learned many lifelong lessons just by watching him.

Beely smiled reverently; it was here that she had learned to pray. Every time her father opened a new book, started a new project, or continued with an exciting experiment, he would close his eyes and say a prayer. He prayed a lot. She would always close her eyes with her daddy, imagining what he was thinking as he silently spoke to God.

Her father had three desks. He was consumed with researching, experimenting, illustrating, and reading. He had quickly discovered that it was important to keep his body from stiffening up from hours and hours of tireless work sitting at the same desk, in the same position, day after day. One desk was so tall that he could stand while working. Beely slid a finger across the dust-covered, hardwood top and immediately sneezed.

She asked herself why she was there. Why now? She had wanted to come back to her father's studio for many moons but never quite felt ready to say a final farewell. Why was today different? She reasoned that perhaps the confirmation from Propo and the salafus regarding the "dry death" was what gave her the impetus to finally go through her father's things. Maybe there was more confirmation in his writings and theories just waiting to be uncovered. She prayed that he had left something to help, something to inspire her to fight the evil that was swirling around her.

Beely was jolted out of her thoughtful paralysis by Reverie jumping onto the middle of the smallest desk in the room, where her father had written his musings and much of his theoretical work. He had always kept pen and paper nearby, but it was at this desk where he had allowed the ideas that kept him awake at night to grow and blossom into beautiful creations.

Beely walked over to a sneezing Reverie. An empachic sneeze—short and high-pitched with a snort—was probably the cutest noise one could ever hope to hear. She carefully picked her up from the small desk, brushed the dust from her fur, gave her a quick kiss, and set her gently on the ground.

"I know you don't want another bath—or do you?"

Reverie squeaked and hurriedly bounced away from Beely. Reverie detested baths, but as she was getting older, she sometimes needed a little extra help with her finicky fur coat.

Beely removed a book from the chair in front of her father's desk. She sat and stared at what was a simple desk with only one drawer, which she absentmindedly opened. The only thing inside was a thin book. It was handsomely bound with fine embossed leather. She had never before seen such detail and attention given to so few pages. She dropped it into her satchel. She would read it later.

She noticed a few loose pages on top of the desk where Reverie had inadvertently performed the job of a feather duster. She glanced over the yellowed pages. It was the first part of a thesis on the political winds of change. Although the only politics in the Five Realms during her father's lifetime were relegated to disputes between neighbors, he had theorized that wherever intelligent creatures congregated, larger political factions would eventually follow.

She read the first paragraph aloud, "Of the four great winds of power that will inevitably bring change to any civilized world, political power is perhaps the most dangerous. All other winds—military, economic, and even religious—will ultimately be affected by the political movements of the culture."

She stopped reading to check on Reverie's whereabouts. No matter how busy Beely became, she could not help but worry for her oldest and most frail friend. She found her hiding under the middle desk. "Reverie, so many people thought my dad was stuck in a fantasy world of his own creation. It seems to me that he was just ahead of his time."

Beely understood why no one had taken her father's theories seriously, especially the ones involving politics. The Five Realms had no need for politics, political leaders, or governments. Each realm had judges that arbitrated according to a law that had been written in the Word and on their hearts. They needed no leader. They still did not need them, as far as she was concerned. That is why she found it so perplexing that Ankur was apparently creating such a stir. The political winds were indeed blowing in the Five Realms.

Like her father had done so many times before in that very room, Beely bowed her head, closed her eyes, and prayed. Unlike her father, who did not allow animals in his studio, she was quickly distracted by her furry companion. Reverie had found something of interest in the middle desk. Standing up on her hind feet, she scratched at one of the drawers.

"What is it, little one?" asked Beely as she walked over and rubbed the excited chic behind her ears.

Reverie continued to paw at the drawer, only stopping to look up to squeak emphatically at Beely.

"Okay. Okay. Let's see what's in there." Beely tugged on the drawer handle of the dark green desk. It would not budge. She looked down, noticing a slot intended for a key. She had never known her father to lock anything. "Well, Reverie, if you want to get into this drawer, you had better start looking for the key."

Beely stopped to consider where her father might hide a key. She picked up her heavy braids and tied them at the top of her head. She usually did this when preparing to work out in the gardens or do anything laborious. It seemed that her time in the studio was becoming both dirty and laborious.

While her most beloved four-legged companion simply curled up in a chair and slept, Beely searched every crack, crevice, shelf, and drawer until there were no more spots to inspect. Beely did not mind the lack of help from her sweet empachic. She knew Reverie's daily medication made her less energetic. It was a compromise—less energy but a longer life. Beely could not bear to think about her "little girl" passing. As her caregiver, she would always do whatever it took to keep Reverie happy and comfortable.

Beely had looked everywhere. She had moved every book on every shelf. Her satchel was now so full of mementos that she had to set it down because her shoulder had begun to ache. She promised herself not to take anything else. The promise did not last long once she came across an unusual puzzle box. A puzzle box was just as its name implied—unique shapes fitting together to form a box. Once the puzzle was solved, secret contents could be accessed inside the box. Children loved them, as did her father. He often made his own. She had no memory of this particular puzzle.

Emotionally exhausted, Beely gave up looking for the key. She gently lifted Reverie and sat down, putting the chic in her lap. She immediately shook her head, pursed her lips, and sighed as she felt something beneath her.

"Reverie, you can be a very pesky little girl!"

Beely held Reverie in her arms as she stood. There, on the chair where Reverie had slept for the last hour, was a key—*the* key, as they would soon discover. It was almost as if the creature had been sitting on it by design, guarding the threshold until Beely was emotionally ready to cross it. Reverie placed her two front paws over her eyes and whimpered.

Beely objected, "Don't pretend you didn't know it was there. You knew! You just like being out of the house. You're not fooling me, little one!"

Before Beely had a chance to open the drawer, there was a light rap on the door. Beely quickly let her braids down and cautiously cracked open the door. An elderly man with long gray hair, too thin to braid, stood meekly before her. He attempted to look past Beely in order to peer into the studio. Plenty of neighbors had inquired with both Beely and her mother about its availability, but most had given up many moons ago. This man must have seen her entering.

Beely knew almost everyone in Pixanese proper, but the elderly man did not look familiar. She glanced over her shoulder to see what he was focused upon before turning back to address him. "May I help you?"

He flinched at the sound of her voice, but quickly rebounded with a warm smile. "I think you can. My name is Eudox. I've been eyeing this place for quite some time. How fortunate I am to find someone home."

"This was my father's studio, but it's not on the market. I'm sure there are other places nearby that might be available." Beely could not help but wonder what this elderly man would need with a studio. All the cliff dwellings on this side of the village were not suitable as living quarters. She did not believe that he had just randomly happened to find her there.

This man had an agenda.

The old man wrapped his long, thin fingers around his gray beard and slowly stretched the curly hairs until they were twice as long. With his other hand, he stroked his beard the way one might pet an empachic. Beely was engrossed by the man's odd nervous habit. He had more hair on his chin than on his head. His eyes were large, deeply set, and expressed much vulnerability, or perhaps loneliness. Yet, he was strong; of this, Beely was sure. This man was not looking to purchase property. He was at the door of her father's sanctuary for a different reason.

After another stroke of his beard, he asked, "May I come in and sit for a moment, just to catch my breath?"

Whether or not it was a good idea, she would not deny the elderly gentleman a moment of respite. "Of course, have a seat here."

Beely quickly made her way to her father's third desk, which was a small reading desk with legs seemingly too thin to hold the weight of a man's arms. A lamp with five octopus-type tentacles sat atop the desk. However, the luminescent organisms that provided the illumination had long since departed. She hoped the lone illumination she had carried with her would be sufficient for the elderly man's vision. She dusted off the chair's leather cushion with her hand.

Eudox, breathing heavily, all the while examining every square inch of the room, eventually made his way to the leather chair and sat. Beely could not help but think that his feebleness was all an act. She felt guilty for such thoughts.

"We don't have long. We are being watched. We are always being watched," said Eudox.

"By whom?" she asked.

"Ankur, of course. The evil one."

"Who are you?"

"I was a friend of your father's. I don't have time to go into many details. He left you with what you would need to know here in his studio—things you will need. I'm sure you have found most of them by now. Nothing is as it seems. You must look deeper, study harder, reason well."

Beely's heart raced, and suddenly her voice sounded a bit higher. Finally, there was someone who understood the severity of what was happening. She was not alone. "How do you know these things? Do you have any proof of any wrongdoing by Ankur?"

She had a hundred questions to ask this man, but she was being distracted by Reverie. Her most shy empachic had taken a liking to the man with the long beard. Beely had never seen her so affectionate with anyone else other than herself. She rubbed and purred as the man stroked her fur.

"What is her name?" he asked.

"Reverie."

"I knew her by another name. She is an old one, this one. Quite a special girl. You have taken good care of her."

"She has taken good care of me."

"Touché." He smiled. "Your husband does not believe you."

She looked at the man incredulously. "Excuse me?"

"Be wary of him, but don't lose faith in him. It has yet to be seen if he will come around, but it is true that he will deceive you." The words felt like a physical blow, colder than the dust in the room. Beely's lip twitched; the idea of Maximilian, her anchor, being a source of deception was almost too much to process.

"What are you talking about?"

"You must stop wasting time. Do what needs to be done." Eudox seemed tired and was still breathing heavily.

"What exactly is it that needs to be done?"

"Take the glouscenshire, the fruit from Okrad, to the person at this location." He handed her a small card.

"Assign the Twelve, of which your husband should not be one. There is no time to waste. Your life will be in danger. If you are wise, you will progress quickly on the path that has been laid out for you. You must act. The time is now." He glanced back at the door, half expecting to see someone knock it down.

"How do you know all of this, or should I ask why I should believe you?"

"You already believe me. You have been shown the sign two times—the salafus and the three streams."

"Three streams?" she asked.

"Three streams ceased flowing right before your eyes."

"You mean the other night on my father's old table?"

"I have no idea how you were shown. I just know you were shown. You will be given a third sign, and then you will not only believe, but you will act upon that belief. I was told by the prophets that when you returned here to your father's place, you would be one step away. The seeds have been sown, but you alone must see to it that they grow. You will need the help of the others. Choose wisely, but I warn you, do not involve Maximilian any further."

He gently set Reverie on the desk in front of him as he stood to leave.

"I knew all of my father's friends. I don't remember you."

"Your father spoke of you often. He wanted to share with you all that he knew, but that was not the way. He left his legacy, and now what was his is yours. You must finish what he started." He turned toward the door.

"I select you as one of my twelve."

The man paused, slowly turned around, and said, "Very well. Perhaps not the choice that I would have made in your position—choosing me before you even know what tasks are ahead of you."

"I know enough. Ankur must be stopped. The water and the way of life as we know it are in jeopardy," she said.

"You know much, but you have not broken the surface. Not even I know all that will be revealed to you."

"Why me?"

"Don't worry, dear. If not you, then it would be someone else. God needs no one. If you do not act, He will find another." Eudox turned away again, placing his hand on the door. "You are your father's daughter. I will be one of your twelve."

Just before he opened the door, Beely asked, "How will I know how to find you?"

"She..." he pointed to Reverie, "...will know. Find the one that hears the empachics."

"But empachics do not speak."

He laughed. "I did not say they speak, I said find the one that hears them. You have much to learn, but you will learn fast." He opened the door and looked both directions before exiting.

Beely looked at Reverie and thought aloud, "I've lived a lifetime and never knew—you've been holding out on me. Who can communicate with an empachic? Who indeed?"

Chapter 8

MARYBAH

"She's obsessed!" Maximilian blurted out as he paced back and forth.

Marybah had been sitting comfortably in her swingsong for the last thirty minutes, listening to her son-in-law vent his frustrations about her daughter. Her feet pushed off the floor, and the swing swayed back and forth, releasing a low hum as the air passed through its fibers. She sipped a cup of ognatia and nibbled on sweets as she tried hard not to interrupt the all-too-familiar rant.

Marybah's home was nestled high in the arms of the most prominent picalo tree in the village of Pixanese. Most of the trees in Pixanese were old and strong, but none were as tall and wide as a picalo. The picalo's circumference could spread as large as fifty Nectarions stretched arm to arm. Marybah's dwelling alone consisted of five separate rooms. It was an architectural vision that incorporated natural elements—

branches for walls, wood for floors, and thatch for the roof. There were also many finer accoutrements, such as her meticulously crafted furnishings and her heirlooms made of glass, ceramic, and various precious metals.

Maximilian's mother-in-law was quite wealthy. She had worked hard her entire life, but she also came from a family of means. The home she lived in was exquisite in location and view, but the only route up a picalo tree was on foot, through elaborate stairs and bridges. Her friends often wondered why Marybah purposefully chose the highest spot—just below the canopy—for her home. It was a simple reason, really, but one that no one would ever guess. With so many stairs, enough calories were burned that Marybah could indulge her ravenous sweet tooth and still remain relatively fit.

Marybah motioned for Maximilian to sit next to her on the swing. "My daughter was extreme—*is* extreme. She has always been obsessed with one thing or another. Why are you so worried now?"

"This is beyond her *normal*. She is convinced that our realms are coming to a slow, painful demise. She's been depressed because of these persistent, pessimistic thoughts. Did you know that she's been meeting under the cover of night with strange people? She even begged me to go to Okrad. Okrad! She thought if I saw what's happening there, I would finally believe that her theories—and her father's—are true."

Marybah suddenly turned from mildly interested to rather contemplative. "Okrad? Hmm. I've heard rumblings about that realm. Did you see anything interesting?"

"I don't know. Everything about her 'theories' is so convoluted. There's no proof for any of it. Apparently, they elected a leader in Okrad. Someone by the name of Ankur. A charismatic man, for sure, but harmless—maybe even well-meaning, as far as I could see."

"Interesting. Well, what would you have me do? I haven't spoken to my daughter in long time. As hard as I've tried to get back into her good graces, she still won't have anything to do with me. What exactly is she worried about that has her so depressed? Is it losing the child, her father—what?"

Marybah worked her way out of the swingsong and joined her son-in-law in the main living area.

Max stared pensively at a portrait on the wall. "If I shared details, you would urge me to have her committed."

"My daughter is strong, independent, and creative. There is nothing you could say that would surprise me." She pulled a pipe from the pocket of her robe. "Do you mind?" she asked as she began to fill it with dried leaves.

"Go right ahead."

He sat down on a soft chair only to sink in so far that he could not breathe comfortably. After fidgeting for a bit, he stood back up and began pacing once more. The floorboards groaned slightly, and the entire room gave a subtle, nauseating tilt as a gust of wind caught the upper canopy of the picalo.

"Well ..." She blew a puff of gray smoke as she waited for an answer.

Max waved his hand to clear the air. "She is convinced that Ankur is literally going to take over the Five Realms."

She coughed before responding. "What do you mean by *literally*?"

"I didn't even know you smoked leaves?"

"I don't—in front of anyone, anyway. Please continue." She took another long drag from the pipe, followed by more gray smoke.

"According to your daughter, he—Ankur—will use every bit of persuasion and power to conquer the Five Realms, should its inhabitants not voluntarily appoint him ruler, and if they do appoint him ruler, their fate won't be much better."

"The Realms will never appoint a ruler. How preposterous." She walked to the balcony and exhaled into the breeze.

"I know that. Beely knows that, or at least she must realize it somewhere deep down. How could one man take over every kingdom and every territory? Furthermore, why would he want to?"

"What is my daughter's theory on the matter?" she asked indifferently. She tried, successfully, to hide her concern. Marybah knew much about the theories that had been tossed around by the Plotists over many moons. She did not want anyone, especially her daughter's husband, to realize just how extensive her understanding was concerning the theories of her ex-husband.

"Now, conceptualize this, if you can. Beely is convinced that his first course of action is to take over all of the water—to stop the water from flowing except where he permits."

Marybah's previously expressionless eyes widened, the pupils constricting as she leaned toward Max. A sharp intake of breath whistled through her teeth, and she quickly turned her face away to stare out over the railing. She almost spoke, but instead slowly raised her hand to her mouth as she walked over to the balcony. She said nothing and instead took another long drag from of her pipe. The smoldering leaves were taking the edge off of her frayed nerves.

"What is it?" he asked.

"Would you bring me that plate of sweet curls, please? You should try some. They're quite good." She pointed toward the kitchen before continuing. "Her father, he—" She stopped mid-sentence, looking concerned, as she gazed out over the village of Pixanese far below.

Max joined her on the balcony. He looked up at the sky through the branches. After taking one of the sweet curls, he handed her the plate and asked, "What about her father?"

"He had such notions. He was part of a conspiracy group known as the Plotists."

"Never heard of them." He took a bite of the curl. "This *is* good. Where did it come from?"

Ignoring his question, Marybah continued. "The Plotists were a fringe group of conspiracy theorists. No one took them seriously. Except perhaps Maliko himself. I used to think that's why I left him. That's what I blamed for the end of our relationship. I'm not so sure now. Maybe I just used his crazy ideas as a convenient excuse. At any rate, I could not deal with his eccentricities any longer, so I left. Beely never forgave me."

"What was different about this group?" he asked. "There are plenty of people who believe in conspiracies."

She laid her pipe in a silver tray before nibbling on another curl. She then took a drink of her ognatia. "The difference was that these men were smart, well-respected, and otherwise grounded. They never made any public proclamations of their ideas, but word got out."

"These ideas—"

"One of them, if I remember correctly, was concerning the springs of the Realms. Maliko was a scholar. He studied the sacred texts. He practically designed and built the Library of Truth himself. First, you have to understand that Maliko believed that the Realms were not the only realm. He theorized that we were but a figment of a place called Adamah."

"What about the springs? What specifically did he theorize about the springs?"

"He said the water of the Realms would all but dry up and that most everything would die. Any living thing remaining would be subject to the whim of an evil dictator."

Maximilian shook his head. "That's where she got it from. She got it from her father."

Marybah shook her head. "She couldn't have."

"Why?"

67

"He made it a point never to involve Beely with such worrisome accounts. I might not have agreed with him, but I can say with complete conviction that he was a man of his word, and he would have never told Beely about such things. I'm not saying he wouldn't have told her eventually, but he died before she was old enough to understand."

"Are you sure?"

"I am."

"Could there be any validity to it? All the water drying up? It's unimaginable. I just don't see how anything of that magnitude could take place," he pondered aloud.

"I could not begin to imagine such a scenario. Has she said anything about the books?"

"What do you mean?"

"Maliko was also convinced that all writings would be banished. Really, the freedom and peace we have now would all but be obliterated. He talked about it endlessly before Beely was born. It used to be an interesting topic of conversation until it became a part of *every* conversation."

"Yes, she has mentioned something to that effect." He paused a moment while digesting the new revelations. "What should I do?"

"You think there is something you can do? And you came to me for the answer?" Marybah laughed as she carried the now empty plate into the kitchen.

He followed closely behind her and demanded, "What's so funny?"

"I left her father for as much. You think I have any answers on how to handle delusions? If in fact they are delusions." Marybah knew much more than she was letting on. She was manipulating the conversation in a way that would shape the outcome to her liking. A more perceptive audience might have noticed this fact, but not Maximilian. He was too preoccupied with saving his wife from suspected paranoia to read the room.

"Of course, they are delusions," he fired back.

"If you are so convinced of that, then prove it. Prove her wrong. Beely is not beyond reason. I'm sure of it."

"How can one prove a negative? How do you prove something wrong if it hasn't even happened yet?"

"Upon what is she basing her beliefs?"

"Signs from God!"

"Well, that's somewhat subjective. What else?"

"Prophecy."

"Do you believe in the prophecy of the elders?" Her voice had softened. She sounded like the most concerned of mothers.

"I guess. I've never really thought much about prophecy before."

"Well, start thinking about it. Look into the ancient texts of the Realms and perhaps even the Biblical texts of the other world. See if any have come true. I'll tell you this. If a prophet has ever been wrong, they cannot be trusted. A true prophet will never be wrong. Start there."

Chapter 9

PUZZLING

Beely thought that the number twelve was probably more symbolic than anything else. She knew the Biblical story of the twelve disciples quite well. She was keenly aware that they were chosen by God, not by a mere person. It struck her as ironic that she would be assembling twelve in her world before the time for the Twelve had even occurred in the other world. She was not clear on how time worked between realms, but she had been taught that the Christ had not yet come. Of this, she was certain. Regardless, finding twelve individuals to unite in a secret effort to stop Ankur from overtaking the Five Realms of Here was a task she was not prepared to undertake.

All she could do was pray for clarity. She was in no hurry to do something so important without first consulting the ultimate source of wisdom. Beely was no stranger to prayer. She, like her father, prayed unceasingly. She knew, however, that prayer did not always bring immediate answers. God, she had been told, works in mysterious ways. Along with prayer, Beely also had to use the wisdom of the Word and seek counsel from other believers.

After many hours of contemplation, Beely had made some preliminary decisions. She would count herself as one of the Twelve. Including Eudox, that left ten trustworthy souls to find. Propo and Duly would make three and four. Contrary to what Eudox had said, she would not count Maximilian out just yet. He was her husband, after all. She loved and trusted him completely. She was uncertain that her goals could be accomplished without Max's support and blessing. She was much less inclined to trust Eudox, yet would do so until proven otherwise. The remaining seven would come in time. She would continue to pray.

As Reverie's steward, Beely was deeply unsettled to learn that a stranger like Eudox knew more about Reverie and empachics than she did. She had never been told that empachics could communicate with people. In fact, it was well known that they were one of the very few intelligent, soulish creatures that did not overtly communicate with others outside of their species. Beely was becoming overwhelmed. The Realms as she knew them were changing, or perhaps they were remaining the same, and she was changing.

Beely sat up against the headboard with her legs crossed. Reverie rested her head on Beely's foot. The curtains were pulled tight, extinguishing any possibility of outside influences infiltrating her private sanctuary. She was not depressed, as her husband feared she had been of late. She had no time for depression. The curtains were kept closed for secrecy. If someone or something was watching, Beely did not want to make it easy for them to see her activities. Maximilian left for work early in the morning. He was often hired to train broraydings.

Beely knew that it was not the broraydings that needed training; it was their handlers that needed it. He would return home from work smelling of sweet hay, wet musk, and the sharp, clover-scented breath of the beasts. Maximilian was good with both people and animals. That was why she had asked him to study Ankur. If anyone could perceive the leader's true intentions, it was Max.

She pulled her satchel up off the floor and opened it wide. She stared deep into the overstuffed bag before reaching in for the cube she was convinced her father had left for her to find. Cubes were not as popular as they once were, but older ones were prized by collectors. The one from her father was not one that a collector would value. It appeared to be just a common box with perhaps a simple solution. She held it up with her thumb and index finger, examining all six sides. It was in pristine condition—no scratches or chips. The box was made of some type of wood and painted a shiny black. She turned it slowly around, catching a glimpse of her face in its glossy finish. She thought she spotted a new wrinkle. She was exhausted, and it showed.

She hesitated before making her first push of what appeared to be the top of the box. She had no idea what to expect. Did her father leave her a paternal message of encouragement or something more diabolic—a warning of inevitable catastrophic disaster? She leaned over and stroked Reverie, more to comfort herself than the chic. She was also procrastinating. What if the box contained nothing of meaning? She then took a deep breath, bracing herself, and began.

The box was slightly larger than her palm. Whatever might be contained inside would be small. She gently rotated a tiny square attachment on the side of the box ninety degrees to the left, but it had no effect on any other pieces. She carefully pushed and pulled at several obvious spots, but still, nothing. For another long span, she slowly turned and flipped the box while pushing, twisting, and sometimes banging it against her hand. She could no longer see her reflection. A dull sheen from her oily skin replaced the once glossy finish. Some boxes were easier to figure out than others. This one was turning out to be rather difficult. Her frustration was growing. She was no longer a child who had time for games.

She exhaled. Depending on the sophistication of the device, it could take hundreds, possibly thousands, of moves to open. She had hoped this puzzle was not so sophisticated. She could have pried it open with a knife, but her father would not have approved. Besides, there was a chance that clues could only be deciphered if opened in the correct order. *Best to play by the rules,* she thought.

After a few more moments of patiently working at the puzzle, she caught her first break. When she turned one of the side pegs forty-five degrees, she was able to partially slide one end past the lowest piece. After turning the only other peg in the opposite direction, the other side slid up as well. She pulled the bottom piece down, and the rest began to fall into place. It took another five minutes, but she had the center of the box exposed. Even Reverie noticed the change in Beely's countenance. The elation did not last long, however. There was absolutely nothing inside the cube.

Her father would have thought of everything. He would have left nothing to chance. She knew there was something valuable about the cube. She stared at the partially dismantled puzzle, shook it hard, and even tapped it on the edge of her nightstand.

Nothing.

Frustrated, she set the cube on the pillow next to her and lay back, closing her eyes. The thought occurred to her that she was attempting to put meaning into things that perhaps had none. Not everything had to be a clue or confirmation. Nonetheless, she would examine the other things she brought home from her father's studio—but first, she would take a much-needed nap. Just as Beely was about to doze off, Reverie sneezed—not once, but three times. Beely sat up and watched as Reverie began sniffing the box. Her sneezing intensified.

"What is it, Reverie?" Beely picked up the cube. She brought it to her nose. There was no discernable odor.

Reverie, in an attempt to get away from the source of her allergic reaction, buried herself under the covers.

Beely reexamined the box. As it tumbled around in her long, graceful fingers, another side of the box loosened. She slid it open the rest of the way. A small, dry, brittle leaf fell onto the bed. Beely gently picked up the crisp sprig and brought it closer to her face until it touched her nose. She inhaled deeply and detected a faint herbal aroma—perhaps too delicate to notice while enclosed in the cube. She pressed the cutting lightly against her tongue. It was distinctively bitter. She knew without a doubt that her father had left her a leaf from the wormwood plant.

She sat in bed, with a small lump that was Reverie not far away, and wondered what a cutting from a fairly common plant could possibly have to do with anything. What message was her father attempting to communicate? Her father had been very much aware of his daughter's fondness for plants and gardening. She was upset with herself for not being able to immediately understand his cryptic clue.

Beely's mind drifted back to a time in her father's studio. There had been a man on the other side of the door. She could not see his face, but she could make out some of what was said.

"This is not a good time. Come back tomorrow, and I will see about it then." Beely's father was standing with his back to his daughter, speaking through the partially opened door.

"This is too important to wait, Maliko."

"Wait, it must. Now, I really need to get back to work."

The man on the other side of the door stuck his foot through the crack and attempted to push his way through.

Maliko glanced at his daughter before pushing the man back. Maliko stepped outside, closing the door behind him.

Beely quickly ran to the door and placed her ear against the smooth hardwood. She knew her dad would not be happy if he caught her listening, but, as was often the case, her curiosity was greater than her restraint.

"What cannot wait until tomorrow?" asked Maliko.

"Do you really want to discuss this out here in the open?" the stranger asked.

"Just be quick about it."

"Fine!" The stranger's voice softened, making it harder for Beely to understand. "Our lives are in danger...is missing...is insisting that he was taken and...we must flee immediately...it's confirmed that your wife..."

Beely cupped her hand around her ear and pressed harder against the door but could not make out any more of what was spoken. When her father came back inside, she immediately sensed he was different. She did not know what to call it, as she had never before seen anyone look that way. Why did the stranger mention her mother? Was her mom in trouble? These were questions she wanted to ask but could not.

"What's wrong, Daddy?"

Maliko put his hand on his daughter's shoulder and drew her to his side. "Nothing for you to worry about, sweetheart. We were just discussing adult things. When you are older, I'll tell you all about it."

"How much older?" she asked.

He looked deep into his young daughter's eyes—she was not quite ten—and knelt down before her. He took her hands in his and said, "I want you to remember something very important."

"Okay."

"Someday this place will be yours." He waved his hand through the air. "If you want, everything here will be yours. All of my research, writings, and inventions will go to you—no one else—but only when you are old enough. You must promise you will never enter without me, or until you are older."

"How much older? I'm already old enough to understand."

"Yes, you are, but you are not old enough to carry the weight of that understanding. Promise me, Beely Rembree."

"I promise." She raised her arms and wrapped them around her father's waist. She squeezed hard and whispered, "I love you, Daddy."

It was not until her father had died under mysterious circumstances that she remembered the incident. So much time had elapsed that she did not immediately connect the man's urgency to her father's fate, but now, sitting in bed examining her father's personal effects, she could not help but wonder. Could the man have been warning her father? Is that why her father chose that day to give her access to his most prized possessions and secrets? She also considered that the man behind the door might have been Eudox. She would be sure to ask him, if and when she ever saw him again.

She placed the wormwood back in its hiding spot. She would take it to Duly later. Maybe he would know what it meant. She had another reason to visit Duly as well; she needed to know if he was willing to become a member of the Twelve. She knew he would, after a bit of protest. He could never say no to Beely.

She opened her satchel once again. She took out her father's leatherbound book. A small painted portrait of two young men fell out. She had never seen it before. She thought one of the young men resembled her father, but she could not be certain. She thought the other man was very handsome, but she had never seen him before. She looked on the back to see if there was an inscription. There was not. She flipped it back over to study it more carefully. She set the small painting on her nightstand and sighed. She was so confused. Just because she found these things in her father's studio did not mean they were intended for her. Perhaps they meant nothing of any importance whatsoever. How could she possibly know?

She pulled a blanket over her head and sank deep down into warm serenity until the realm above disappeared, and she could only feel Reverie next to her. She ran her fingers through Reverie's soft fur. The chic immediately began to purr. That is when it struck her. The look on her father's face after he had spoken to the stranger. It was fear.

Beely could have stayed under the covers for the rest of the day. She did not want to face the insurmountable tasks before her. Thoughts were spinning wildly in her head, but the more Reverie purred, the more comforted she felt. Everything would be okay. All would be well. She kept repeating that mantra over and over.

Chapter 10

BOOKS

She could hear him speaking to the books before she had even stepped foot into the Library of Truth. Beely admired Duly's love for words. She herself revered the Word of God, and she respected the philosophies of the wise, but she wished she had Duly's passion. She sometimes felt guilty for opting to toil in her gardens rather than spending more time in God's Word. For Beely, seedlings represented new beginnings, hope, and possibilities. They also marked the passage of time and memories, reminding her of her own inevitable mortality. She saw God's story through His living creation, but she knew nothing could tell the story better than the Word itself.

Before she stepped over the threshold of the library, Duly had scurried over with a pair of foot coverings. He handed them to Beely and exclaimed, "I know you have been out in the dirt with those plants of yours. I wish I had something big enough to cover your entire body! In fact, that's my next project—to come up with a way to clean people like you, people

that bring foreign particles of decimation into my sanctuary!"
Duly stopped to think. He twirled a finger into the air before
ending with a snap. "A suction tube of some sort. Something to
suck up the filth!"

Beely scowled and said, "Well, it's good to see you, too!
You're certainly in a mood." She sat down on a wooden bench
next to the entrance and began placing the coverings over her
sandals.

"My mood is no different than it ever is, which must mean
you are the one who is in a mood." Duly diverted his attention
away from Beely in order to toss foot coverings to another
patron.

"So, this is standard now? These foot robes?" asked Beely.

"Until I figure out a better solution, yes. Creatures are
absolutely filthy; you know that, right? All beings…parasites on
them, in them, around them."

"My goodness. I must truly be in a bad mood!"

"What is that supposed to mean?"

Shaking her head, she turned and began walking. "Come,
let's go to your quarters. We have lots to discuss." Beely was
dressed in her finest attire, wearing her best copper headdress.
Her braids had never looked better, and she had even applied a
bit of face tint—a rarity indeed. Whether Duly knew it or not,
Beely had great respect for the library and its caretaker.

Duly's legs were only a third the size of Beely's, but he
speedily passed her by, making it to his quarters first so he
could clear a path from the door to the sitting area. Beely
arrived just in time to see him spraying floral incense. She had
no idea what the incense smelled like because the offensive
odor of a Braewicker's home was impenetrable. It was a thick,
stagnant scent of dirty rags, moist parchment, and the lingering
pungency of decaying food scraps.

Beely carefully maneuvered around the books, teacups,
plates, clothing, and other personal effects as she found her way

to the only chair free of the same. She slowly lowered herself onto a tufted feather chair. She looked around the room as Duly banged and clacked his way to a piping hot pot of ognatia. He poured two servings, placed them on a tray, and brought them over to Beely.

"What brings you back to the library so soon?" asked Duly.

"You'll need to sit down first."

Duly obliged and took the seat right next to Beely, ignoring all the clutter as he eased into the chair.

Beely reached into her bag, pulled out the black puzzle cube, and handed it to Duly.

Duly brought the cube so close to his face that his breath left a mark on its polished exterior. After a few moments of very superficial inspection, he handed it back to Beely.

"What do you make of it?" she asked.

"Either someone stored this in a cupboard with bitter herbs or there's a piece of wormwood in there—but why would anyone put wormwood in a cube?"

"That's what I want you to tell me. My father left it for me to find. What significance could it have?"

"Wormwood?" Duly looked over at his prized bookcase. After a moment, he jumped down off his chair and quickly retrieved a book from the lowest shelf. He wet a finger and leafed through the pages. He mumbled, "Revelation 8:11." Finding what he was looking for, he sat back down, never taking his eyes off the page. "The name of the star is wormwood. A third of the waters became wormwood, and many people died from the water, because it had been made bitter."

"My father left that for me long ago. How could he have known what seems to be happening today?"

"I have no idea what you are talking about," said Duly.

"Of course you don't, but you will soon enough. That brings me to the other reason I am here today. I need you to join the effort to protect our kingdoms."

"Since when have the kingdoms needed protecting?" asked Duly.

"There will be a great battle."

Duly poured more ognatia as he contemplated how to respond. "I'm not entirely sure what battle is to come, if any at all. I do know my calling is to these books. That's all, nothing more."

"There's always more. This cube was my third sign. I am convinced that Ankur of Okrad plans on unifying the Five Realms under his sole control."

"Ah. That is what Maximilian warned me about. You have succumbed to delusions of grandeur. Our sweet, sweet Beely."

"What has Max been telling you?" She stood, towering over Duly, her copper headdress catching the lamplight with a sharp, metallic shimmer as it emitted a faint, authoritative *clink*. Duly's shoulders drew inward as if bracing for impact. His breathing grew shallow and quick. She lowered her voice into a sharp, cold tone. "I tell you this, Braewicker, heed *my* warning. The Five Realms of Here are in danger! Life as we know it will cease to exist if we don't act soon."

Duly raised his arms, shielding his face, his fingers trembling, and shrank back in shock. Beely, steely-eyed, continued to stare down at the stunned sniblet.

Beely withdrew back to her overstuffed chair. Her eyes grew large, and her voice softened. "Oh goodness. I'm sorry, Duly. I didn't mean to startle you. I was just trying to get your attention, and my fear got the best of me."

Duly slid to the floor, holding his belly, laughing uncontrollably. "You could never scare me, Beely, and neither could that husband of yours. He wanted me to try and talk some sense into you. He is most worried about your health."

Beely looked at Duly with disdain. She did not appreciate his mockery. "Don't worry about Max, and don't worry about my health. I am fine. I have had three signs. Three signs in themselves are a sign. I know I am right."

"What were the signs?"

"To begin with, the fabled tiny salafus is no longer a fable. I saw one. It showed me a vision of darkness and death over every kingdom. Then, there was the water on my table at home. It should have rolled off the table, but it miraculously stopped flowing. It sounds crazy, I know, but it was a sign. Now the wormwood. I can't ignore where all of this is leading."

Duly sighed. "The last time you were here you were going on and on about the books. That someone or something was going to destroy the written word and that I must protect them. So, which is it? The water or the books?"

"Why can't it be both? Both—and more."

"Do you believe that your God is sovereign?"

Beely did not answer right away. The only sound between them was the faint bubbling of the teapot and the soft settling of books on their shelves. Duly held still, watching her, waiting.

'Of course I do."

"Then what can you do to stop His sovereignty? 'Wherever a tree falls, there it shall lie.' That's from the book you follow."

"You and I are part of His sovereignty. He knew the choices we would make before we ever existed."

"Beely, you know I don't care for the living. I can't stand anything that doesn't simply let things be. Most creatures are selfish, dirty, and contrary. Why do you think I like it here so much? The books don't cause problems unless they are opened—or remain unopened as the case may be. It's not until readers interpret the books that the problems begin. Books are quiet unless I choose to listen to them."

"Would you agree that everyone, whether you like them or not, should have the same choices as you—to open the books, to interpret them, to act upon them?" asked Beely.

"I don't stop anyone who enters. They are welcome to read as they please as long as they obey the rules."

"How would you feel if Ankur said that no one, including you, could do anything without his approval? If Ankur controls the water, he controls everything. The people, the food…the books. Nothing will be out of his control."

"All right, all right! If I say I believe you, will you stop trying to convince me?"

"I don't need to convince you. It will become evident soon enough."

"I will do only one thing if I join you on this Plotist agenda of yours."

"Any support you give will be appreciated. There are very few I can trust."

"I will see to it that the books are protected. I'll make it my mission that the Word of your God will survive any treasonous effort by this Ankur, or anyone else for that matter."

"Thank you, Duly. You are one of my trustworthy twelve. I know the library is in good hands with you."

"Now that that's settled, will you stay for dinner?"

Beely looked over at Duly's messy kitchen and could not think of an excuse fast enough to get out of dining, but if Duly was willing to suffer for the cause, she thought she could do the same. "Dinner sounds marvelous, my friend."

While Duly began to clear a spot off the table, he asked, "Who are the other eleven?"

"Well, maybe you could help me with that."

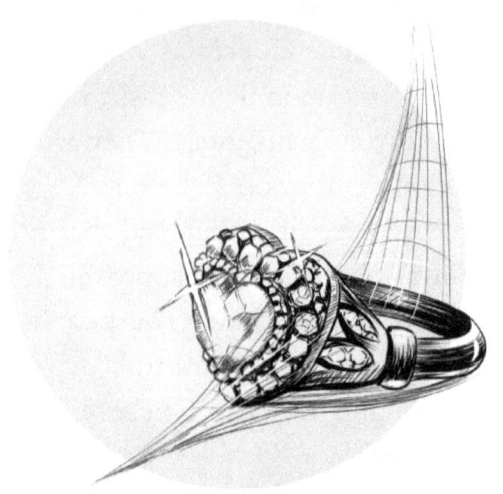

Chapter 11

BROKEN

(three turnings earlier)

High within the ancient timber of Okrad sat Ankur's dwelling, a residence of singular prestige. It boasted a grandeur that even Marybah's famed Picalo home could not match, yet it lacked its soul. In place of Marybah's organic textures and wood-spun harmony, Ankur's home was a gallery of the artificial. Clad in ornate, fabricated embellishments and shivering panes of synthetic glass, the structure felt alien—a cold, molded shell that had long ago traded the warmth of the forest for the precision of the machine.

His had once been a tasteful home, but it had become garish with gold curtains, oversized bronze sculptures, and more taxidermied animals than one could count. Many who visited the house of Ankur questioned its ostentatiousness. He remarked on more than one occasion that the space was intended for the family he planned to have once his efforts for Okrad were fully realized.

Everything Ankur did seemed to be for the benefit of Okrad. He was well-regarded by the inhabitants, and very few questioned his high standard of living. Everyone in the community was living better and toiling less; they were prosperous as never before. Life had become much easier due to their leader's tireless efforts.

This was Athaliah's first time dining at her cousin's house. She was both excited and nervous for her fiancé to meet the only family she had—aside from her parents. Her anxiousness manifested as hiccups, which she managed to subdue before arriving, though her sweaty palms proved more difficult. Sweaty palms always seemed to plague Athaliah at the most inconvenient of times. Ankur had invited her and Nicholas to dine shortly after Athaliah returned from her less-than-successful trip to the Land of Mana.

"I'm amazed at how you got such a large and ornate dining table so high up in this type of dwelling," said Nicholas. He and Athaliah sat on the opposite side of the long, polished table from their host. Nicholas was dressed in his finest attire, which included a dinner jacket. He had even abandoned the standard Okrad sandals for a new pair of fully enclosed shoes he had acquired just for the occasion. He was honored to be dining at such an influential man's home, but more than that, he wanted to show respect to his fiancée's cousin.

"It was built right where it stands. All of the materials were brought up separately. In fact, most everything of any substantial size had to be built on-site," said Ankur.

"That's amazing, sir. It's very beautiful," replied Nicholas.

Athaliah only heard part of the conversation; she was too preoccupied watching the servers bring out the most exquisite food she had ever seen, much less tasted. She finally worked up the courage to take a sip from her drink without fear of her glass slipping. Her nerves had calmed, and so had her sweaty palms.

Ankur stabbed a piece of meat off of a serving tray with a large knife as he looked at Nicholas and asked, "What is it you do for a living?"

Nicholas jumped at the sound of the knife hitting the tray. He was taken aback by Ankur's aggressive table manners but quickly regained his composure. "I'm a curator of antiquities."

"What type of antiquities? Do you have a specialty?" Before Nicholas had time to answer, Ankur looked at Athaliah with a hint of disgust and said, "You're using the wrong utensil." He shook his head as if disappointed. "When the main course is served, you use the larger instruments."

"Oh, I'm sorry," said Athaliah.

Nicholas answered, "I studied art, but I have a natural affinity for books."

"He's very good at what he does," said Athaliah.

"What exactly do you do, Nicholas?" asked Ankur, never bothering to acknowledge Athaliah.

Nicholas rubbed Athaliah's knee under the table and replied, "I research and maintain a catalogue of works that have had a substantial influence on various clans, villages, and kingdoms. I focus primarily on works of art and literature."

Ankur snapped his fingers and pointed at the not-quite-full glasses on the table. A server instantly topped off their drinks. "I had no idea such qualitative data was collected. Interesting. Does it require a lot of traveling?" inquired Ankur.

Athaliah answered, "Yes. It's amazing really. I've actually gone with him on one of his more remote trips. Nicholas is a lot like you; he has a great rapport with strangers." Athaliah and Nicholas looked at each other affectionately. Athaliah's face flushed, and she could not hide her love for the man she would soon marry.

Ankur shook his head ever so subtly. He ground his teeth and slowly turned his head away from Athaliah. He disapproved of her interruptions, but she was not getting his hints to cease. He looked directly at Nicholas and asked, "Who do you do this curating for?"

Nicholas was surprised but pleased with the attention he was getting from such a successful person as Ankur. Most people found his work boring and rarely asked questions. "There are quite a few sponsors actually. I don't know them all. It's a very wealthy group. At some point, someone thought it was important to maintain the integrity of our most valuable artistic and intellectual properties. A committee was formed, and I was fortunate enough to be in the right place at the right time, I suppose."

"You're much too modest, Nick." Athaliah turned from her fiancé to her cousin. "He's the absolute perfect person for this type of work." She put her arm around Nicholas and kissed him on the cheek. "They are lucky to have you."

"Well, it's nice to know you are good at something," said Ankur.

"Excuse me?" asked Nicholas.

"Not you. Your admirer," said Ankur without looking up from his plate.

"I don't know what you mean," said Athaliah.

"Of course you don't, dear," responded Ankur, still not bothering to look at his cousin.

The conversation continued in much the same vein throughout the rest of dinner. Athaliah's palms had never been so damp. She nervously and repeatedly rubbed them on her dress until eventually excusing herself to visit the restroom.

She walked around the large trunk at the center of Ankur's house, running her fingers along the textured, unbroken bark while contemplating her cousin's caustic behavior. He had been harsh since her return from her last assignment, but tonight he had been downright mean. She feared he was angry that she had not spoken with Ekrad Oren when he had first asked. Athaliah was furious with herself. How could she have been so naive as to trust that meddling willow tree?

She let herself into the restroom and quietly closed the door. She had never been in a bathroom so high in a tree before; only the wealthiest citizens lived in such extravagance. She felt the cool, rubbery skin of a Vessel-Vine that ran along behind the sink and toilet. It was a specialized plant that thrummed with the faint, rhythmic pulse of water being carried into and out of the residence. Athaliah was surprised that the plant grew so far up into a house like this.

She did not need to use the restroom. She only needed a few moments alone. She looked deeply into the reflective glass hanging above the sink. The face looking back at her was almost unrecognizable. Without any warning, tears began to flow. Athaliah tried hard to repress the raw emotion erupting from deep within her. She could not risk Ankur hearing her weakness. He was already so critical of her every move. The harder she tried to stop the tears, the more they seemed to flow.

She sobbed as quietly as possible, only stopping when there was a rap at the door. Athaliah quickly wiped the tears from her eyes. Behind the closed door, a servant asked if everything was okay. Athaliah assured her that she was fine.

Athaliah took a deep breath, straightened her hair, and pinched her cheeks for a little color. She vowed to find the inner strength to face her cousin with confidence. She opened the door and started toward the dining room. She was quickly stopped by a firm grasp on her shoulder. It was one of Ankur's helpers.

"Yes? May I help you?" asked Athaliah, startled.

The woman spoke so softly that Athaliah had to turn her ear and lean in. "Your cousin does not have your best interests in mind. You must be very careful." She was oddly solemn, and a bit unsteady as her eyes darted back and forth.

"Do I know you?"

The servant seemed to relax a bit. "No, I am one of your cousin's servants." She carefully moved a strand of Athaliah's hair back into place and smiled. "I know who you are, though. Rather, I knew your mother. She was a lovely lady."

"You knew my mother?"

"Yes. We studied together for a while at the same school. She was a strong voice—always stood up for those who had less. I remember she was a great storyteller. She was funny and always passionate. Most of all, she was kind—so young to be so kind."

"What's your name?"

"Jossie. I was not a close friend, but I think she would remember me."

Something in Athaliah's thoughts brought about an abrupt, harsh response. "Well, perhaps you should not be observing things that are none of your business! My cousin has been very good to me since I moved here." Athaliah was surprised at her own rude tone, as well as her defense of her cousin who had been anything but good to her of late.

"I am sorry. What you say is true. I should not meddle in other people's affairs. Please accept my apology." The servant may have been cautious at the start of the conversation, but now she seemed almost remorseful. "Please, don't mention to your cousin that I spoke. I am not well. I sometimes speak when I should not."

Athaliah was unsure how to respond. In the end, she simply shrugged her shoulders and nodded. The woman rushed off before Athaliah could ask any more questions. She wished she had been less abrasive. Athaliah had not felt like herself lately. She could not remember the last time she spoke to someone so harshly.

When Athaliah found her way back to the dining table, her fiancé and cousin were no longer there. She looked around the room but saw no one. She scanned the adjacent rooms until noticing two lights illuminating the hanging bridge connecting the main house to the dining hall. She took a light from the sconce and walked out to join them.

"Ankur was just showing me the view of the city lights. It's quite beautiful up here, isn't it?" asked Nicholas.

"It sure is," answered Athaliah.

"Someday the two of you can have a place like this. It's like living on the very air itself." As if on cue, a wind current pushed the bridge, causing it to gently sway.

Nicholas grabbed Athaliah in his arms to hold her steady. "Guess what, dear?"

"What?" asked Athaliah.

"Ankur has asked me to come work for him."

Athaliah stifled her surprise, but her response was stiff. "Oh, really?"

Ankur smiled and nodded. He took a step forward, subtly positioning himself on the bridge so that he stood between Nicholas and Athaliah, effectively claiming the space next to the young man. "Your gentleman friend here has quite an impressive resume. I could use someone like him in the Realm of Many."

"Doing what?" she asked.

"Procuring antiquities, what else?" answered Ankur.

Athaliah looked from Ankur to Nicholas. "The Realm of Many is so vast and far away, and we are to be married in less than a cycle." She tried not to sound desperate, but it was futile. She had a very bad feeling.

"Don't worry, sweetheart. We can postpone the wedding for just a bit. It's not like we were having a big wedding with lots of guests. This is a great opportunity for me—for us."

Ankur quickly jumped in. "Besides, maybe you should have a larger wedding. I could help you with that."

"I don't want a larger wedding. We've had this planned. You proposed to me, remember?"

"Oh, come now, child," said Ankur. "Don't start the marriage with so many demands. That couldn't end well." Ankur laughed smugly and patted Nicholas on the arm.

Athaliah had become irreversibly flustered. She was shocked at how the evening had progressed. Her mouth was dry, and her throat constricted, rendering her speechless. The two men in her life seemed to be considerate of everything but her. She did not want to make a scene without understanding their exact motivations and intentions.

"Well, I guess we could make a go of it someplace else. A little more time before the wedding is not the end of the realms," she finally managed to whisper.

Ankur was quick to respond. "I need you here, Athaliah. Things are not settled in the Land of Mana yet, remember? Don't worry. We will work out all these wedding details later. Come, let's have a drink to celebrate the new careers for you both. You're headed to a prosperous future!"

Ankur put his arm over Nicholas' shoulder as they began walking the rest of the way across the bridge. Athaliah stood behind and watched the two happy fellows excitedly discussing a future that felt increasingly foreign to her. Nothing, it seemed, was what she had expected.

Perhaps Jossie, the servant, was right. Maybe Ankur did not have her best interests in mind. She wiped her palms on her dress one last time and followed after her increasingly hazy future.

Chapter 12

THE PLOTIST

The Five Realms of Here might seem like an imaginary place to those from other worlds. There were no wars in the Five Realms, and no one went without food. Everyone who wanted a home had one. All basic necessities were met because almost every able body willingly worked and contributed to a stable economic system. All creatures were able to pursue careers wherever their gifts or their hearts led them. Along with a strong work ethic, a high moral standard resided deep within the consciousness of nearly every citizen. However, it was not a perfect world filled with infallible inhabitants. Although a typical lifespan in the Five Realms was nearly five hundred turnings, there was still death and illness. Relationships were not always perfect. Sadness and loneliness, though not common, were far from foreign. There were just enough obstacles to keep those in the Realms striving toward the pursuit of better.

Maximilian and Beely were not exactly the most typical couple in the Five Realms. Beely lost her father when she was very young. His absence was complicated by the fact that her parents were estranged before his death. Marybah and Maliko had not spoken long before he passed. They had often relied upon Beely to convey necessary information between them. It was this role that eventually caused a rift between the daughter and her mother. Max's family had also suffered an unexpected loss. His only brother died at the age of eighteen from an accident involving a brorayding. Maximilian cherished his older brother; there was no one he looked up to more. He was the one who had taught Maximilian the mysteries of the greatest beasts in the Realms.

Beely and Max had an instant connection from their very first encounter. Nothing could have quenched the spark that had been so impetuously ignited. They fell in love and married in record time by Five Realm standards. They were two broken souls who found comfort in their empathy for one another's heartache. They also shared a passion for the Word of God, art, and nature. Even with all that they had in common, however, it would always be a relationship with frailty as its cornerstone.

Several turnings after their marriage, Max befriended his mother-in-law. He had hoped Marybah's insight might help him better understand the sometimes-tenuous relationship that had developed between him and Beely. Until recently, he had only met with Marybah a few times. He knew his wife would not be pleased if she discovered he was discussing their relationship with "the enemy," as she would put it, but it was a risk worth taking—or so he thought. His intentions were not entirely self-serving. He also considered that a friendship with Marybah might one day help with a reconciliation between mother and daughter. Unfortunately, all hopes of any reconciliation were soon to be irreparably shattered.

It had been days since Beely and Max had spoken more than two words to one another. Avoidance was not hard between two busy people, but there was something that had been eating away at Max for many moons. In the end, he simply took a direct approach. "I heard you have been meeting with Propo." He extended a cup of ognatia to his wife.

She paused at the sound of his voice. Beely was in her shade garden tying vines to a trellis. The vines needed no tending, but the activity calmed her and allowed her to think more clearly. "Yes, I have seen him a few times recently. Once was to give him a gift from my father. My father loved him dearly." She accepted the warm drink, which released a sharp, spicy aroma that cut through the damp scent of the garden, and sat on a nearby bench that had been carved from an ancient stump.

Max sat next to her. "Yes, you have told me how much your father thought of Propo, but do you think it wise to be seen with him?"

"What? Do you think he might soil my reputation? You know very well I couldn't care less what gossips have to say. Besides, Propo is a good man."

"A good man he may very well be, but he is also a plotist, and everyone knows it."

"How has that word escaped my vocabulary?" She set her drink down and returned to weaving vines through the trellis. "It seems like everyone is aware of plotism but me."

"Plotist."

"What?" she asked.

"It's not 'plotism.' It's 'plotist.' It's referring to people who plot."

"Yes, I realize that. I was simply using the word in its broadest philosophical form."

"I see."

Beely sat back down and put her hand on her husband's knee. "What would you have me do? I know bad things are happening, and no matter the curious ability of others to hide their heads in the thick branches of the picalo, I must act. Something must be done."

"Why you? Can't someone else do whatever it is that needs doing?"

"Let me ask you this. If you knew with complete conviction that what I have been saying is true—that Ankur plans to control the water, ban the written Word, and unite the Five Realms under his sole authority—would you not want me to do something about it? Better yet, wouldn't you join me and the other plotists in the battle?"

"Your father was under some of the same delusions. You know that, right?"

"How would you have come to such a conclusion? You don't know anything about my father's theories on the changing winds."

A look of confidence overtook him. "Ah, so you admit it, then. You suffer the same delusions."

Beely kept her outward composure, but underneath, she was boiling. "They were not delusions. Everything he theorized has started to happen."

"Really? What's happening, Beely?" Max walked over to a hand pump and began to pump water out of an underground spring. He cupped a handful of water and angrily flung it over the garden. "What is this coming out? Is it imaginary water?" He gestured sharply toward the flowing stream. You have books with the Word of God all throughout the house. Ankur can barely keep his own realm united, let alone all Five Realms."

"Have you ever heard of birth pangs, Max? Change does not happen all at once. There is an order to it all."

"What order? There is no evidence of your father's premonitions coming true."

"You know as well as I that no realms have ever had leaders. God is our leader. Ankur and Okrad are blasphemous. It all starts small and grows."

"If the people of Okrad want a leader, that's their business. It's up to them, and it has nothing to do with us. Furthermore, I think you have not been completely honest with me in regard to Ankur."

"What do you mean?"

"I saw the picture you just put on your nightstand—your father and Ankur standing side by side. Beely's breath caught in her throat, her hands going suddenly still against the vines. You knew all about Ankur before you sent me to spy on him."

"What are you saying? That the man in the portrait is Ankur? My father never mentioned anything about him."

"Oh, come on, Beely. Stop it! Now you're lying to yourself. Enough already."

"I promise. I didn't know that was Ankur. I just found that little painting in my father's studio. I don't think he intended for anyone to see it." Beely stood up and looked out over her garden, lost in thought.

"I've been speaking to your mother."

Beely tried not to sound surprised, or worse, hurt. "Why?"

"I'm worried about you. That's why."

"How could speaking to my mother help you with that?"

"She's dealt with this before."

"Excuse me?"

"With your father. I thought she might have some advice."

Beely threw up her arms in exasperation. "And did she?"

"She did, but you're not going to like it."

"What I don't like is you conspiring behind my back—my own husband. You, of all people, know how I feel about her."

Max walked behind Beely and paused, his hands hovering just short of her shoulders. For a brief moment, he seemed uncertain, as though weighing his words—and himself. Then, he gently wrapped his arms around her. "I love you. I would do anything in this world to help you, even if it means conspiring with the enemy."

Beely pulled away from him, obviously hurt. "I just need you to have faith in me, to trust me."

"Of course, I trust you." He took her hand and pointed to their house and all the land surrounding it. "Look at what we have done—what you have done with no help from your mother or anyone else. We are a team. No matter what happens, never forget that."

Beely turned into her husband's embrace and quietly wept. She felt overwhelmed and unsteady. The mission before her was barely underway, yet she was already feeling lost. Was her father actually affiliated with Ankur in some way? Was her own mother trying to interfere with her life once again? She needed her husband's support. She needed him to believe her. Maximilian held her in his arms until she pulled away, wiping the corners of her eyes. She did not like it when others saw her vulnerability, not even those closest to her.

"If we are a team, and you love me as you say you do, meet Propo and me tonight. I took the fruit that you brought to me to be analyzed. We can both see the results together. If I'm wrong, and it turns out to be nothing, I will give up my pursuit of this."

"You promise?" he asked.

"I do."

Chapter 13

PROOF

"It has been genetically modified. How, I cannot say." The man in the strange outfit held his mouth open, gripping his chin between two fingers and a thumb. He moved his jaw back and forth in a circular motion. "Een moa so, I cahn ell yew—"

Propo interrupted, "Excuse me, but we can't understand you when you're doing that thing with your jaw."

The man lowered his hand and continued. "My apologies. My jaw gets extraordinarily tight when I'm stressed. Why am I stressed, you ask? My wife says it's because I work too much." He took a deep breath and exhaled slowly. "I'm almost two hundred turnings old with eight children still at home—"

Beely took her turn to interrupt. "I'm sorry—or should I say congratulations? Eight children is quite a blessing." She glanced at Propo and grimaced.

"Oh, that's not all of them; that's just the ones still living at home. Why do you think I need to do extracurricular activities like this?" He flicked his fingers as if counting imaginary coins.

"We are in a bit of a hurry. If you could just give us your findings, we'll pay you and be on our way," said Propo, not concealing his growing impatience.

The man took no offense at Propo's frankness. "Of course, I understand. Busy. We are all busy. Busy, busy, busy." He looked back down at the object on the table. "I don't know why anyone would want to modify food in this manner."

Propo and Beely listened attentively to the scientist while he poked and prodded the souring specimen. According to his own introduction—in which he never gave his name—he was a genius superior to all geniuses. Neither Beely nor Propo had heard of him before. He was recommended by Eudox, the man Beely had met at her father's studio.

"What does it do?" asked Propo.

"What does what do?" repeated the self-proclaimed genius as he removed his spectacles.

"What are those two square-framed glass things you had covering your eyes?" asked Beely, pointing to the spectacles.

"These help me focus up close. My own invention. I'm going to call them focals."

"You have issues with your sight? No one in the Realms has eye deficiencies," said Propo.

"Did I say I had eye deficiencies? I did not. You need to listen better." The man rotated his left shoulder in a full circle and then repeated the motion with his right shoulder. "*You* need ear focals, I do believe. Yes, I should invent focals for the ears to enhance hearing." He raised his focals and shook them in Propo's direction. "These help me to focus better. I can see the minutest of details without the use of a handheld magnifier."

"Okay, that's all you had to say," protested Propo.

Beely quickly got back on topic. "What is the modification for? What effect does it have on those who eat the fruit?"

"I would need to keep it longer. Conduct some experiments," he responded.

Beely kept flexing her fingers. It was something she did when nervous or agitated. Watching the scientist continuously stretch his own stiff joints was making her own tic worse. Her nervous habit did not go unnoticed by Propo. "What's wrong with you?"

"What do you mean?" she asked.

"You're as nervous as an empachic in a room full of crying children," said Propo.

"You noticed?" she asked.

"Of course I noticed."

"I need more conclusive evidence!" she shot back.

"You heard the man. He said he would do more experiments. Try to relax."

"No, I need more evidence now. Tonight."

The scientist interjected, "I don't think it will take long, but I certainly won't have an answer for you tonight, dear." He placed his hands on the lab table, leaned forward, and began to stretch his calves.

Propo gave a puzzled glance toward the scientist and then turned to Beely. "We've been gathering evidence for a few cycles. What's a few more days, Bee?"

"I promised Max that if I could not find any proof, I would give up my pursuit of the changing winds. He still doesn't believe that any of it is true."

"Was that wise?" Propo asked. He tilted his head toward the fidgeting scientist. "What if he can't find any proof based on this one sample?"

The man cleared his throat and pushed between Propo and Beely on his way to retrieve the bag that he had left sitting on a small metal desk. "If there is anything to be found, I will find it."

"I told him we would have solid proof—tonight," implored Beely.

"Lie to him," suggested Propo.

"I would never lie to Max. We might have our problems, but trust is not one of them. I won't betray our relationship."

"Come...look at this." The scientist, wearing his focals, leaned over the specimen holding a syringe that he had just retrieved from his bag. He placed the syringe in his mouth to free his hands. He then made a small incision in the center of the fruit's white flesh. He took the syringe and suctioned a small amount of liquid from the area of the incision.

"What are we looking at?" asked Propo, leaning over Beely's shoulder for a better view.

"You are looking at an incredibly clever genius. I mean, I'm not just a genius. I'm an artist."

Beely's excitement over the good news superseded her growing annoyance with the person discovering it. "What is it?"

The scientist moved away from the table. "I wouldn't want to contaminate the specimen." As he unzipped his protective apparel, he moved over to the desk and sat. "It's a drug. I've only seen it once before. When it enters the body, it self-replicates until—or unless—the host takes an antidote."

"What's the antidote?" asked Propo.

"I have no idea. I guess you still need those hearing focals. I've only seen this drug once."

"Where did you see it before? How do you know that it replicates?" asked Beely.

The scientist pulled out a long chewing stick from his front shirt pocket, which he promptly let hang from his mouth. The stick moved up and down as he chewed. He casually put his feet on the desk. He finally responded as his two eager clients looked on impatiently. "A colleague happened upon it. He asked me to take a look. It was many moons ago. The only reason I remembered was because of the way the chemical moved. It's rare that this type of chemical moves at all, but the way it moves is even stranger." He sat up in his chair and scrawled something in the desktop dust with his finger. Motes of gray dust swirled in the dim light as his finger traced a path.

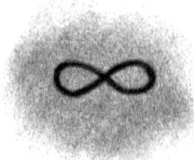

$$\frac{a}{(1-r)}$$

Propo tilted his head to the left and then to the right. "That looks like some sort of equation."

"It seems we have two geniuses in the room." The man rolled his eyes and turned toward Beely before continuing. "The drug, or virus I might say, moves like this." He drew a figure underneath the equation as he continued to explain what it meant. "See how it turns back in on itself? It's called a lemniscate. Like a snake eating its own tail, only it never finishes the meal. Each time it crosses its own path, it creates another molecule. This repeats into infinity."

$$\infty$$

"I don't know if the how is as important as the what. What does it do to the host?" asked Beely.

"I couldn't venture to conjecture. It's a drug. Whatever it does is precisely calculated and meticulously manufactured."

"It's not natural," added Propo.

"Genius!" The man looked at Beely and asked, "Where did you find this one?" He continued, "It is not naturally occurring in the fruit. It has been introduced."

Propo ignored the man's jab and addressed Beely. "Is that enough to satisfy Maximilian?"

"I certainly hope so." She walked to a window and pushed the curtain just enough to peek out. "He should have been here already. He knows the location." She quickly closed the curtain as if she had seen something troubling. She whispered to the scientist, "Are you expecting company?"

"Only you. I did this as a favor for Eudox. This is not my lab. No one knows I'm here."

Propo took a quick peek through a crack in the curtain. "Then who are those thugs sizing up the place? They're wearing thick, dark uniforms, and one has heavy restraints hanging from his belt."

Beely's eyes quickly darted around the room. "Is there another way out of here?" The man nodded affirmatively and pointed down a dark hallway.

"What's wrong, Bee?" asked Propo, still speaking in hushed tones.

"I have a very bad feeling. You stay here and see what those men want. Meet me at our special location in two cycles." She turned and asked her host to lead her to the other exit. He sensed her urgency and quickly obliged. He gathered a few things, including the specimen, and rushed with Beely toward the rear of the building.

There was a hard rap on the door. Propo waited a few moments to make sure that Beely had made her escape. Once satisfied she was safely on her way, he opened the door. "May I help you?" He stared up at two large men standing before him. Up close, their uniforms looked official, perhaps private security, and their grim expressions promised zero tolerance for resistance. Before either of them had time to answer, Maximilian pushed between them, and walked through the door.

"Where is she?" demanded Maximilian.

Although surprised to see Maximilian, Propo tried to play it cool. "Who?"

"My wife. Don't play games with me, Propo."

"She's not here. She left some time ago. She said you were supposed to have met us. What's with the entourage? She didn't mention inviting anyone else."

"Look, Propo. Beely is not well. If you care about her, you'll tell us where she is."

"Not well? What in the Realms are you talking about?"

"It's not just me. Her mother agrees. She has fallen to the same delusions as her father. It could be genetic."

"Genetic? Since when is a set of beliefs genetic?" asked Propo, more sincerely than he thought possible.

"I just want to help my wife, keep her safe, that's all."

Propo looked down at the paperwork in Maximilian's hand. "Oh, wow. You got her mother's signature to have her committed, didn't you? It only takes two—the two most important people in her life: a mother and a husband. Who are the Plotists, now?"

Max resented the remark but did not react. "I'm not having anyone committed—just evaluated, that's all."

One of the men interrupted, "Mr. Wren, would you like us to look around?"

"Please," answered Maximilian.

"You might be interested to know that the fruit turned out to be genetically altered with a manufactured chemical. Beely was right. Delusions don't usually come with evidence, do they?" Propo was trying hard not to show his anger. He needed to salvage any possibility that Maximilian might join their effort to stop Ankur.

"You have proof? Well, okay, where is it?"

Propo looked around helplessly, the realization slowly hitting him that any proof that may have existed moments earlier had left with the scientist.

"Well?" asked Maximilian.

"If you had trusted your wife and had been here like she asked, you would have seen the evidence. As it is, you and your thugs scared the scientist away."

"What's his name? I'll give him a visit."

"I don't know his name. He never gave it to us."

"Interesting. Not a problem, really. We know where he works. I'll just come back tomorrow."

Propo scratched his head and ran his fingers through his graying hair. "It gets more interesting."

"Really, how so?"

"This isn't his lab."

"Yes, more interesting indeed." Max shook his head in disbelief.

"Look, Max, I know you don't like or trust me. That's perfectly acceptable. You don't know me, but I would think if there was anyone you could trust for the truth, it would be Beely."

"You're right on both counts; I don't know you, and I don't trust a man who spreads misinformation. You're right on the third count as well. I have trusted Beely, and as soon as Beely is well, I will trust her again."

"I'm afraid trust goes both ways. I don't think she trusts you anymore," Propo said, with a little more bravado than he had intended.

Max angrily took a step toward him. Propo squared off for the return. Both men were prepared to come to blows.

Fortunately for Propo, as Max was much larger and younger, the other two men came back into the room. One of them shrugged his shoulders, indicating they found no one else in the building. The tallest of the two men signaled for the other to go outside to continue the search. He then looked at Max and said, "We'll look around outside, but we're not trackers."

"I understand," responded Max, flatly.

"If you need us again, let us know."

"I will." Maximilian walked over to the lab table. He examined the remnants of the fruit left behind. He looked around for any clue that might reveal something about the scientist who was using the facilities—if, in fact, he was a scientist at all. Max had his doubts.

"Was this the same fruit that I gave to Beely? The one I brought from Okrad?"

"Yes."

"What did this *scientist* have to say about it?"

"He said that it had been modified with a chemically manufactured drug. How or why, he couldn't say."

"What does this drug do?"

"We don't know yet, and with your interruption, we may never know," responded Propo with a little less attitude. Propo could not help but notice the intensity in Maximilian's eyes.

What Propo did not know was that Max had tasted the fruit after Beely sliced it open the night before. A sudden, sour mucus crept down the back of his throat, and a subtle twitch started deep in his jaw muscle—just like the scientist. If what the Plotists believed was true, was it possible he had already been infected? He had no time to think about hypothetical scenarios. He needed to focus all of his energy on finding his wife. He was shocked at how an otherwise normal life could spiral out of control so quickly.

C h a p t e r   1 4

ΛTHΛLIΛH

The two vultures soared in circles above the picturesque landscape.

"Do you see it?" asked Screech.

"I don't need to see it. I can smell exactly where it lies. The aroma is so delectable—unmistakable—and it rises from below like a gift from above," answered Gawker. She was slightly smaller than her male companion, although both birds were large and formidable with beautiful amber feathers. The pair had met while feasting on a rotten crolquet, something closely resembling a pumpkin in both looks and flavor. Their meeting may have been a chance encounter, but the two young birds had traveled as an inseparable pair ever since.

Birds of prey were superfluous in the Five Realms, as the Realms experienced slow rates of decay, and death was not common. Meat, the vultures' preferred choice of sustenance, was always in short supply. When fleshly beings did die, they were quickly buried and kept off-limits to scavengers. This only made the birds' craving for carrion all the greater—a craving seldom satisfied. Screech and Gawker had to make do with less appealing offerings.

Today was different. The smell of meat and death permeated the air.

****

Athaliah had always possessed an exceptionally beautiful physical appearance. The gentle way she interacted with others gave her a radiance beyond what exterior beauty alone could reflect. The way she moved her hands and arms while speaking, though never demonstrative, was as if she were painting with the delicate brush of an artist. Her smile expressed a shyness and an honesty that endeared her to anyone who saw it.

Her magnetism was perhaps most evident in her manner of listening. She only spoke when a smile or a gesture could not impart the necessary sentiment. Her words were few, chosen carefully, and uttered just loudly enough to avoid the need for repeating.

Because she was raised alone, in one of the most remote areas of Okrad, she rarely interacted with people like herself. The native creatures of Okrad were her only friends. Most of the various species around her could use language, but with Athaliah, they rarely needed words. They all loved to be near her. Her favored pals were the chiropters. Chiropters were bats, and they were very misunderstood by almost everyone. The small bats were distant relatives of the much larger broraydings, although they looked nothing alike. The only obvious similarities were their ability to fly and the fact that they were both mammals.

Perhaps what initially endeared Athaliah to the chiros was that they were outcasts. They had few friends outside of their own species. Mostly nocturnal, they were agile and fast in flight. They ate mostly fruit, but they were not opposed to the occasional insect. Her association with these creatures would someday impact her more profoundly than she could ever imagine.

It was no secret that Athaliah grew up a lonely child. As she grew older, she longed for connection. She wanted a relationship as special as the one her mother and father had enjoyed. She longed for someone to laugh with and for someone to share her passion for the creatures of Okrad. She might not have understood fully what grown-up relationships were all about, but she saw how happy and affectionate her parents were. If they had found each other, surely she could find someone too.

When she eventually left home for an apprenticeship with the Institute of Cave Cartography (ICC), it did not take her long to meet someone special. Nicholas worked as a curator in the building next to the ICC. Their meeting was entirely by chance, and it was literally love at first sight. Nicholas had grown up in a large, busy village and had never met someone as sweet and sincere as Athaliah. He could sense her gentleness, a trait he greatly admired, the moment he looked into her eyes. The usually confident and boisterous man stood frozen, his vocal cords paralyzed, as he stammered out the most awkward greeting ever to be witnessed by a group of people waiting in line to order lunch.

Athaliah was unaware of just how oafish Nicholas' attempt at an introduction was. She was also oblivious to the fact that everyone in the cafe was watching them. In her short time in the village, other men had taken notice of her beauty, but she never took notice of them in return. This time was different. As she stared into Nicholas' piercing green eyes, she too was speechless. Of course, Athaliah did not need words to convey her thoughts. She smiled, took her order from the counter, and walked in a way that said, "Follow me." The two had been together ever since.

Nicholas proposed after just a short time. They were in love. The wedding was to take place at her parents' home. Life could not have been more perfect for the once-lonely girl from the remote countryside. She had a successful career in an important village, a wonderful apartment, and a loving relationship that was leading to marriage.

Athaliah had never been happier.

Looking back, she was amazed at how quickly things could change. In the time it had taken to eat one dinner at her cousin's house, her engagement had been disrupted, leaving Athaliah feeling insecure about her relationship with the only man she had ever loved. Nicholas had accepted Ankur's offer to work for him. In a matter of two days, he had resigned from his job, packed most of his belongings, and naively told Athaliah that even though he was postponing their marriage, once settled, the two of them would be much better equipped to start life as a couple.

Her fiancé insisted that instead of a small, intimate wedding, the generous salary from Ankur would allow them to afford an opulent wedding unrivaled by that of any of their friends or family. She believed that he believed the altered plans were for the better. She could not really blame him, she thought. His parents were not well off, and he had no powerful contacts to help his career. That had all changed when he met Ankur.

He would travel the Five Realms, working for a wealthy, powerful man. He would quickly establish a name for himself, gain wealth, and then marry the woman of his dreams, all while Athaliah waited in the wings. She did wait. In the first six cycles of his new employment, Nicholas came home to visit his soon-to-be bride exactly once. She may have been naive, but she was not stupid. Yes, she continued to wait on her love, but she knew it would never be what it could have been before Ankur was involved. She even had the thought that her cousin was purposeful in the demise of her happiness. She would not have been wrong.

Blind ambition often mitigates the sincerest of intentions.

Athaliah clung to the hope that Nicholas would return for her. While she waited, she continued her attempts to gain her cousin's approval. Athaliah was smart and worked diligently at every task given to her. She had never struggled to impress others. Success and affirmation usually came readily for Athaliah, so why did Ankur treat her with such disdain? Was he testing her? Were his demeaning actions simply an attempt to strengthen her already resilient resolve? If so, he was failing.

She began doubting herself. With few friends in the village, no other family nearby, and her sweet chiropters unable to offer comfort, she felt lost. She began acting in ways that were foreign to her. She began to hate herself.

Eight cycles after Nicholas left to begin his new career, Athaliah decided to take matters into her own hands. In order to gain control, she felt the need to gain power. She needed her cousin to trust her. She requested that he meet her in the town square by the water fountain. There would not be many people around, and the jetting water would make it hard for anyone nearby to hear their discussion.

"Athaliah, I'm a very busy man. Why could you not have simply come to my residence?" Ankur sat on the edge of the fountain. His dog sloppily lapped water with his tongue. Most things the dog did were sloppy, as far as Athaliah was concerned. She had never met an animal that she did not like, until she met her cousin's mastadonian.

"I did not want anyone to overhear what I have to say." Athaliah stood pensively, about a foot away from her cousin and his dog.

"My home is secure. Nothing you say there is at risk of being overheard or—worse—repeated."

She moved closer to him. "That's just it. I don't think your people are as loyal or your residence as secure as you might believe." The dog jumped into the fountain, splashing water on Athaliah. She stepped back, trying not to show her frustration.

Ankur stood, looked up into the sky, and shook his head. "What are you going on about, dear girl?"

She stepped closer again. "Do you remember the night you met Nicholas?"

He nodded impatiently.

"Well, when I went to wash up, one of your servants addressed me," she paused.

"And?"

"She warned me."

"Yes?" Ankur was growing more impatient. He waved his dog over to his side. On the way to obeying the command, the large, clumsy beast shook the water from his thick coat, drenching Athaliah, who was standing between the dog and his owner.

Athaliah did her best to ignore the smell of wet dog all over her beautiful, white attire. "She told me that I should not trust you, that you were not an honorable man."

If Ankur was surprised, he did a good job of concealing it. "Her name?"

"Jossie."

Ankur stopped to leash his dog. It gave him a moment to think without being obvious. "Why are you just now informing me of this if you felt I was being betrayed?"

"I wasn't sure how to go about it, and I wanted to know if the other stuff she told me was true."

"Other stuff?"

"She said she knew my mother. I have since found out that part was true."

"Yes, that's why I initially hired her. She was a friend of the family. Great credentials. What else did she say to you?"

"Nothing. I told her that she should mind her own business and that you had been nothing but kind to me since I arrived."

Athaliah was getting better at telling lies.

"You've done well. I appreciate you telling me this." He paused a moment to give his next statement emphasis. "I really feel like we're starting to bond. I need someone like you, someone that I can trust completely, without reservation. Being both family and confidant makes for a strong ally."

Athaliah was secretly embarrassed at how much she prized her cousin's affirmation. It was an odd feeling to be both ashamed and grateful at the same time. She felt lower than the dog leashed at her cousin's side. She convinced herself it was a fleeting emotion, and she would gain the respect she deserved soon enough.

"What will you do about Jossie?" she asked.

"Don't you worry. A little betrayal is easily dealt with. It's not the first time, and it won't be the last."

A few days later, miles away, nestled in a deep, shadowed canyon, Screech and Gawker folded their broad wings. They looked down at a figure who had been picking berries just moments before—a woman whose life had ended as abruptly as a snapped vine. They began their descent.

Athaliah had eventually heard about the discovery of a dead body which had been half eaten by vultures. The remains were identified as Jossie. No conclusive evidence remained of how her untimely death came about. Most assumed it was an accident from falling down the canyon she had been known to frequent.

Athaliah wondered if she was the only one that thought it odd the vultures ate just half the body. Why would flesh-starved vultures carry the remains where they could be seen by passersby? It sounded very un-vulture-like to Athaliah. Of course, she was avoiding the real question. Did Ankur have his servant killed? She had thought there would be repercussions for Jossie's betrayal, but was her cousin capable of murder? She dismissed the idea immediately. She could not allow herself to think someone could be so evil, especially a family member. Such things were unimaginable in the Five Realms.

Her cousin's actions and her own growing connection with Ankur were changing Athaliah. It was as if a poison were surging through her veins. She had to admit, the excitement and intrigue were powerful narcotics. She wanted more. She was a good person, she kept reassuring herself. If things got too crazy, if Ankur were really responsible for Jossie's death, Athaliah would back away. She could stop and change course at any time. She still had full control. It was a statement she would keep repeating to herself over and over and over. "I'm in control. No one can make me do anything that I don't want to do."

As she walked through the garden that evening, a small group of chiros took flight from the trees above. For the first time in her life, they did not swoop down to greet her. Instead, they silently veered away into the darkness, as if the girl they once loved now carried a scent they could not trust.

Chapter 15

FAITH

"For His invisible attributes, namely, His eternal power and divine nature, have been clearly perceived, ever since the creation of the world, in the things that have been made. So they are without excuse." Duly closed the heavy, oversized Bible with a thud.

Propo leaned against the doorframe of the mostly hollow room in which Duly stood at a lectern. "Beely said you didn't believe in the Bible."

"I believe in your belief." Duly snorted as though clearing his throat to say something profound. "I believe in possibilities."

"Just not God, the One who created the opportunity for possibilities. You choose not to believe in Him?"

"I probably know more about Him than you do. I live among His words. I read them. I find them most entertaining. But here in this world, as you know, we are mere figments—or so I've been led to believe. We don't have the advantage of verifiable proof like those in the other world."

"Proof? All you need is faith, my friend."

"Test everything that is said. Hold onto what is good, says your Bible. Your God is not opposed to you examining the facts. Supposedly, in the other world, there is archaeological evidence, scientific evidence, and of course the prophetic evidence—purportedly all verifiable if one studies and digs deeply enough."

"My dear Duly. Faith is not an evidence problem; it's a heart problem. We all know, including you, that God is real. His moral law is written on our hearts, and His creation is proof enough, in any realm. What are you holding onto so tightly that you can't seem to let it go?"

Duly stepped down from the lectern, quickly scuttling past Propo to polish an empty shelf. After a moment of moving the rag in a circular motion on the already shiny surface, he turned back toward Propo. "Do you think you are the first?"

"The first what?" asked Propo.

Duly set his rag and polish down on the floor. For a Braewicker, everything was easier to reach when placed there. He moved away from the wall to give himself more space, and without saying a word, he performed the most disjointed, fidgety, spasmodic dance ever witnessed by Propo. His knobby joints clicked like dry wood with every erratic movement, and his warty fingers drummed a frantic, hollow rhythm against his own chest. When Duly abruptly stopped—and the only thing left moving was his stomach, heaving from heavy breathing—he asked, "Do you think this is my first dance? That you're the first to ask me these questions?"

Propo smiled wryly. "You call that a dance? I see the problem now." He laughed.

"Don't waste your time. Beely is a far wiser and much more convincing believer than you, and if she hasn't changed my mind by now, you surely won't!" Duly turned on his heels and returned to polishing the bare shelves.

Propo wisely changed the subject. "What are you doing? What is this place?"

"As one of the Twelve, I suppose I can tell you. Come all the way in and close the door behind you."

Propo did as he was asked. After the curious visitor shut the door, Duly quietly tiptoed to the right and then to the left. Once he was convinced that no one else was in the room, he walked back to the lectern, where the huge Bible still lay displayed on top. With his knobby finger—the only one with no warts—he motioned for Propo to stand beside him.

"What?" asked the perplexed Propo.

"Open the Bible," responded Duly, rolling his eyes and raising his palms.

Propo moved the step stool that Duly had used to reach the top of the lectern out of his way. He then shrugged and opened the cover. As the heavy binding creaked open, a faint, sharp scent reached Propo's nose—a metallic tang mixed with a hint of sun-dried citrus. "Now what?" Propo asked, sniffing the air curiously.

"Turn past the opening page. Turn to the middle of the book. OPEN THE BOOK!" Duly yelled the last few words but then stopped quickly to look around. He did not want anyone to overhear.

Although his patience was growing thin, Propo obliged the testy little sniblet. He opened to the middle of the book. He looked down, seeing nothing but a blank page. He flipped through a few more pages and saw more of the same. The entire book was blank. He thought for a moment and then pretended to read a Bible verse from Hebrews that he had memorized in his youth. "Now faith is confidence in what we hope for and assurance about what we do not see."

Propo would never forget Duly's reaction. The Braewicker's face first contorted between a look of confusion and anger but quickly manifested into disbelief as his short legs promptly marched over to Propo. Rather than taking the time to position his step stool, he jumped onto Propo's back, pulled himself up to his shoulders, and leaned over to get a good look at the Bible. Propo felt the rough, sandpaper texture of Duly's warty palms gripping his neck for balance. The small creature reached around and flipped a few pages before sliding back down to the floor.

Propo would have laughed, but the shock of the Braewicker's acrobatic back-climbing skills gave him a temporary paralysis.

"That was a good one. Beely failed to mention that you had a personality," said Duly, dryly.

"So, it used to be a Bible. Now it's just a bunch of bound blank pages."

"Wrong. It's still very much a Bible. The words are there. You just can't see them. They're invisible and will only reappear with the correct organic compound." Duly had intended to whisper, but the excitement of sharing his creation got the better of him.

"For what purpose?"

"Look here. Are you part of the Twelve, or aren't you? You two cockamamie quacks seem convinced that the Realms are being taken over by evil and that the Word will be banished." By "two cockamamie quacks," he meant Propo and Beely.

"And the water," added Propo matter-of-factly.

"And the water, of course. One mustn't forget that we are all going to dehydrate to death because the water will disappear."

"What? You decided to get a jump on erasing the Word from public view by making it invisible?"

"In a sense, yes." Duly excitedly pushed his step stool next to Propo. He climbed on top, because even a step stool was too high for a sniblet to easily mount—and once standing fully on his tiptoes, hurriedly flipped through the blank pages. He rubbed his hand over a few of the pure white sheets as if he were caressing pages of gold.

"You see, there are no words to banish here. It's not only the other world that has prophecy. We have prophecy too, and ours speaks of distant travelers visiting here, to save both our world and theirs. They will bring back the words to these pages, and if the prophecy is true, they will save all of us from the evil that Beely is sure will befall us."

Propo rubbed the back of his neck. "But why erase the words at all?"

"Are you seriously that much of a nitwit?" Duly eased himself off of the stool and raised his arms as he twirled around in a circular motion. "If there are no words here, in this soon-to-be secret room, who would come seeking them? You can't banish something that does not exist."

A slow smile crept across Propo's face. "You're truly brilliant. Beely was right about you. That's—it's genius."

"*It's* not genius. *I'm* genius."

"What's the organic compound needed to make the words reappear?"

Duly wagged his only non-warty finger at Propo and exclaimed, "Nope! No one but me is privy to that information."

"But I'm one of the Twelve."

"No one but me!" he repeated sternly.

"Fine. I get it. You don't trust me. Which brings me to the point of my visit here today. The only one you do trust—have you seen or heard from her?"

"Not a word. Pardon the pun."

"What pun?" asked Propo.

"Really?"

Ignoring Duly's attempt at humor, Propo continued. "I don't know what to do. I'm most worried about her; not only for her but for our mission. We can't finish the work we need to do without Beely."

"We can keep at our tasks. We do what she has left for us to do until we hear otherwise. Beely is resourceful. I have to believe she will be okay."

"So that's what you choose to have faith in: something we literally have no verifiable proof of whatsoever."

"Touché, my friend, touché. Now grab that book and bring it back to my quarters. This room is not yet ready for the treasures it will soon hold."

Chapter 16

SALVATION

Beely gripped the brorayding's horn so hard that her knuckles turned stark white. They were soaring above the lush green valley, far higher than she ever thought possible. It was not the first time she had ridden a brorayding, but never before had she ridden one alone, and never so far from home.

She had always refused to ride such a formidable beast on her own, but the distress caused by those following her surpassed even her fear of flying. Beely could not be sure about the intentions of the men who showed up at the lab, but her instincts told her to flee. She was still unaware that her husband was behind the intrusion. Had she known, she might not have risked returning to their home to commandeer his prized brorayding.

Once Beely felt secure, seated atop the massively winged raptor, she was surprised at how exhilarating flying through the air on such a formidable creature could be. The brorayding pushed through the atmosphere with ease. The power of his muscular wings sent chills through Beely's limbs. She had never felt freer, her troubles slowly melting away with each surge forward.

She commanded the stealthy beast to go faster. For the first time, she understood her husband's passion for flying. She shouted, "Faster," once again, and the brorayding immediately flapped his huge gray wings, surging upward toward the Empyrean Realm—the uppermost realm of the Five Realms. The light became so bright that Beely was forced to close her eyes momentarily. Using her hand to block the glare, she managed to catch a glimpse of what she thought might be a foghorse. Little was known about the mysterious creatures other than the fact that they looked like tiny horses made of something nearly translucent.

The reclusive foghorses had no cause for concern. The two intruders descended even faster than they ascended, so fast, in fact, that Beely felt her legs getting lighter. Butterflies filled her stomach. She began losing her grip on the brorayding's horn. A sudden panic struck as she struggled to maintain her position. She had no rope or saddle to secure her body to the rapidly descending beast. She had only her hands and legs, which suddenly felt far too light. She could not manage to give a command or even scream.

It was too late to scream.

She futilely reached for something to hold onto, but it only took an instant for Beely to slip off the brorayding's leathery, smooth hide. The whistle of the wind became a deafening roar in her ears as the stabilizing pressure of the beast's back vanished. She was a leaf in a gale, tumbling through empty space where the air felt too thin to catch her.

She found herself freefalling, hurtling downward, clutching nothing but her satchel and rucksack as if they would somehow cushion her fall. The ground was a blurred mosaic of distant greens and browns rushing up to meet her with terrifying speed. It was then that she found her ability to scream had returned. Her voice rang out in terror. Tears streamed upward from her fear-filled eyes. Beely's entire life flashed through her mind. She felt remorse for not having made up with her mother, for not hugging her father more often and longer, for not allowing her husband to fully know her, and for failing to convince Duly that God was real. She thought of her plants, her home, and her dear sweet Reverie. *Who would take care of Reverie?*

She closed her eyes tightly and prayed. The prayer was an incoherent mess of jumbled words, but she knew the Holy Spirit understood. She once had heard that believers felt a calming peace just before death. All she felt was panic.

Perhaps the feeling of peace would have come soon enough, but she would never know. The brorayding slid under Beely with such precision and grace that she did not even need to hold on—although she wasted not a moment in doing so. She seized the brorayding's horn as if her life depended on it. She suddenly remembered how to breathe. After fumbling with her pack and repositioning her satchel, Beely muttered a quick thanks to the Lord. She was astounded at how quickly things could change as she was once again soaring through the air. Her faith in her flying companion could not have been stronger.

After a short distance, she loosened her stranglehold on the brorayding's horn. Her imprint looked as though it might be permanent. There was no reason to fear with such a gallant creature in control. She realized she had never truly been in any real danger. After she took a few deep breaths, her heart rate began to slow, and she thanked the brorayding with a few soft pats for saving her.

It did not take long before Beely became angry with herself. She had become too arrogant. Her overconfidence could have been her end. She vowed never to make the same mistake again. She had too much to do for the Five Realms of Here. Her life was more than her own. She had to serve God's people. She had to complete her mission.

Even though this brorayding had a secret name only known to her husband, Beely would give him a special name as well. A brorayding usually only imprints on one rider for their entire life, but Beely had a rapport with animals that could make them act in extraordinary ways. Animals understood Beely, and they trusted her. "I will call you Joshua, because you are a strong and willing deliverer." She stroked Joshua just below his horn and whispered, "Thank you, friend."

Beely quickly brought her thoughts back to the task at hand. In one of her father's journals, he had detailed a secret hiding place in the Realm of Many. The Realm of Many was the largest of all the Realms. It contained many diverse people groups, animals, and flora, as well as a unique and heterogeneous geography. She had never before been this far into the realm and hoped she would not need to stay long.

Her father described a small shelf-like plateau deep in the canyon. On that plateau, he wrote, sat a singular, tall, thin butte. The plateau was halfway down from the top of the deepest section of the canyon. Her father stated that the monolith-like butte was so striking that it stood out among all the others. He wrote that it was far taller and much thinner than any other butte in that area of the canyon, making this plateau shelf uniquely identifiable.

The entire canyon itself was gorgeous, Beely thought. It was not simply a large crevasse with a river and dirt walls on either side. There were many levels and tiers of mesas and plateaus. There was the occasional cozy cove along the riverbank. There were many green, red, and blue trees, with flowering vines hanging off of them. Some of the vines hung from the rim of the canyon all the way down to the canyon floor, reaching into the beautiful white-capped water flowing below. There were waterfalls all around. Under many of the ledges was an iridescent reddish moss that glowed brightly even when the sun was shining. There were birds and butterflies of every shape and color. It was a spectacular sight.

"There," she shouted to Joshua as she pointed. Not far in front of them was the singular, tall, thin butte her father had described. It stood majestically on a shelf plateau about halfway from the top of the canyon. There was no mistaking it. It was even thinner than she had imagined—so thin, in fact, she wondered how it had remained so beautiful for so long, standing tall with orange at its base and brownish-red at its top. Beely thought it was amazing that something so thin and fragile had withstood the test of time.

Joshua landed as smoothly as expected. Beely stepped off her new friend and immediately took in their surroundings from a terrestrial perspective. The ledge was small, perhaps only thirty paces in each direction. Unlike other ledges, there was little vegetation. According to her father's journal, which she had studied in great detail since finding it in his office only a few days earlier, there was a secret entrance to a place that no one could find if they did not know the proper way.

Beely began to get excited, much like a child in a secret garden all her own. "If what my father says is true about this place, Joshua, you are in for a real surprise. I believe this butte was created by God Himself for such a time as this. Do you know what I mean?" she asked.

Joshua released a big blast of air through his nostrils, and because a brorayding's nostrils are located on its underbelly, he stirred up much dust in the process.

"I'll take that as a yes." Beely smiled and patted Joshua on his thick hide. "If all goes as my father foretold, I will be back soon. If you must leave, for whatever reason, please return at the same time tomorrow. I can't stay here long. There is much for me to do in Pixanese."

Joshua released another large gust of air followed by another cloud of dust.

"And whatever happens, bring no one else here. This is our secret place." Beely turned to face the tall monolithic butte. They had arrived just in time for the shadow crossing. A long shadow fell between the monolith and the canyon wall. According to her father's journal, the shadow access would only last a few moments. Beely closed her eyes and jumped over the shadow.

Joshua reared back, flapping his large wings. Beely had just disappeared right before his eyes. She was nowhere on the ledge. She was gone.

****

Once on the other side of the shadow, Beely found herself on the same ledge, with the same monolith. There was one singular difference. On the ground was a stone with a clue engraved upon it.

"Have no fear. You are here, but should you choose another step, my dear, make sure you know true scripture, or you shall never reappear. If in doubt, do not pout, simply turn and step back out. Through the next shadow, you shall see a word that is truly divine. If you know the answer, more answers there you'll find."

Beely's father had always promised that a good understanding of the Bible would never fail her in times of need. Beely confidently stepped over the next shadow, and, again, everything seemed the same except for another message on another stone.

"One thing in common these things have. Say it aloud, and you will pass. Heed this warning before you speak, or a worse fate you will meet. Once your hand is on the stone, you've just one chance and one alone, or rest forever with the bones. This was in the beginning, This became flesh, and This was God."

Beely grinned from ear to ear. Her father was right: her knowledge of the Bible was about to bear fruit. She gently placed her trembling hand on the sandy pillar, for even though her mind was confident, her hand had yet to catch up. She whispered the correct word required of the riddle: "Word." Another shadow instantly appeared. She wasted no time in stepping over the final shadow.

But alas, there was no amazing moment. She had not been transported to some safe distant land or another time before all her troubles began. She looked around for another message or clue, but there was none. Beely sighed in frustration and turned away from the colorful monolith.

She was wrong—at least in part.

She had indeed been transported, but how and where, she was uncertain. Everything was almost the same, but not quite. For starters, Joshua was still nowhere to be seen. Secondly, there was a door in the cliff wall opposite the monolith. She was positive there was no door when she arrived only minutes ago with the brorayding. The air was oddly still, and there was no ambient noise.

She let out another sigh as she whispered a prayer under her breath, "I'm sorry, Lord. My doubts will yet keep me from seeing Your full glory. Your ways are not my ways. I need to see what can't be seen. Help me believe in all that You have done and all that You are doing."

Inside the door, attached to the canyon wall, was a cave. The cave was made to look like a typical home one might see in Pixanese. The rooms—how many she had not yet ascertained— were illuminated with beautiful and ancient bioluminescent plants. There was furniture and even a desk with several items one might expect: writing instruments, paper, and a tray to hold odds and ends.

She walked further into the sparsely furnished hideaway, checking for dust along the cave wall with her finger. Surprisingly, the cave behind the shadows was dust-free. Yet she had the feeling no one had been there for a very long time. She stood in front of a storage room full of preserves and dried food. She continued down the only passageway and found other rooms with beds and small chests, perhaps for clothes or personal items.

Before she could make a full inventory of the various rooms, she became distracted by the unmistakable sound of trickling water. The cave had been made into a bunker with everything necessary for survival, including its own fresh-water source.

She walked back into the main cavern and set her rucksack on a small leather chair. The rucksack was filled with food and water, which she would soon add to the other reserves she had found. Someone was way ahead of her—a fact both comforting and a bit unsettling. She placed her satchel on the desk before slowly easing into a chair woven from the soft and supple limbs of a tree with which she was unfamiliar.

She was exhausted but could not rest for long. She allowed herself a moment to admire the beautiful cave. There were several columns, similar to the butte that had led her there, reaching from the floor to the ceiling. The entire room reflected the colors of the soft amber sandstone that made up the walls.

Absentmindedly, she tied her braids on top of her head. They had become frayed and tousled with all of the flying and falling. She wished she had time to take a much-needed bath. Too tired to get up from her chair, she took her foot and opened the middle drawer of the desk in front of her. Unable to see inside from her reclined position, she sat up and peered in—finding exactly what she had hoped for: a puzzle box.

It was much simpler to open than the previous one her father had left for her to find. This box only took seven straightforward moves. She reclined into the comfortable chair while unfolding the single sheet of paper found inside the puzzle box. The message was from her father. She recognized his handwriting immediately, even though it was the tiniest script she had ever seen.

"If you're thinking I'm the one who did all of this, you are wrong, my sweet girl. There were many who gave of themselves to further the cause. What happens now is largely up to you. You, my daughter, have shown several gifts of the Holy Spirit, but your most obvious gift is fortitude. I have no doubt that is why God chose you to carry on my work. The Book that tells of our Lord is not a book from our world, as you know, but the Words therein speak to us, nonetheless. There is only one Creator God, of all the realms. He has called us to inspire some of those in the Earthly Realm. You have heard the word figment. Perhaps that is what we are. I do not know all of the answers. I do know that God is sovereign. He wishes none should perish.

If you have found your way here, you know enough to continue without any help from beyond the grave; that would be me. I'm only leaving you this message to tell you that I love you, to encourage you onward. Continue reading the Word, pray, and seek others like yourself. May these words from Paul in the book of Ephesians encourage you: "Then we will no longer be infants, tossed back and forth by the waves, and blown here and there by every wind of teaching and by the cunning and craftiness of people in their deceitful scheming. Instead, speaking the truth in love, we will grow to become in every respect the mature body of him who is the head, that is, Christ. From him the whole body, joined and held together by every supporting ligament." *Or perhaps figment, I would add.* "Every supporting ligament grows and builds itself up in love, as each part does its work."

I wish I could be there to help you. I can only pray Propo has survived. You can trust him. Be well, my daughter, be strong, and be blessed."

Chapter 17

DEBAUCHERY

Along the walls, from floor to ceiling, were cages stuffed with animals too cramped to freely move. Feet, legs, noses, mouths, and tongues stuck out between cold metal bars. Other than the occasional low growl or dry bark, the mastadonians had given up complaining long ago. No one was coming to save them. Their fate had been sealed, and they had resigned themselves to certain death, as death was all they smelled of their kindred beyond the closed doors, in the other rooms.

The smaller containers held winged creatures of differing species, but most were chiropters. From these smaller cages came hissing and an occasional ear-piercing screech. There was one wall where the containers remained silent and from which no movement was found. These crates were filled with glouscenshires.

Workers were moving and shuffling cages and crates from one room to another. The fruit was being moved outside. Transport animals waited while workers filled their empty cargo containers with Ankur's "gifts" to the other realms. The entire facility was chaotic. The chaos increased when the workers caught sight of Ankur.

He began barking orders left and right. "Line that up," he pointed. "Stack that there," he demanded. "Clean this mess!" Ankur did not like disorganization. Everything had to be in its place.

Ankur made his way through the long corridor where two large hermetic doors had just been opened, welcoming him into a place he had spent many moons imagining into existence. His dream was finally a reality. This place was the culmination of long labor and careful design, which he believed would secure his place among the greatest minds in history.

Once he was through the doors, two security guards closed and secured them with a large metal beam. The entire room was bathed in soft light. There were several lab workers dressed in ivory-colored hides. Their work obviously required much concentration because they failed to notice their benefactor's entrance. Their heads were down and their hands were busy with precision tasks. This room, unlike the outer rooms surrounding it, was perfectly ordered and pristine. The only noises were the hum of a centrifuge spinning and the occasional word between technicians.

A middled-aged, studious-looking man entered from the rear. He was surprised to see Ankur standing in the lab. His countenance immediately changed from singularly focused to wide-eyed and nervous. He began frantically wiping a layer of cold sweat from his upper lip with the back of his hand. He handed a clipboard to the nearest technician and quickly made his way to Ankur. "I'm sorry, sir, we weren't expecting you today."

Ankur walked within reach of a glass lab table. He examined the specimens, and without looking up, said, "A surprise visit is the least of your problems. What should trouble you greatly is the utter lack of progress being made here."

"Correct. You are fundamentally right." The awkwardly nebbish man tapped himself lightly on his temple. "Of course, you are right. Who else would be right but you, right?"

Ankur snarled. He then patted the man on top of his thinning brown hair. "You are a sweet one, aren't you, Haberstitch?" Ankur turned his attention to the specimen on the table before him. "Why is this dog just lying here?"

Haberstitch tapped his chin with his index finger and blurted out, "It's dead. Absolutely dead. So dead. Very dead." He waited for a response from Ankur, but after getting none, he added, "Dead."

"I can see that. The body cavity is wide open and there are no internal organs."

"Yes, you saw that. Of course you saw that. I mean, *you* would notice that. Everything. Nothing gets by you unnoticed. Right?"

"How can someone so illiterate with speech be so brilliant with genetics?" Ankur muttered aloud. One of the other lab techs snickered at this remark. Ankur immediately looked around to see which one it was. He turned his attention back to Haberstitch. "Look—is this feasible or not? I've given you every resource available, and there has been very little progress."

"Giving a mastadonian wings has never been done, sir. In fact, I don't know of any genetic splicing to have ever been achieved of this advanced nature. Actually, I know of no attempt in the matter." Ankur glared down at the nervous man with total indignation. Surprisingly, Haberstitch was able to continue. "We have made potential advancements in grafting, but in changing the actual genetic composition, well, that's another matter entirely. Absolutely entirely completely a different thing altogether." Haberstitch stopped only to catch his breath.

Ankur placed his hand on the geneticist's shoulder and smiled. "Relax, Haberstitch, there is still time. Just keep working." Haberstitch was the man's last name, but it was a name Ankur found fitting for the mad scientist. It suited the uptight genius, he thought, and since he could not ever remember his first name, it stuck.

Haberstitch smiled. "I have some good news, however. Follow me, if you will."

As they walked back to the farthest nook, they passed open cages with the limbs of bloody corpses hanging out. There were creatures whose wings had been surgically removed. There were several large mastadonian dogs with rib cages exposed and one that was missing its head. Ankur, for one tiny fraction of a moment, seemed disgusted.

Haberstitch noticed his boss's discomfort and offered, "These are on the way to the incinerator, sir. The unfortunate cost of progress—right, sir?"

Ankur did not say a word. The smell was enough to keep anyone from opening their mouth any more than necessary. He held his breath as they walked the rest of the way to the abortorium.

The abortorium had its own set of hermetically sealed doors. This lab was very different from the one where the animal experimentations took place. It was bathed in natural warm light. The walls were mostly glass. The ceiling was vaulted several stories high. Glass panels were supported by metal beams. Tables and shelves were lined with a sundry of different plants, some of them flowering. A few were brown with shriveled leaves.

One section of the room had an active mister. There were tubes lined up and down the walls. They carried water and nutrients to the various pots and planters below. There was one attendant too busy to look up at the intruders. He was analyzing the various readings from differing instruments protruding from various plant specimens.

Haberstitch addressed the attendant, "Leslie, would you mind giving us a few moments of privacy?" The attendant nodded and exited the abortorium excruciatingly slow. Had Ankur been holding a shock prod, he would have used it.

Ankur looked around before commenting, "Why did you bring me here?"

"It's incredible. Exciting. I, myself . . ." he stopped to tap himself on his temple "I am unable to process the emotional response from what has happened."

"Which is?"

"It took a full season, but it's confirmed. That small tree in front of you is a modified glouscenshire. We did it. We no longer need to chemically inject every single fruit. The tree itself will produce them."

Ankur stepped closer to the specimen. It was an unsettling sight. Unlike the graceful original, this tree had thick, oily leaves that seemed to weep a dark, viscous sap. Its bark was a sickly shade of bruised purple, and a cloying, sweet scent hung in the air around it—a smell that was far too pleasant to be natural.

"You have tested the fruit? You know this for certain?"

"Undoubtedly. No doubts, I mean. Absolutely. For sure. You are not going to believe this." Haberstitch pulled a sheet of paper from his lab coat pocket and handed it to Ankur.

After taking a moment to look it over, Ankur responded, "These results. They are incredible. If this is true, the chemical in the modified fruit is even more effective than what we can produce in the lab."

"If you want to see the test subjects, you are more than welcome. Well, of course, you are welcome. You can do whatever you want. It's all yours. Everything here. Yours. All yours."

"How many people have you given the naturally grown fruit to?"

"I'm not sure I would call it natural. I mean, it sort of is natural now as opposed to what we make ourselves. The tree is actually producing it on its own. So, there might be an argument that it is indeed natural."

"Haberstitch!" Ankur's patience had been exhausted.

"Ten. Exactly ten. Of which there are nine still living. The one death was not because of anything we did. The person's heart failed. I assure you it had nothing to do with the glouscenshire."

"I want you to send all nine subjects to this location." Ankur handed Haberstitch his own piece of paper. Haberstitch looked at it and handed it back to Ankur.

"You may keep the address, Haberstitch."

"I've committed it to memory, sir." He again tapped himself on his temple. "But what good are the subjects to you? They are all catatonic. All nine are exactly the same."

"Can they take orders?"

"They will obey simple commands. In fact, they are good at performing the most rudimentary of tasks. Quite good, according to the tests."

"How many of the modified trees do you have?"

"Currently, only two. One is already producing fruit. Of course, it is producing fruit, or we would not have had the fruit to test on the subjects." Haberstitch would have continued to stammer on *ad nauseum* had Ankur not interrupted.

"Do you know if the tree will cross-pollinate?" asked Ankur.

"Not only will it cross-pollinate with its own, but preliminary tests seem to suggest that that the drug may spread to other fruiting plants. The tree itself, as ugly and pitiful as it looks, is quite aggressive. It grows quicker than the original specimen."

"I want you to give one to Athaliah. I will send her over in the morning to retrieve it. Instruct her on how to plant it."

"Can I ask what you will do with it, sir?"

"Of course, you *can* ask, Haberstitch. You are one of my most trusted people."

Haberstitch stared blankly at Ankur until it finally dawned on him to ask the actual question. "What do you plan to do with it?"

Ankur pointed sharply at Haberstitch. "None of your business. Now get me out of here before my sinus cavities start a revolt."

Chapter 18

MAXIMILIAN

"It's beautiful. She did all of this?" asked Marybah. She stood at the highest point in her daughter's garden, overlooking an extraordinary array of plant life. Her head moved slowly from right to left until her eyes rested on a patch of low golden ground cover abutting a thin, winding creek. The slow-moving water trickled over smooth, dark blue rocks, winding its way downhill until it disappeared into a large crevasse lined with colorful tree ferns. A faint, sweet floral scent drifted on the air, momentarily catching Marybah's attention before vanishing as quickly as it came.

Maximilian sat on a bench in front of his brorayding stable. It was one of the few places on their property that Beely had not transformed into a green oasis. He often trained riders in the adjacent clearing, which offered a safe and unencumbered place for the large broraydings to land.

"Yes. She spends countless hours in these gardens. I always thought it was to get away from me, but I soon learned that she genuinely adores watching things grow."

"I could have told you that. She learned it from my mother. She would follow her around for hours, listening to the folklore about the plants of Pixanese." Marybah inhaled deeply and looked toward Max. "I didn't realize your property had a flowing creek."

"That's a fairly new addition to the landscape. Beely insisted that we bring up a spring to flow on the surface, out in the open. She claimed the land was thirsty—that the creatures and plants needed the water more than we did. I never understood the effort she put into it, but she wouldn't rest until this particular spring broke the surface."

"You haven't heard anything from her for three days?"

"Not a word. I even sent out several of her favorite messenger birds, but none returned with good news. She came home the night I visited the lab. I know because some of her personal things were missing. But when I saw Reverie, I thought nothing of it. She would never leave Reverie for long. Not if she could help it."

"I remember Reverie. She's been around for a long time, that one."

"She's holding on. A roofah brings her medicine daily. Three days is the longest Beely and I have ever gone without seeing one another, but she would never leave Reverie for this long. I'm worried. My personal brorayding is missing. I find it hard to fathom that Beely might have taken him—but…"

"You really do love her, don't you?"

"I know we have had our problems, but, yes, I have grown to love her, deeply."

"Love is a distraction."

"How would you know?" He immediately regretted his retort, but she ignored him.

"Could she have heard about what we did? That we signed her sanity away?"

"There's little possibility she could have known on the day I showed up at that lab. Propo figured it out after I arrived, but he claims not to have seen her since."

"And now? Does she know the extent of our actions by now?"

"Your guess is as good as mine. Why else would she be gone for so long? Someone must have warned her."

"I hope so," she said.

Max appeared confused. "Why?"

"Because the alternative would be worse. If she's not hiding, she's in trouble. She needs to eat of the fruit before Ankur meets with her. If Ankur finds her to be a threat and not under the influence of his drug, he will make her disappear. Perhaps not immediately, but at some point, when the time is right, he will do the unthinkable."

Max stood, brushed the dirt from his pants, and began walking to the entrance of the stable. "Follow me."

Marybah followed closely behind.

He stopped at the farthest stall just after retrieving a bottle from a nearby cabinet. He sat on a stool and whistled. A very young and energetic brorayding effortlessly glided mere inches above the ground until it reached Max's ankles. It began a series of high-pitched snorts that, to Marybah, at least, sounded a bit musical.

"How adorable. I've never seen or heard one this small," said Marybah.

The baby brorayding, or dingding, as they are often called, moved swiftly up Max's leg to his lap. Broraydings have no feet. On the underside of their bodies and wings were thousands of tiny cilia, hair-like appendages that move in unison. When not flying through the air, they use these cilia, making them appear to glide over surfaces.

"Would you like to feed her?" He extended the bottle to Marybah.

Marybah shrugged as if questioning if he were serious. He nodded reassuringly. She took the scarf hanging over her shoulders and tied it around her thick, singular braid of hair. She held the bottle low to the ground. In only a few seconds, the dingding slid out of Max's lap and rushed over to Marybah.

Marybah awkwardly gripped the bottle as the dingding began suckling. She tried, without much success, to see the baby's mouth, which was flush with the underside of its body. Two soft, rubbery flaps on both sides hindered her view. The dingding gave off high-pitched snorts as it drained the milky liquid from the bottle. Somewhere beyond the stable walls, leaves stirred without wind.

Max looked both ways to make sure no one could be listening. In a world where even the plants could hear, secrets were hard to keep. "I had to tell Ankur about Beely. He knows everything."

"Everything?"

"He knows that Beely is convinced he wants to control all the water and ban the Word. I even mentioned her awareness of the tainted fruit."

Marybah handed the now empty bottle back to Max as she took hold of a nearby post to assist her in standing upright. "I only agreed to your scheme under one condition—that you not tell Ankur until Beely herself ingested the chemical."

"I'm sorry. I thought, and still do, that she is safer. Ankur needs Beely. He won't harm her."

"You don't know Ankur like I do. He needs no one. He is ruthless. If he finds my daughter before we do, her life is in jeopardy."

"I will find her before he does, I promise."

"Even if you do, there is no guarantee she will come around to our way of thinking. Beely is stuck in the old ways. She is her father's daughter. The winds are changing, and we either change with them or we get blown away."

"I'll make her eat the glouscenshire. She will have no choice."

"It doesn't work that way. She has to choose to eat the glouscenshire of her own free will. As we both did."

"I don't believe that superstitious spiritual stuff. It's basic science. It's a drug—nothing more."

"It's both. I'm not here to argue with you. Things are changing quickly. Ankur will not wait around forever. Find my daughter, and make sure she remains safe."

Marybah and Max should have learned more about plants from Beely. If they had, they might have understood that the elderflower vine need not be near in order to hear. The elderflower could decipher whispers carried on the wind for many miles. Beely's elderflower was, in fact, only mere paces away from the stables. The vines were very loyal to their caretaker, and although they had never intervened in the affairs of humans before, they, too, knew that the current times demanded change.

It was not long before the flowers disseminated the secrets shared in the stable to the fast-flying birds that regularly partook of their nectar. It was a fair trade: get the information to Beely as soon as possible, or there would be no more nectar. The bargain was not really necessary. The birds loved Beely, too, and they would have freely gotten the message to her, if they could.

Chapter 19

The Political Winds

It was as dark a night as Beely could ever remember. Even so, the brorayding flew effortlessly just above the canopy of the thick forest. The trees were motionless in the eerily serene environment. Joshua coasted and soared, avoiding the use of his strong wings whenever practical, just in case any of Ankur's minions were lurking about below.

Beely held tightly to the antler-like appendage on top of the brorayding's head. She inhaled deeply to calm her nerves. As good as she was with animals, she was not adept at flying upon them. Fortunately, when the brorayding was not asked to do any aerobatics, the antler was enough to keep Beely firmly in position. Regardless of her apprehension, she was able to appreciate the fresh night air flowing through her now unbraided hair. With no one to help with her long, thick locks, her hair had become an unruly mess, something she would need to get used to with the changing winds. Vanity was soon to be a thing of the past.

In the satchel, securely resting over her shoulder, was a list of the final members of the Twelve. Her husband's name was there, but it bore a cautionary note that read: "Do not inform or involve until I say otherwise." Even under the threat of being captured, it was important to get the names to Duly as soon as possible. She could not stay hidden away in the shadows forever. There was work to be done.

Beely leaned forward and whispered near Joshua's ear. "As soon as you drop me off at the Library of Truth, I want you to go home. Tell no one who is not a part of the Twelve of the shadow cave." Beely was unsure if Joshua understood the names that she had read to him earlier, but he would learn who they were in time. "You must go back home, Joshua. I don't want you in harm's way on my account. There will be a time when danger will be inevitable for all in the Five Realms, but that time is not yet upon us. I want you to be safe for as long as possible." She gently patted his smooth, leathery body.

Joshua let out a low, long, vibrating snort, acknowledging Beely's concern. Although broraydings did not communicate verbally—choosing instead the occasional nonverbal response—understanding beings that used words came easy to them.

The uncomfortable position of kneeling on the brorayding made the flight seem longer than it actually was, but they had finally arrived. Joshua flew around the library several times before choosing a place to land. The bioluminescent lights made the building easy to spot from high above, but the ground around it was all the darker by contrast. Beely was amazed at how gracefully Joshua could land in a place in which he had never been before.

As Beely slid from his back, Joshua did not turn to leave. Instead, he brought his tail forward, uncoiling the long, leathery appendage until it gently lay upon the palm of her hand. He looked at her with an intensity that went beyond animal instinct; in that silent exchange, it was clear he had made his choice. He was no longer a mount from a stable—he was hers.

Duly was none too happy to greet Beely in his sleep attire. Hiding his knobby, hairy knees under his short night dress was impossible. He clutched a tattered copy of *The Chronicles of Hitherland* to his chest, looking as though he had been robbed of a vital organ. He wasted no time addressing Beely in an accusatory fashion through the partially open door.

"If what they say is true and Ankur is indeed after you, you mustn't come here anymore," beseeched Duly. "I was just at the part where the Great Invemid falls, and here you are, bringing the very chaos I was trying to escape!" Looking more disgruntled than usual, he opened the door fully and pointed. "What is that thing doing here?" He stared incredulously at the brorayding.

"That's Joshua. So much for hospitality. You can trust him explicitly, but he won't be staying long, and neither will I!" exclaimed Beely. Duly was not the only one in a foul mood.

Beely had yet to understand just how loyal broraydings could be. They were highly instinctual beasts that had no difficulty discerning good people from bad. Joshua would not be returning to his home anytime soon. Serving two masters was out of the question. Beely would now be his only commander.

Beely left Joshusa, assuming he would follow her instructions, and followed Duly all the way back to his private quarters. "I don't plan on hiding from Ankur. I cannot be effective in the shadows. I must confront him face-to-face."

Beely sat while Duly steeped a pot of ognatia tea. She tapped her foot nervously against a table leg and squirmed restlessly. When Duly gave her the tea, it did not go unnoticed by him how Beely held her cup. She embraced it gently with both hands, as if she were caressing the face of a long-lost friend. She ran her finger around the rim, inhaled the fresh, steamy aroma, and then pressed the warm cup to her cheek.

"You don't plan on coming back, do you?" Duly accused more than asked.

"Of course I plan on coming back. Why would you say such a thing? I have a plan. Ankur will find me one way or another. I plan on finding him first. On my terms, not his."

"You have a plan? If you had a plan, I would know it. You have no plan. What are you up to, Bee?"

"My specific plan is not important. What is important is *our* plan. Tell me, what have you done to preserve and protect the Word? No matter what happens, the Five Realms will always return to what is right and good. I must believe that. The Word will always be important to those who are victorious."

"Changing subjects—very poorly, I might add—will not allow for your escape from the pertinent questions. You need not worry about *our* plan. It is well under way."

"Do tell."

Duly cleared his throat. "Every book of importance, and even duplicates of the most important, are soon to undergo a transformation. I explained it all to Propo."

"I haven't spoken to Propo in days. Bring me up to date, please."

"I have created a secret room that will hold all of the chosen books. But first they must be erased."

"Erased! That's exactly the thing we want to avoid."

"Simmer down, young lady. Simmer down and smell the ognatia."

Beely shook her head in doubt and gave a side glance before revealing a faint smile. She inhaled the steam from her cup, and her shoulders sank a bit as the tension eased.

Duly pointed his crooked finger near her face. "There's the Bee that I know, the one that trusts me completely. I read Esther again, as you mentioned the last time we spoke. You are correct about how perfect I am for this job."

"I'm listening."

"Once the books have had their content removed—or should I say hidden—they will all be placed into the room I am having constructed—nearly complete, I might add."

"Tell me more."

Duly coughed and gurgled as a bit of phlegm constricted his ability to speak. He took out a dirty cloth from under his seat and spat. "All of the words will be made invisible to the naked eye. They will only reappear with the proper chemical compound. Once that process is completed, I will place them into the hidden room, a room that can only be entered by those who know the way." He placed the dirty cloth back under the chair, causing Beely to wince.

"Intriguing. What is the chemical compound?"

Duly leaned in, his voice dropping to a dry rasp. "I will not reveal the secret, even to you. But know this: it is a substance as common as breath, yet will become as rare as a pure heart. It is something found in the deepest part of the garden, where the Word and the soil are one." He cleared his throat once more before continuing. "I have read every prophecy written about these changing winds from the books of the Five Realms. If the prophecies are true, the right ones will come, and they will not only have the correct way to the room, but they will also possess the correct organic compound."

"Genius. The evil ones in our world will not know how to correctly interpret prophecy. As much as I have read and studied, I'm not sure I would even know. I've never been gifted with interpreting the prophecies."

"Obviously, none of this will work if the prophecies are not true, but then it wouldn't matter anyway, if the prophecies are false, am I right?" Without waiting for an answer, he continued, "Of course, I am right. I am almost always right." He coughed again and reached for the cloth under his chair.

Beely raised her arm in protest. "Please don't." She went behind his kitchen counter in search of something clean for him to use. After finding nothing, she reached into her satchel and handed him a clean cloth. She sat back down and said, "When I leave here—"

"In the morning. You will stay the night."

Beely glanced around at the very messy, overcrowded room, which had more stacks of books than usual, and attempted a sincere smile. "Thank you. I will accept your offer."

"Gee, don't sound so overjoyed. You could do much worse." He attempted to hand her back the now soiled handkerchief, but she refused. "So, what is your plan?"

"I'm going to Okrad. Ankur knows that I am well liked in Pixanese. My father was much beloved, and Maximilian's family has much respect, and because of them, I will hold some political power of my own. He has already convinced so many to follow him, but not those in Pixanese. I can convince others to agree to his leadership, if terms are met."

"Political power? There are no politics in the Realms. There are no governing bodies. We have no need."

"I'm surprised. You actually do read all of the books in here, don't you? There are so very few that understand politics or the changing winds."

"I am fascinated by the concept. In the Old Testament books, there is much about politics in the earthly realm."

"Indeed. Now that Okrad has a leader, all of the Realms will need some way to deal with the repercussions. We will all need leaders as well, or at the very least, designated representatives, to deal with the demands that will come."

"Demands?"

"Never has a leader existed that did not make demands on those less powerful."

"What if Ankur decides to just do away with you?"

"You mean kill me?"

Duly scooted his chair closer to Beely and lowered his voice, as if someone else might be listening. "There has been an increase in sudden deaths, or have you not heard the rumors?"

Beely had heard that sniblets had atrocious breath, but their short stature rarely put them face-to-face with those as tall as Beely. She was overwhelmed by the odor but did not want to insult her host by moving away. "I've heard. No doubt the rumors and the deaths are related to Ankur and Okrad."

"You are no good to us dead." To Beely's delight, Duly moved his chair back to its original position.

"Dead? Have you always been so blunt? Never mind, don't answer that. He won't kill me. He needs me, at least in the short term. He needs me to convince Pixanese to conform."

"He knows you would never agree to that."

"His pride hinders sound reasoning, especially when it comes to the potential of adversaries. Creatures who, to him, are seemingly weaker, less important—like me."

"I hope you are right."

"Don't hope, pray."

"Other than praying, which is highly doubtful, and getting a message to those on the list, what else would you have me do?"

"I'm glad you asked. There is one named Willow. She is in the orchard with Ekrad Oren. She has much influence and is well beloved by all, including Oren himself. I need you to get a messenger to her, one that is empathic, that can communicate the dire circumstances manifesting all around us."

"The roofah bird. There's no better choice."

"Excellent thinking, my little Braewicker. Explain all that you know to the roofah. The bird must tell no one else but Willow."

"What would you have this Willow do? We don't know specifics about any of Ankur's plans."

"I wish I had all of the answers. I don't. Willow is clever, with the wisdom of many turnings. She is pure of heart and would give up her life for the truth. My father told me many stories about her. There is no stronger ally we could have on our side."

"Very well. I will make sure she hears all of the theories we have come up with: the drought, banishment of the books, and the politics and poison as well. She will hear of all the conspiracies."

"Thank you, my friend."

"Now, we must get some rest. It is late."

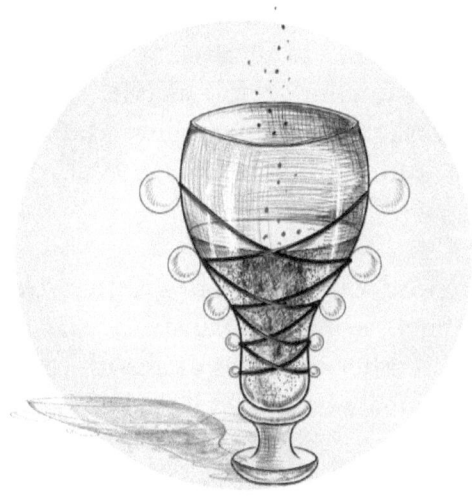

Chapter 20

UNF⊙RGIVEN

"I'm surprised to see you back here so soon. Ankur said you were not due for quite some time," said Athaliah.

The last person Nicholas wanted to see was Athaliah. Yet, there she was, proudly seated behind Ankur's desk. It was too late to turn around and make a dignified exit. The encounter was obviously uneasy for him, but he tried his best to be genial. "I wasn't aware that you would be here, Athaliah. Where is Ankur?"

"Away…meeting with his newest followers. It's amazing how easily he has convinced so many to join him. Don't worry, though; I can help you with whatever you need," she answered coldly. Athaliah had just recently been elevated to Ankur's second in command, and she wasted no time flaunting her newfound authority.

Nicholas fidgeted with his hands as he awkwardly found a seat on the opposite side of the room from his ex-fiancée. "Something strange has happened. Many of the historical acquisitions I've made over the last few cycles have disappeared. I only know because I wanted to do an accounting of the ancient biblical texts. They are very rare, as you know—irreplaceable, in fact. They're all missing."

Athaliah was as uncomfortable as Nicholas, but she refused to show him the slightest vulnerability. Her fingers tightened once around the armrest, then released. "Will you excuse me for one moment?"

"Of course."

Athaliah stepped out of Ankur's office, closing the door behind her. She leaned against a nearby wall and absentmindedly used her overcoat to absorb the sweat from her palms. She then wiped what might have been the beginning of a tear from the corner of her eye. For a fleeting moment, the memory of his laughter—unguarded and sincere—rose unbidden, tightening her chest. Her jaw clenched. But the hesitation passed as quickly as it came.

Her purpose for the abrupt exit was much more diabolical than simply concealing her emotions. The passion she once had for her first and only love had been replaced by hatred. Athaliah had learned that hate possessed far simpler objectives than love.

She reached into the lining of her jacket and retrieved a capsule of white powder. The small capsule had been hidden in a pocket next to her heart for days. She had not been certain if she would ever have a chance or the will to use it. Her thumb hovered over the seam, trembling just slightly, as though her body remembered something her mind refused to honor. But once she stared into the face of betrayal, she could not stop herself.

Athaliah had taken the capsule out of its hiding spot no less than three times in the hour before her once betrothed was due to arrive. She brought the small, encapsulated poison into the light one last time. It was odd, she thought, that something so small and seemingly insignificant held so much power.

A servant with a tray of refreshments startled Athaliah, who quickly hid the pill from sight. "It's all right; you may go. I can take it from here," said Athaliah, still leaning against the wall. Without saying a word, the servant nodded, handed Athaliah the tray, and quickly descended the staircase.

Athaliah set the tray on a small table. She twisted the capsule in two, careful not to lose any of the contents inside. If any of the powdery poison were to become airborne, it could find its way into her lungs. She slowly turned the first half upside down and watched as it disappeared into Nicholas's favorite drink. The powder vanished without resistance, leaving only a brief shimmer on the surface. She turned over the second half and waited until it, too, completely dissolved. She was utterly unaware of her own hissing as she methodically stirred the cup of revenge.

Athaliah pushed the office door open with her back, revealing a warm smile as she turned around. "I'm sorry it took me so long. I thought you should at least have something nourishing after traveling so far." She placed the tray on the desk and returned to her chair directly across from Nicholas. "Please, help yourself; don't be shy."

Her eyes lingered on his hands for half a second longer than necessary. Nicholas mistook the look for lingering affection. She knew he could never refuse his favorite drink. "The servants know how much you love this, and they made it especially for you." He accepted the tainted refreshment without reservation.

"Thank you, Athaliah. I must say I am relieved at how well you are doing since—"

"Since I was abandoned by my only love." She paused just long enough for him to feel ashamed. "I am very glad that you are relieved." She took a sip from her cup. "I'm only jesting. Yes, Nick, it has taken time to heal, and little things bring me encouragement with every new day that passes."

Nicholas noticed the slight tension in her shoulders, the rigid way she held the cup, and wrongly assumed it was the strain of unresolved emotion—proof, perhaps, that she still cared.

"I'm sorry. I didn't mean it that way. 'Relieved' is the wrong word. It's just that I was really worried about you," he said.

"Really? Because I've barely heard a word. I haven't even seen you for may moons—just reports from Ankur about how well you are doing in your position."

He took a long drink, more from nervousness than thirst. After a moment, he finally responded. "I was wrong to have left you…the way that I did. My ambition was blind—heartless really. But we were—are—so young, Athaliah. Perhaps too young to rush into marriage so quickly. I am sorry. Can you ever forgive me?"

"You sent a letter by courier. Do you know what I remember most about that letter? It wasn't even sealed. Anyone along the way could have read it—and probably did. The poor fellow who gave it to me couldn't even look me in the eyes."

Nicholas took another long drink. He began to perspire, something he attributed to his inability to make an easy exit. As he set the cup back down, his fingers betrayed a slight tremor. He tightened his grip on the glass, assuming it was merely the weight of his guilt causing his hand to shake. He stood and walked over to one of the open-air balconies as he tried to say something that would appease his boss's cousin, or at the very least, distract her.

What came out instead was less than he would have hoped. "Do you realize how negative you are?"

Her eyes narrowed, her head tilting just slightly. "What?"

"Do you think the only reason we didn't work out was because of this job?"

"I wouldn't really know, now would I? You never told me," said Athaliah with undisguised disdain.

"Fine…so you want to hear the truth? I'm not sure you realize this about yourself, but no matter what anyone says, you almost always respond negatively. Your first reaction is almost always the opposite, definitely negative." He walked over to the table in front of Athaliah and downed the remaining liquid in his cup before placing it firmly on the tray.

"Remember when I brought you that small sculpture of the two moons and you said you preferred it when the larger moon rested in the night sky alone? You didn't even bother to ask where it came from, who made it, or what it might have meant to me."

She sighed. "What could it possibly mean?"

"I had it especially made for you. It represented our relationship: two souls illuminating the night sky more brightly than one moon alone. As it turned out, I was simply blinded by what I thought was true love. I did love you, Athaliah. But I eventually discovered that you don't love yourself. You aren't capable of loving anyone. I hope that I'm wrong. I want the best for you, but it was never going to work out between us. This job with your cousin was just an easy way for me to spare telling you of all the harsh realities."

"Odd, some say that the truth hurts, but I'm too numb to feel anything. Of course, in your perfect world with your perfect personality, I guess someone like me, from the middle of nowhere, could never meet your standards," said Athaliah.

"I'm convinced that you don't know pain because you've never known real love, and you don't know love because you've never known real pain. Perhaps you're right about me, too. I'm too much sometimes. Maybe I expect too much." Nicholas paused and took a deep breath. "Look, there's no reason to fight. I'm sincerely sorry. I am."

"You're right; there's no reason left to quarrel. It's all over."

There was an awkward silence before Nicholas bid his final farewell. "I've got to be going. I need to meet my mother for dinner before leaving on my next assignment. Can you please relay a message to Ankur for me?"

"Absolutely, and I'll try my hardest not to be too negative. I don't know why you couldn't have just sent a letter by courier, though." She flashed an insincere grin.

Nicholas shook his head as he walked toward the door. "This information was too sensitive to send by courier." He paused to let his piercing words sink in. She would not show it, but his harsh words struck her like an arrow through the heart.

He continued, "Tell Ankur that I have located the painting, the one he most wanted to find. I have it hidden away in a safe place."

"Where?"

"No, information about things of consequence is for his ears only. I've heard rumors about this painting, that it holds much power. I'm not sure it should be trusted with anyone at this point. I won't have its destruction or misuse on my conscience."

Athaliah rose from her chair, her face reddening as her voice intensified. She knew how important this painting was to Ankur. It was the only thing he spoke about as of late. All of his most recent plans centered on the painting. "Excuse me?"

"You heard me. I have the painting, and it's hidden. Only I know where it is."

Athaliah would remember this moment as the angriest she had ever been. She was positive he could see her face turn into an inferno. She instinctively clutched her breast so he could not witness the intense pounding of her angry heart. Before she knew it, she had positioned herself between Nicholas and the door.

He was somewhat taken aback by her reaction, although it pleased him. She, after all, had all the power up until that point. Ankur was quickly becoming the strongest presence in all the Realms, and Athaliah was his second in command. It was nice to have her groveling for a change.

"My cousin won't be happy with your insolence. Tell me where the painting is." Athaliah could not hide her desperation. If he did not tell her soon, the whereabouts of the painting could very well be lost forever.

Nicholas smiled, reached around Athaliah, and placed his hand on the door. He gently pulled it open, nudging Athaliah forward as he did. They were face-to-face as he said, "I'll tell Mother you said hello."

Athaliah attempted to push the door shut, but her strength was no match for his. In that moment she knew she had made a tactical mistake, but she would not give him the satisfaction of hearing her plead. She looked at the man she once loved with a stare that could have melted ice. She hissed as he stepped over the threshold. "One last bit of advice: if you want to see your mother, you'd better hurry."

He was not sure what to make of her last comment, and he would not spend any time worrying about it either. He was soon to be done with Athaliah and Ankur forever. He had not only come to share information concerning the painting Ankur so desperately wanted to find, but also to hand in his resignation. He had heard the rumors about his boss. He wanted no part of Ankur's questionable plans.

He was soon to be a free man, or so he believed. Free to start over again.

Chapter 21

FORGED ALLIANCES

Athaliah was alone on the wooden vessel. There was no one to see her cry. The oarsman, under the water, could hear muffled sobs, but oarsman mind their own business and ask no questions. As long as the land dweller brings something edible, the oarsman remains a loyal and confidential guide. On this day, Athaliah paid her way to the Land of Mana with a glouscenshire. Appropriate, she thought, since she was transporting a seedling of the only known hybrid that could produce the pharmakeia version of the glouscenshire.

The canyon walls slowly receded the closer they came to the Lake of Prosperity. Athaliah had been too preoccupied with her own self-pity and sadness to notice the colorful fauna growing on the shore, or the intricate flowering vines cascading from above. She did not hear the winged creatures fluttering by, some even singing songs. Athaliah tucked bad memories behind thoughts of what she had to accomplish on her current visit to the Land of Mana.

She bent down, leaned over the side of the boat, and dipped the tail of her black trench coat into the water. She patted the cool, wet cloth on her cheeks, erasing the paths of her tears. She wanted no sign of the last remnants of her outward display of weakness. She vowed never again to cry over anyone—especially a man.

She knocked on the bottom of the boat, an indication for the oarsman to head to shore. She did not enjoy the idea of relying on someone, or something, she had never seen or spoken with—like the oarsman. She had to trust that the guide would remain close to shore for when she was ready to leave because there was no other way home but on the river. Athaliah trusted no one, so once on land, she tossed another glouscenshire into the water, hoping that would buy the oarsman's loyalty.

The hike up the hill to Ekrad Oren would be farther from this point of the river's edge, but she wanted to visit someone else first. She could see the sweeping arms of the weeping willow from where she stood. She walked up a steep incline carrying her pack. She traveled light, with only the sapling and a few nibbles. Ankur had admonished her to be very careful with his live cargo. The success of her cousin's plan depended on the proliferation of his carefully cultivated speciation.

With each step she took, she noticed how fertile the soil was in the Land of Mana. It was no wonder the orchard grew so well here. The Land of Mana was the perfect environment, with multiple water sources, healthy soil deposits, and ideal seasonal temperatures. Athaliah assumed these were the reasons her cousin wanted to bargain with Ekrad Oren. There was no better place to grow an army of his hybrids.

"Hello?" Athaliah stood a few paces away from the willow tree. She had heard of trees that were sentient and could communicate, but other than Willow and Ekrad Oren, she had never interacted with one before. "Hello?" she called out again, but there was no response.

Since the very first time she met Willow, Athaliah had developed an odd fascination with the tree. She felt something deep within her—a need to understand Willow. She was compelled to speak to her, but she was not sure exactly how the process worked.

She set her pack on the ground and surveyed the land around her. Even though she had studied the area extensively back at Ankur's residence, she wanted to make sure it all made sense in real time. The old tree, Ekrad Oren, was a few thousand paces to the north of where she now stood.

Two round browns, taking advantage of Athaliah's diverted attention, crept up to the pack that she had placed on the ground. They were called round browns because they only consumed dead, brown leaves, and their excrement always formed perfect round balls. The cute creatures resembled a cross between a large beetle bug—with hard, iridescent green shells—and a furry-faced shrew. Round browns had long, pointed snouts and four short legs with pink feet. They could move unbelievably fast and were as quiet as mice.

One of the round browns, the one with the Crooked Ear, worked its way into Athaliah's pack, while the other stood guard watching Athaliah. When Crooked Ear crawled back out of the bag, the top of the hybrid emerged with him. The little creature let out a sharp, jagged hiss, recoiling from the sapling as if its very scent were a toxin. It scurried back several feet, shivering with a primal disgust that even Athaliah could not ignore.

"Hello, Athaliah. Welcome back to our land," said Willow abruptly.

Crooked Ear and his friend quickly scurried away as Athaliah turned around to face Willow. They had done their job, revealing the intruder hidden away in the visitor's pack.

"Thank you, Willow. I was beginning to think you might not be happy to see me again."

"And why would you think such a thing?"

"Because you didn't speak when I first got here."

"Please forgive my slumbering. I'm not as young and spritely as I used to be." The truth was that Willow had no intention of speaking to Athaliah ever again—until the sapling was exposed. The new life being introduced to the land in which her roots were buried had to be reckoned with. "What brings you back so soon?"

Athalia was unaware that a roofah bird had recently visited Willow with a great deal of interesting facts, a few rumors, and all the tidbits in between. Willow had already heard about some of the changes happening in the Realms, but the roofah's news was daunting. No one was really aware of just how far and deep Willow's roots traveled. The truth was that she knew more about the underworld than anyone. She knew more about Ankur's plans than even Athaliah.

"Ankur wanted me to meet with the old tree in the center of the orchard one last time."

"I know why you are here. You have brought an abomination with you."

"What do you mean?" asked Athaliah.

"That sapling, in your pack, it's not natural. It's a disgrace—an abomination."

"What would make you come to that conclusion?"

"I am sorry you have chosen this way. The choice was yours, and the options were many." Willow used her limbs and leaves to form a face of sorts. She wanted to appear more personable to Athaliah. "I suppose you could change course at any time, but the farther one follows hate and ambition, the harder it is to see the alternate paths."

"I'm sorry you feel that way. Ankur and I only want to make every kingdom stronger under a united togetherness. Things are already happening, and it'll be good for all the villages, clans, and creatures, you'll see."

"The old tree will grant your request to accept that abomination into his fold. He will do it with the condition that the water that feeds the Land of Mana will not be diverted."

"How do you know this?"

"Ekrad Oren—I have not spoken that name in a century—has his own resentments. His heart has had time to grow much colder than yours. Ankur knows that the fruit he requires will grow nowhere but here, and there will need to be abundant water." Willow abruptly stopped speaking, and the image of her face faded. "Come under my branches, near my trunk, so we may converse in private."

Athaliah parted the branches and followed the large aerial roots leading to Willow's trunk. Along the way, she passed a myriad of happy mushrooms. Round browns were scurrying about, making sure the path was clear of any fallen leaves. When Athaliah moved the occasional low-hanging branch, its leaves made a noise that could only be compared to giggles. There were also a few flying insects, singing as they passed by to inspect the visitor.

All of the joy underneath Willow's arms began to annoy Athaliah. She had serious work to do and had no time for silly fungi, singing bugs, or giddy leaves. As a cluster of mushrooms let out a soft, musical chime near her boot, Athaliah deliberately brought her heel down upon the tallest one. It let out a tiny, wounded sigh as it was crushed into the loam. Athaliah did not look back.

After a long walk under Willow's canopy, she finally arrived at the trunk. The enormity of the colossal tree could never be ascertained from the outside, unless it was from the clouds looking down. Athaliah was impressed with yet more evidence of her cousin's genius; there could be no land more fertile to grow his prized trees. She bent down to pick a mushroom. Willow quickly loosened one of her branches on top of Athaliah's head. It landed a little harder than Willow had intended, perhaps.

"Ouch!" exclaimed Athaliah.

"Pardon me, dear. My branches sometimes have a mind of their own." Willow once again formed an image of a young motherly face with long flowing hair.

"What secrets have you to tell? What don't you want Ekrad Oren to know?" asked Athaliah.

Willow was put off by Athaliah's growing boldness. Who was this mere girl to speak to an ancient being like Willow with such disregard? Willow answered, nonetheless. "I hear you are no longer engaged. What has become of your lost love, may I inquire?"

"You may, but I have no idea what has become of Nicholas. I haven't seen him since he resigned from my cousin's employ." At this, Willow's leaves rustled and twisted as if a violent wind had penetrated under the canopy.

"Surely you know of his passing, don't you, dear?"

Athaliah felt a sudden, icy needle prick in the center of her chest. A phantom chill washed over her, and for a split second, the air seemed to taste of the white powder she had stirred into his cup. She pushed the sensation down, hardening her gaze. The mushrooms closest to Athaliah let out an airy wheeze and shrank lower to the ground.

"It seems as though you have frightened the wee ones," Willow said.

Athaliah gave a disgruntled look down and replied, "Why would you be scared of me? You're just smelly little funguses. I have no need of you." She looked back up at the image of Willow. "I know that you are the wisest one in this orchard. I know you are cleverer than even Ekrad Oren." She glanced down at the bag she was holding with the sapling sticking out. "You and I both want the same thing."

"Which is?" asked Willow.

"As you said, Ekrad Oren will accept the deal my cousin has proposed. He has no other option, really. If he doesn't, every bit of life will die here, just as it will in the other realms."

Willow responded, "Ankur has positioned himself quite well in Okrad, where many aquifers reside. The underground springs are more easily manipulated than anyone would ever know."

"They will know, soon enough."

"He will never have control of all the springs," said Willow matter-of-factly.

"He won't need all of them. He has every water source that matters. The Realms will be unified under our control, have no doubt," replied Athaliah.

"So, what is it you want from me, dear?"

"Ankur does not believe in prophecy."

"Do you?"

"Let's just say I'm not the betting kind, but if I am forced, I like to cover my bets, if possible. One of the prophecies speaks of the branches that will turn toward the light, defeating the evil roots of darkness. Most anyone reading that might consider Ekrad Oren as the center of that future outcome, in one way or another."

"Perhaps. He is regarded as the highest reaching and most deeply rooted of all the trees."

"In a literal sense, sure. But when has prophecy ever been literal? You're the one the prophecy is pointing toward. It's you, is it not?"

"Now how would I know the answer to that? Even if it was referring to me, the events are future. None of us, me, you, nor Ekrad Oren, may even be alive when these future events unfold."

"Nonsense!" exclaimed Athaliah.

Willow's branches rustled once again, the mushrooms gasped, and a few of the flying insects feigned an attack, prompting Athaliah to thrash her arms futilely about her face. They had never before witnessed anyone being so disrespectful to Willow—their friend and protector.

"None of us know the day or the hour," replied Willow.

"No, but we can see the signs. All of the indications are that this is happening now. It's now. I have no doubt, and I would bet you don't either."

"I thought you weren't the betting kind?"

"Only if I'm sure I'll win."

"How do you want to win this one, Athaliah?"

"Will you promise me that my mother and father will have food and water when their village goes dry and the trees die everywhere else but here?"

"I could ensure their ability to enter and leave the orchard unharmed. It would take some effort on my part. What would I get in return?"

"You tell me. If it's within my means, I will do whatever you require," answered Athaliah.

Willow already knew what she wanted even before the request was made. She did not trust Athaliah, which was the only reason she was willing to bargain with her. Trees, although resilient and wise, were not immune to evil deeds. Willow was not the only remaining willow tree because of happenstance. Hundreds of turnings ago, there was a fire in the orchard. All of the trees but two were burned to ashes. It was not a naturally occurring spark that caused the devastation. Willow was determined to make sure another such event never took place.

Willow rustled before she spoke. "Make sure that the abomination gets planted six paces north of my farthest limb."

There was a pause. Athaliah was surprised by the request. "That's it? That's all you want?"

"I'm in need of nothing. That thing you carry, however, will be in need of much. I shall keep it close."

Athaliah knew the sentiment behind keeping your friends close and your enemies closer. She had no idea what Willow had in mind, but it did not matter. The tree would grow, and it would produce many offspring. The agreement between Ekrad Oren and Ankur would remain regardless of Willow's intent. Willow would not impede progress; of this, she was certain.

"Fine, I shall plant the tree myself exactly where you have requested," said Athaliah. She did not need any further guarantees. She knew Willow would not go back on her promise. Athaliah's parents would remain safe during the impending chaos and death that was soon to visit most every living creature.

Chapter 22

BETRAYAL

"So, as far as you're concerned, it's a foregone conclusion that death and mayhem are inevitable, and everyone is going to die—except Ankur, of course." Max said this as if he were reciting it from memory, his voice carrying no emotional weight.

Beely lowered her arms, releasing the loving embrace of the man she called her husband. She placed both of her hands on his chest. Her face remained mere inches from his. "You *still* don't believe me."

"What did you think? That you would come home, after being missing for days, and we would make love, and I would somehow miraculously come around to your way of thinking? I love you, Beely Rembree-Wren. I always will, but that doesn't mean I'm going to give up my sanity in return."

Beely patted her husband on the chest, pausing to feel the beat of his heart. She then gently pushed him away with the palms of her hands. "Changes are coming, whether you see them or not."

She moved to the end of the bed and retrieved her dress from the ottoman. She suddenly felt as if she were a guest in her own home. She glanced around the room, and an unexplainable sadness reached deep down into her soul. Reverie sensed her emotional struggle and sat on the bench beside her. She looked up, with one eye peering through her matted fur. Her sides fluttered with a shallow, uneven breath, and a faint tremor passed through her small frame before she settled.

Beely gasped. She had never seen Reverie—or any empachic, for that matter—look so solemn. Reverie was not able to comfort Beely because of her advanced illness. After slipping the dress over her head, Beely picked up Reverie and held her tenderly. She stroked her fur, resulting in the faintest whisper of a purr.

Max stood in front of the window, looking out over the beautifully manicured gardens. The sweet, cloying scent of the half-eaten glouscenshire lingered in the room, its floral notes almost overpowering in the still air. "She hasn't been the same since you left. Visits from the roofah seem to make no difference."

The subject of Reverie's illness was too hard for Beely to discuss, so she promptly introduced another topic of conversation. "I know why you've been meeting with my mother."

"Only for the purpose of your well-being."

"She told you why I married you, I suppose."

"She did."

"She was never one to keep a secret, especially when it could hurt me."

"She didn't tell me to hurt you. She actually thought it might help our relationship if I understood the terms. Even back then, before we were married, you believed in the prophecies and your father's wild conspiracies. Was it worth it—marrying me?"

She set Reverie down on the bed and walked over to her husband. She placed her hand on his shoulder right below his neck. It was his most tender spot. She gently rubbed his muscles.

"I married you to gain favor in the community. This is true. Many loved my father. His following was loyal and true. When I married you, I not only gained the respect of the few who opposed my father, but even more from those who already admired him. It was a strategy that worked better than I could have hoped. Your family was always respected, and I think the only person more charismatic than you is Ankur himself. Or so I've heard."

Max turned from the window to face his wife. She could see the hurt in his eyes. "I'm glad you accomplished your goal. For a society free of politics, you have done wonderfully well in solidifying a political base, and the people don't even know it. You're their next leader."

He sat on the bed to put on his sandals. Two empachics immediately came to his side, pulsing with a soft, rhythmic vibration as they pressed their warm bodies against his knees to absorb his rising anxiety.

"I know you're not blind, Max."

"What do you mean?"

"I may have married you for political reasons, but no reason could stop me from falling madly in love with you." She knelt down at his feet and secured his remaining sandal. "I love you. I always will. Perhaps I always have."

He refused to give in to further sentimentality. He stepped around her, walked over to the dressing area, and began to weave his copper headdress through his braids. "I wish I could believe you. I want to believe you. I have spent our entire marriage praying for God to move your heart and convince me of your love—whether it was real or not."

"I do love you. I wanted you to be together with me in everything, always. Just as I can't make you see what is to come, I can't make you see my love for you. I also can't blame you. My motives were not always pure. It was the Realms I was thinking of—neither you nor me, but all those who live here."

"Why did you come back here last night?"

"It wasn't to spend the night with you, if that's what you were thinking." She paused to consider her words carefully. "I was hoping that you might have changed your mind. Perhaps in my absence you would see how important it is to stop Ankur."

"Ever since this started—I don't mean with your mother's declaration or your father's conspiracies, but when you saw the water spill onto the table—something in your eyes told me it was over."

"What was over?"

"Our marriage. As much as I loved you, and no matter how much you may have loved me, you were always going to put Pixanese and the Realms first. My ability to deny that fact was gone in an instant. It would have taken more faith for me to believe we could go on than to believe what you were saying was true."

Beely made sure to lock eyes with her husband before continuing. "Please, before I go, can you just tell me that you know that I love you?"

Max quickly moved closer to his wife, sweeping her up in his muscular arms. For a fleeting instant, his resolve faltered. If he said nothing—if he held her just a moment longer—everything he had set in motion might still be undone. The thought terrified him more than losing her. He held her close and whispered in her ear. "They are watching us. You must go, quickly. I'm sorry, my love, but I sent word that you were here."

She held onto him tightly, not wanting to let go. She whispered back, "I know, Max."

Max lowered her a few inches back to the floor. With mounting desperation, he quietly but urgently said, "You have to go, leave through the kitchen and meet me in the barn. The broraydings are ready; their massive wings are already stretched wide in the shadows. One of them will carry you safely above the treeline."

She kissed him lightly on the cheek and said, "This is what must happen."

"What are you talking about? I've made a terrible mistake. Right or wrong, you don't deserve this. These men are going to take you before Ankur."

"I know."

"You have heard the rumors about the strange deaths. I wasn't sure at first, but now, I don't know." He nervously looked out of the front window and paused to listen for intruders.

"Never lose faith, my love. And pray. God will have victory regardless of what happens to you or me."

The last thing that Max saw, moments before the men came in to forcibly remove Beely, was the half-eaten glouscenshire sitting on his wife's nightstand. He suddenly felt great remorse. He was confused. The one thing he knew for certain was that there was nothing he could do now. Somehow, he had played right into Ankur's hand. He did the unthinkable by betraying his wife.

It was only minutes ago that he was confident in his plan of action, and then, in the blink of an eye, his heart sank and his world came crashing down before him. It was the fruit, he thought. His mind felt encased in a thick, floral fog, and his thoughts moved as if through honey. The power of the chemical was stronger than he realized. It was making him do unthinkable things, like betray his own wife.

Beely carefully placed Reverie in her husband's arms before whispering in his ear. "I forgive you."

Two large men began to escort Beely out of the room. They said nothing. There were more men waiting outside. Beely did not protest or express any animosity toward them. When she got to the bedroom door, she turned one last time to her husband. "I know you will take care of Reverie. Remember the book of Job; God does all things twice, three times with a man to bring his soul back from the pit, that he may be enlightened."

Reverie buried her head in the nook of Max's arm. Beely was gone—her fate unknown. He sank into the heavy quiet, clutching a dying creature and a hollow prayer, realizing too late that the pit Beely spoke of was not where she was going—it was exactly where he had chosen to stay.

Chapter 23

THIRST

Not long after Ankur's men led Beely away, Max hurried to the stables, choking down his last ration of glouscenshire on the way. He waited for the calm to hit, but the relief would not come; he only grew more anxious by the second. He expected to find Greatest—the Brorayding Beely had renamed Joshua—waiting nearby, but the paddock was empty. No matter his name, the creature was nowhere to be found. Max scoured the favorite grazing spots, but his calls went unanswered. It was not like Greatest to be more than a whistle away, but with no time to solve the mystery, Max had to push on toward Marybah's.

Fortunately, there were three other broraydings in the stables. One was a pup, and two were being trained for other riders. As Beely often declared, broraydings hardly needed instruction; it was their owners who needed training. He quickly mounted the fastest of the two adolescents. Her name was Searing, a beautiful specimen with graceful agility and mature intuition. She was larger than most females, and her coloring was a light shade of emerald gray. Her horn was tall and darker than the rest of her body. Max gave the call to rise, pressing his fingers on the soft portion of her lower horn to indicate the direction he wished her to travel. She responded in an instant.

Marybah's picalo tree was not far. It took only minutes to arrive on the back of a brorayding. Searing was as wide as three grown men, making landing problematic amongst so many trees. Max gave the call for the descent. Searing saw an opening in the canopy, but when she reached it, it was not wide enough. Even so, she obeyed her rider's command and attempted to clear the ragged treetops. Her tender skin was torn by a thick branch. She immediately lifted, retreating back above the canopy.

"I'm sorry, Searing. Your epidermal fibers have evidently not toughened up quite yet. We'll find another way."

Had he been on his own brorayding, he would not have been hesitant to try an aerial drop, but Searing was not as experienced. Time was of the essence, and Max made the choice to descend anyway. His half-cocked rush to land was putting them both in danger of injury. He applied pressure on the right side of Searing's horn with two fingers. She moved to the right, following his command. He then rubbed his hand in a circular motion right behind her head, above her horn. She immediately lowered and hovered. They were now less than ten feet above Marybah's treetop balcony. Max gently patted her right wing. She tilted slightly, and he carefully slid off.

He landed harder than expected, twisting his ankle in the process. He winced in pain but could only think of what an outstanding job his young trainee had done. He shouted and gave a signal for her to return to the barn. He was not sure if she understood him, but he was fairly confident she would know to go home.

All of the commotion had brought Marybah to the highest point in her home. She was startled to find a man limping toward her, but she relaxed when she realized who it was. "Max, what in the Realms are you doing here? And why didn't you just come up from below like a normal guest?"

Max let out a painful moan and gingerly found his way to the nearest chair. "I've made a horrible mistake."

"I'm sure it wasn't the first and it won't be the last." Marybah sat in the chair next to her son-in-law. She looked him up and down. "You look awful."

"I feel awful."

"Talk to me."

"They took her. Like you and I agreed upon. She showed up last night, and I was able to send a message to Ankur. His men were there this morning. She didn't seem surprised."

"Did she try to run?"

"That's the weird thing: she was more at ease than an empachic. I think she knew, or perhaps was hoping for a similar outcome. I don't know what to make of it."

"My daughter has resolve, and she has always been at ease under pressure. However, I doubt she was hoping to be forcibly taken to the man she claims to despise?"

"I agree."

"So, what's the problem, Max?"

He rubbed his ankle. The throbbing was beginning to intensify. "I have doubts about betraying my wife. Is that so surprising? I have doubts about everything. The rumors about Ankur and the deaths of his servant and then that young man, Nicholas, I think his name was. What if Beely was right?"

"You look very weak and exhausted. I think you must be hungry. Perhaps thirsty as well. Do you think you can make it down to the kitchen?"

Marybah was not one to wait for a response. She immediately began her descent down the stairs. Spiral staircases were a beautiful and necessary feature of every picalo tree home. The natural wood steps wrapped around the thick trunk, winding their way up from the ground all the way to the balcony. Max's limp was more pronounced than before as he followed her down. He paused to briefly rest his ankle at her bedroom one floor below the balcony.

It was obvious that Marybah was not expecting company. The room was very disheveled, with books and empty food trays scattered carelessly on the nightstand, bed, and floor. The normally meticulous Marybah had even left unfolded clothing in a pile on the floor. Of course, he had never been higher than the living room; perhaps the clutter was normal. He paused for a moment as something on the dresser caught his attention. He quickly glanced back at the staircase to make sure Marybah was not in sight. He ventured off the stairs further into the bedroom.

He froze. Resting prominently on the dresser was a small portrait. He picked it up, drawing it close to his eyes. He recognized Marybah immediately—she was much younger, radiant, and seemingly much happier. Next to her, with his hand draped possessively around her waist, was someone who looked hauntingly familiar. Though the face was younger, the features were unmistakable; it was the same image of the man that Beely had found in her father's studio. It was Ankur.

Marybah yelled from below, "Do you need help? Is your ankle hurting much?"

Startled, he dropped the picture. He quickly retrieved it from the floor and placed it back on the dresser. His clumsiness frustrated him. He looked around the room as if he might find some other nugget of information that Marybah had hidden away in plain sight. When he got to the stairwell, he yelled down, "I'm fine, just had to rest my ankle." He looked at the room one last time before descending the stairs.

"What took you so long? I thought I was going to have to summon the roofahs," joked Marybah.

Max took a seat at the dining table as Marybah placed a drink in front of him. She sat across from him, and the two were silent for an awkward moment before she pushed the drink closer and said, "Here, you must be thirsty."

Max had begun sweating. He took a cloth and wiped the perspiration from his forehead. "How can you be so sure Ankur won't harm Beely?"

"If I thought he was capable of hurting my daughter, I would never have convinced you to alert him when she came home."

"How long have you known this man?"

"Long enough."

"And in what capacity?"

"Why these questions now? I thought I answered all of your concerns these last few moons."

"I thought so too. But—"

"All you need to know is that Beely is right about one thing: Ankur will be the leader of the Five Realms. That was inevitable. He is a man who always gets what he wants. It was in her best interest to meet with him. Everything will be fine, you'll see. Just be patient."

Max picked up the drink in front of him and asked, "What is this?"

"It's the fruit from Okrad—juiced. It'll make you feel better. Have some, and then go home and wait. Everything will be just fine. I promise."

Max finished the drink. She was right: it calmed him better than any elixir. As he tilted the cup back, the edges of the room seemed to soften, and the harsh sunlight filtering through the Picalo leaves took on a warm, honey-colored glow. Before he could ask for seconds, Marybah had refilled his glass. They never mentioned Beely or Ankur again.

On his trip back home, which took considerably longer without the wings of a brorayding underneath him, he was feeling much better. His limp was barely noticeable and lessening with every step. He even found himself happily humming. He chose to take the long way, walking down the main street where he and his own mother often traveled when he was a child. Passing a storefront, he saw a young family enjoying fresh baked goods. He paused, remembering how he loved eating the crust from his mother's spiced-chury curls. They were crispy and sweet, one of his favorite childhood treats.

"Good afternoon, sir Wren," said an older man walking his mashon as he passed by Maximilian. The creature moved with a precise, high-stepping gait, making it look as though it were walking on soft grass rather than the uneven cobblestones. Mashons were pets for those who did not care for empachics. The creatures, with oddly long, thin legs, were related to the mastadonians, but they were much smaller and did not suffer from the same debilitating inbreeding.

Max turned down a narrow alley, walking past several small shops. He delighted in the smells of homemade food and the colorful custom-tailored clothing. It had been so long since he had been on these streets. As he continued down the alley, he heard children laughing behind him. He turned around to find the smallest of the bunch cheerily waving at him.

Just outside of the town square, he briefly chatted with his old schoolmaster, Beechum Salifars, who lived in a house covered in yellow moss and purple grass. The home was well known, as it had been in the Salifars family for hundreds of turnings. Not many Nectarions lived in such antiquated houses anymore. They were sturdy, but usually rather small and always reeking of mold and dirt. In time, as the trees grew taller and wider, people built entire communities in them that connected by swinging bridges. Up in the trees, the air was fresh and the views amazing. Still, others moved into the sides of the canyon, where it was more temperate and serene.

Max was amazed at how his countenance had changed so quickly. His ankle felt much better, his perspiration subsided, and best of all, his mind was no longer jumbled with thoughts of betrayal, murder, and certain doom. He was focused again, and he felt that everything was going to be okay. He even heard the song of the pitchfork dragonfly. He had not heard or seen one of those since he was a very young man. The pitchfork dragonfly preferred areas with lots of people, as they were very social. He wondered why he had not come to town more often, if for no other reason than to hear the song of the pitchfork.

He, like Beely, loved Pixanese and all of its people and creatures. That was why Max gave in to Marybah's notion to appease Ankur. It was ironic, to say the least. Beely was fighting for Pixanese by opposing Ankur, while Marybah and Maximilian were convinced the only way for their fair realm to profit was to work with him and not against him. Max knew that Beely suffered under the same delusions as her father. He was convinced that the only way to heal his wife's escalating paranoia was for her to come face-to-face with her demons—as she would discover they were only in her imagination. Max was not convinced that Ankur was nearly as powerful as Beely thought. Ankur was simply a man who wanted everyone to have a better life. If they worked together, if each realm compromised, Max was certain harmony could be achieved.

Rarely had a man ever been so wrong about so many things. What he did not realize at the moment was that the more fruit he consumed, the more juice he drank of the glouscenshire, the more complacent and agreeable to Ankur's plans he would become.

Chapter 24

ST⊙LEN

It did not take long for news of Beely's capture to travel far and wide. Nothing even remotely like it had ever happened in the Five Realms, let alone in Pixanese. The first thing that Duly noticed after the news had spread was the sudden increase in the number of visitors to the Library of Truth.

When Propo arrived, he found Duly and his helpers scurrying about with dustpans, brooms, and rags. With more patrons came more dirt and debris. Duly, it seemed, had become even more obsessed than when Propo had last seen him. Propo stood near the entrance for several minutes, watching Duly bark orders at everyone.

At Duly's request, Propo removed his sandals and clanged them together in a futile attempt to remove all the loose "filth," as Duly called it. There were no more booties available, and clanging would have to suffice. After obliging, Propo sat and waited impatiently for Duly near the library entrance. Only four visitors came through the doors while Propo repositioned his copper headpiece for the third time. *Not exactly a stampede*, he thought.

When he mentioned the small number of patrons to Duly later, Duly explained that in recent times, the Library of Truth had not been as popular a destination as it once was. The recent number of visitors was a notable increase compared to the last few seasons. With the news of Beely's predicament, among other rumors, folks had become concerned about the current times; they wanted to brush up on the Word—specifically prophecy.

"I think you've become obsessed with dirt," Propo said.

"Quite the opposite, my fellow. It is maintaining sanitary conditions in a public space that I am obsessed with, and you should be too." Duly covered his face with his hands and sneezed. He briefly fumbled through his bag for a tissue, but after finding none, he wiped his hands on his own tunic—none of which went unnoticed by a bemused Propo.

"Follow me!" Duly demanded.

Propo followed Duly back to his private quarters. It was only the second time he had been invited into Duly's home within the library, but he had been thoroughly debriefed by Beely on the sniblet's poor housekeeping skills. He had not, however, been informed of the extreme hoarding talents of such a diminutive creature. Books were stacked from floor to ceiling. Every flat space was being utilized to store books. Between the stacks—the only place where one could walk— were dishes, clothing (dirty, it was presumed), and numerous bottles of mysterious liquids.

"What's with that expression on your face?" asked Duly.

Propo immediately shook the judgmental look of disgust from his face and smiled. "I didn't realize I was expressing anything, other than maybe my delight at seeing you, my friend."

"The plumdinger didly dinger you didn't. You looked as though you were about to regurgitate your last meal. And we're only friends because of Bee. Have a seat there."

"Where?"

"Where? Really? Anywhere! That's where."

Propo, not wanting to agitate his host a moment longer, sat on the nearest stack of books that would somewhat reasonably accommodate him. "What's with all the books? Don't they belong in the library?"

"Yes, they do. They all belong to the people. But now that Beely has been snagged and dragged away to the abyss, I'm beginning to regret my slow progress in getting these jewels of knowledge locked away in the secret room. The pages and pages of words have yet to be erased, but we shall have it done before the night is over."

"You are going to erase all of these pages by tomorrow? I don't think it possible."

"I'm not doing it all by myself. I have help. Besides, it's not as if we need to do it word by word or even page by page. You, apparently, did not pay attention when I explained the ingenious process I have developed. We are not erasing the words, but rather hiding them. They just need to be misted with the special chemical, and the words will disappear as if the pages had never been touched."

"If Beely had faith in you, so do I. How can I help?" asked Propo. He could no longer see the Braewicker. He could, however, hear him coughing and hacking as he maneuvered his way through a tunnel of books on his way to the tiniest of kitchens.

"You can help by freeing our dear Bee. She needs the help, not me," Duly yelled so as to be heard through the voluminous towers between them. He then tossed a book off the stove, over the stacks in front of him, nearly hitting Propo in the head. Duly was obviously distressed, as he had never before treated a book in such a demeaning manner.

"I have no way of helping Beely." Propo paused for a reaction and, after getting none, raised his voice further in case he was not being heard. "She will have to figure this one out on her own. If the prophecy is true about Ankur, she will need to think of something clever to save herself."

Three books, one after another, came hurtling toward Propo. He managed to dodge all but the last, which struck him on his shoulder blade. "Ouch! What are you doing back there?"

"Making ognatia. It was Beely's favorite."

"Please be careful with the books. I'm not as durable as I used to be."

Duly returned with two cups of steaming hot tea. "I always leave water on a warmer just in case someone stops by for a visit." Propo took the cup, though not intending to drink it, and immediately scanned the area for a place to set it down. After holding the cup in midair for an awkwardly long moment, Duly snatched it from his hand, poured the contents into his own cup, and tossed the empty vessel onto the floor—breaking it into several pieces.

Propo looked down at the pieces on the floor and back to his host. "Do you entertain many visitors?"

"Never. The only two people other than my helpers who have seen these walls are you and Beely." They both looked around, noting the irony that no walls could be seen through all the books. Duly took a sip of tea before asking, "Why are you here? Do you think it wise?"

"I don't. It's not wise at all. It will be my last visit. None of the Twelve should be seen together from this point on."

"That should not be difficult. We have no leader, no plan, no mission. I'm not at all sure what Beely's purpose in having such a group of twelve was for in the first place."

A sudden metallic clatter echoed from somewhere deep within the library. Both of them froze. Dust drifted lazily through the stale air, carrying with it the sour smell of old paper and something faintly chemical. Duly tilted his head, listening, one finger raised. When nothing followed—no footsteps, no voices—he exhaled sharply and resumed pacing, his bare feet slapping softly against the stone floor.

"Do you really expect me to believe that you, of all people, haven't researched and analyzed the significance of the Twelve?" Propo asked.

The Braewicker made an attempt to conceal his interest in the number, but the longer he spoke, the more animated he became. "If you mean the significance of the number twelve in the Bible—well, I did spend a little time reading up on it."

"You don't say."

"Beyond the obvious—the disciples—the number twelve is prevalent throughout the Old and New Testaments. It seems to represent authority and completeness. There were, of course, the twelve tribes of Israel, representing God's chosen people in the earthly realm, and the twelve gates in New Jerusalem, which, by the way, are named after the twelve tribes of Israel." Duly stopped to look at Propo. "You do know about Israel, right?"

Propo nodded affirmatively, but would not offer Duly anything else.

"That's good. Very good. There was also the twelve-year-old Jesus, the twelve baskets of leftovers, the twelve stars adoring the woman's crown as mentioned in Revelation—"

"I get it. You've obviously been reading a lot lately, but let's focus on the obvious implications, shall we?"

"Yes, yes." Duly nodded. "I thought you would come back around to that. The simple-minded always like the obvious, don't they?"

"Yes, yes, obviously!" Propo did not know whether he should be losing his patience or his mind, but fortunately, he found the Braewicker somewhat entertaining.

"The disciples, all twelve of them, were expected to share the Gospel, but also to become companions with Christ Himself, always learning about their Creator and testifying to His miracles and His teachings—" Duly paused mid-sentence and sniffed the air. The tea in his cup had gone untouched, its surface now filmed and still. Somewhere nearby, there was a— tap, tap, tap—each sound echoing too loudly in the cramped quarters. Propo shifted his weight, the stack of books beneath him groaning in protest, and for a brief moment neither of them spoke.

Duly shrugged and continued where he left off. "I must therefore assume that Beely chose twelve as a symbolic image. A good one, I might add."

"More than symbolic, my fellow. Each member of our group has a skill set that will help ensure that evil fails and truth prevails in our own realms. If you've researched the names of the Twelve, you already know of their diverse skills and talents. We will undoubtedly save the Word for its prophetic return, and we will plant seeds everywhere we can to make sure a framework will grow out of the ashes for the remnant that remains. Ankur may think he is in charge, but those ignorant of the Word will fall upon it like a sword."

"Wow!" exclaimed Duly. "Maybe you're not such a simpleton after all. You are correct. I have researched all of those chosen by Beely, and they are quite diverse in their expertise, skills, and locations within the Realms."

"Things are in motion. Beely and I were right. We were right about everything, so it appears."

"Of course, her father deserves the praise. If it weren't for him, we would all still be in the dark."

"Not true, Duly. It is God who really gets the glory. If we don't carry out His will, He will choose others. As it stands at this moment, we are the ones."

"What more must we do? We will have the books cleared and safely stored by the next moon."

"We must warn as many people as possible."

"No one will believe a word of it—not until they see for themselves. The Plotists are not deemed credible. I'm not even sure I believe any of it, even though I'm seeing it unfold before my very eyes. The curse of my heritage as a Braewicker, I can only presume. Braewickers are a notoriously untrusting group."

"Then why are you helping us?" asked Propo incredulously.

"I am content because of Beely. I owe her my support. She always believed in me, and so I choose to believe in her. It's as simple as that."

"Now that Beely has been captured, don't you see the evidence?"

"Look, it's one thing to think Ankur a power-hungry madman, but how in the Realms could one man divert all the water in the Five Realms and convince the entire populace to follow him? It's unfathomable. Why would any being follow someone who destroys their very lives? It makes no sense."

"They have blinded their eyes and hardened their hearts. They cannot see or hear the truth," said Propo remorsefully.

A loud crash was heard just outside of Duly's quarters. Duly quickly jumped to his feet. Before Propo could even stand, Duly hurried through and around the claustrophobic piles of books and clutter until he made it to his front door. Even for the fast sniblet, it took a full minute to work his way through the maze. It was another minute until he returned, breathing heavily and with a crazed look in his eyes. "Follow me!"

"What's going on?"

"There's no time to explain. Come now or suffer the consequences." Any other Braewicker would have left Propo to fend for himself, but Duly was starting to like the mild-mannered man. Duly worked his way over and under books, furniture, and other oddities. Propo followed closely behind, knocking over dishes in the process. Being small worked to the Braewicker's advantage in the cramped space. "Did anyone follow you here?" whispered Duly.

"No. At least I don't think so. I'm pretty good at traveling unnoticed."

Duly, followed closely by Propo, crossed out of the living room into a long hallway. It was not all that far, but at several points they had to remove books in order to continue. Propo felt like he was trudging through a thick forest with tons of undergrowth. He tripped not once but twice. He crawled over toppled manuscripts, none of which he recognized. The thought occurred to him that he should read more.

Duly finally stopped moving forward. He began tossing books back toward Propo. Propo, now on his hands and knees, did his best to dodge the colorfully bound missiles coming his way. It was the last pitch—a rare copy of a thinly bound book of ancient poetry—that almost took off Propo's right ear. "Watch it! Must you throw them *at* me?"

Duly ignored Propo and continued. "There's a small door to the outside under here. I hope you can fit through. Hold this..."

Duly handed Propo a bottle of his mysterious liquid as he proceeded to kick a portion of the wall. Nothing happened. "Help me move these." Duly pointed to his right. Both of them quickly tossed everything out of the way until nothing but the wall was exposed. Duly again began to kick the wall, but this time a small square door opened. No one would have ever known it was there. It was perfectly camouflaged.

"I can't fit through that!" insisted Propo.

Duly looked him up and down and then back at the opening. "Sure you can. You're not as big as you think you are. Might I suggest legs first?"

After several minutes of pushing, pulling, and the horrible smell of sniblet feet, both Propo and Duly made it through the small opening. They were outside under the darkening sky. The light was fading quickly, but it was still bright enough to see large creatures flying overhead. One after another of these nearly human-sized winged monsters flew over as if they were in a tactical formation. They were screeching loudly, but none of it made any sense to the two observers below.

Duly stayed crouched on his hands and knees but still managed to point up into the air. "What are they carrying? Look—each one of them is grasping…oh no. Please tell me it's not—"

"Books! They're taking all the books," said a mesmerized Propo.

"There must be hundreds of them." Duly could not take his eyes off the evil thieves. "I've never before seen such creatures. Have you?"

"Never."

"What'll we do? We can't let them take the books," said Duly.

Propo's face turned pale. "Surely you hid some of the more important ones, right?"

"No, we didn't have time. I told you we would have had them all secured by tomorrow. Just one more day is all I needed. One more day!"

Propo lay back on the soft sandy soil as if he had just taken a sword to the heart. They were hidden from the thieves above by a canopy of several large trees. He looked up and rubbed his head where Duly's feet had helped push him through the small trap door moments earlier. He let out a long sigh and then chuckled quietly to himself.

"Are you laughing?" asked Duly, trying hard to suppress a sneeze.

"Sort of." Although Propo was undeniably nervous and perhaps even a little frightened, he was also proud. He and Maliko, as well as Beely, of course, were right. They had been ridiculed as plotists for so long—especially Beely's father, who was more than likely killed for his beliefs. Now the time had come; the evidence was all around. The prophecy was unfolding right before his very eyes.

Duly crawled toward Propo and turned over on his back. He coughed up a huge wad of phlegm before speaking. "Well, it would seem as though you and Beely should have been a little quicker. I mean, you had all of this information about Ankur and the plots he was devising, and you waited until it was too late to do anything."

Propo turned his head toward Duly, who was now mere inches from his face, and spat out, "You can't be serious!"

"Shh...Quiet. Those ugly bat things may very well swoop down and carry us off too."

"Duly, did Beely ever tell you how I ended up here?"

"Behind the Library of Truth?"

"No. How I ended up a plotist, a theorist, a crusader, if you will."

"She said you worked with her father, that he counted you as his most loyal and brightest contemporary."

"That was the result, not the beginning."

"What do you mean?" Duly asked.

"Neither my father nor mother believed in God or the prophecies. They were like you, I guess."

Duly squinted his eyes in disbelief. "Yet, you are such a faithful believer."

"Not always. They encouraged me to read, study, and investigate all sides. At first, I was envious of the other world, the realm in which Jesus will eventually go and be crucified. I thought maybe that's why my parents didn't believe, because God is sending His son somewhere else...to another land, for another people, in another time...to die for them...to show His love for them. God is going to sacrifice His only Son for them, but why not us, why not here, in the Five Realms?"

"I understand." For the very first time, Duly felt a genuine sense of camaraderie with someone other than Beely. It felt wonderful to have another friend. He inched closer to Propo until they were side by side. "I mean, I would be upset myself if I believed in God and that same God treated me as a second-class citizen…an afterthought."

"That's where I was wrong though. We were never afterthoughts. God makes no mistakes. He loves all of His creation. He will be crucified as a sacrifice for the sins of everyone. There are people in the other world, so I've read, living now, that will never see the Christ, yet they will be saved because they believe in the saving grace of the Father. It's not too much different than us here. We have a purpose. We will serve a purpose for such a wonderful and loving God."

"And what's that?"

"I don't know everything. But I can tell you this. Did you know that we were always going to lose the Word here? The evil one was always going to take it away no matter what you, I, or Beely did to try and stop it."

"Then why try?"

"Because we believe, we pray, we do. God works out the details. We always fight for what is right and good. God will always work out things for good for those who love Him."

"I know that verse. It's in the Book—the one those vile creatures are carrying away."

"We still have work to do. We can't stop the good fight, my dear friend and brother, Duly. Our prophecies—not the ones in the Book, but the ones for our world—speak of a time when visitors from the other world will bring Good News. We, in turn, will strengthen their faith. We are all tied together: these realms and those. I don't know how exactly, but we must carry on the best we can."

The skies were completely dark now except for the light from the new moon. Duly jumped to his feet. "I think it is dark enough for the evil flyers not to see us but light enough for us to continue our escape."

"Agreed. Should we try to assess the damage?" asked Propo.

"No, I don't think that would be prudent. They don't just want the books. They want everything that is good. That includes the Twelve. We should leave from the back, avoid the front."

"We don't know where these sands will lead. Has anyone left the library from anywhere other than the front entrance?" asked a concerned Propo. In the Five Realms of Here, the Library of Truth did not reside in any realm. Its sands moved by miraculous means. The moving sands connected the Library of Truth to the other realms in mysterious ways. Although architects, mathematicians, astrological engineers, and even philosophers studied the phenomenon, no answers were ever conclusive. It was accepted that the place where the library resided moved at will. That was the same way every creature arrived at a destination—always moving—by will. If someone desired to visit the library, all they needed to do was sincerely desire it in their hearts. What they did when they arrived there was up to them.

"I have left by this way before. I can't promise where we will end up, but we will be safe. The library never spits a follower out into danger. In fact, between you and me, this is probably the safest way to go."

"Interesting, we finally found something you trust. Totally blind to where you'll end up, but you trust it."

The sniblit wrinkled his already crumpled brow as he headed away from the library. He glanced back at Propo, who was following closely behind, and snorted an incomprehensible response. Propo thought nothing of it. Braewickers were seldom good company, but they were experts at maneuvering their way through shifting sands.

Chapter 25

THE DRY DEATH

The sun and moons turned many revolutions. The seasons changed and the winds grew cold—not in temperature but in temperament. Creatures, both human and otherwise, had spread into lands that did not belong to them. Tensions and confusion grew as cultures clashed. Everyone was in search of answers and resources, yet found little of either.

Willow felt the weight of these seasons in her very marrow. Her bark had thickened into a gnarled armor, and the river she drank from had receded, exposing smooth, white stones that looked like bleached bones in the moonlight.

The Plotists, as it turned out, were indeed correct in their understanding of the prophecies. Literature—books, art, and anything written or printed—had been seized or destroyed. Confiscations initially affected only material related to spiritual matters but quickly expanded to encompass all material. Every

185

book, every written word that could be found, and most artistic expressions of antiquity were either destroyed or locked away in Ankur's dungeons. The Realms had grown quiet and illiterate, as if the collective memory was being methodically erased.

Undoubtedly, the most harrowing reckoning affecting every struggling creature was the Dry Death. The evil one had diverted all of the surface streams to Okrad. He had even managed to stop the flow of many underground springs. Exactly how he managed this remained unclear, but the result was quite evident: the Realms began to dry up. Because water did not fall from the sky as it did in the other world, those who did not have working springs had to relocate to areas that could quench their ever-increasing thirst. Trees, plants, and all things bound by sediment shared but one fate—death.

Entire towns became devoid of life. Families left their homes and belongings in search of living springs. The wealthy were able to buy their way into "wet towns," as they were called. People and creatures of less means had to sell everything they had, and many became indentured servants to those who took ownership of the few remaining springs, which were usually just a trickle of their former glory.

Willow was fortunate. She had all the water her roots desired. She wished there was a way to share her fortune with her timber friends far away. Before the drought got too severe, she still had an ever-dwindling number of visitors informing her of the demise of the water-poor realms. Many birds, insects, and other creatures lamented the fate of the great forest above Pixanese. The trees were all dead or dying. Vultures remained for those creatures that chose to stay behind or could not leave. Of course, the trees had no choice. Most had lost all of their leaves and were near death.

The news saddened Willow. It also made her angry. The death did not stop with the trees. Entire species of flowers, fruits, and vegetables were in danger of being lost forever. There were some who had the foresight to begin collecting seeds, just in case the winds of change came on stronger and lasted longer than anyone dared to imagine.

Ekrad Oren eventually convinced a colony of thorny briars to form a barrier between the Land of Mana and any travelers who tried to enter. There were many water thieves, as Oren called them, when the Dry Death first began. Other than Okrad, the Land of Mana had more water than anywhere else. In order to protect his treasured resource, Ekrad Oren orchestrated the impenetrable thorny briars to surround his land.

The streams and springs that Ankur had diverted to the Land of Mana not only grew his pharmakeia fruit, but also made the native specimens large, beautiful, and enticingly aromatic. Some say the water was cursed, and when the plants of Mana drank it, their fruit became just as tainted as Ankur's chemically altered glouscenshire—the proof of which would come in time.

For her part, Willow convinced Ekrad Oren to have at least one secret passageway into the Land of Mana. As it was, only Ankur's flying creatures could come and go. Ekrad Oren finally relented because he knew he had to stay on good terms with Willow. He was older and stronger, but she was clever and trusted by all. He chose not to alienate, or worse, aggravate her. They might not have agreed on helping Ankur, but they were both still trees, and they were family, like it or not.

Willow, unlike the prideful old tree in the middle of the orchard, knew prophecy. Prophecy told that creatures from the other world, where water fell freely from the sky, would break the spell cast on the Land of Mana. If the prophecy was true, thought Willow, they would know the Word of God as well as—if not better than—herself. The secret passageway could only be discovered by someone who knew the Word of God. It took a long time for Willow to plan and implement its construction, but it would take far longer for the prophecy to be fulfilled.

As the days passed, Willow worked on the secret entrance while she watched the planting and harvesting of Ankur's wicked abominations. The original, from which all the seeds came, was planted very close to Willow. She tried her best to communicate with the twitchy tree. Either it could not—or would not—speak to Willow. Once it reached the height of a tall man, it stopped growing. Its ability to produce fruit was unparalleled. In no more than fifty cycles, it had produced thousands of offspring. They were all planted in the orchard between where Willow stood on the river bank and where Ekrad Oren resided in the middle of the orchard. Ankur's flying creatures returned often to harvest their fruit.

With little to no water to grow crops, the people of the Five Realms grew dependent on the fruit from the Land of Mana for sustenance. It was delivered to them in abundance, and they were grateful to Ankur, their ruler, for his foresight. They began to call Willow's home the Land of Indulgences. Ankur was heralded as a hero. So many of them had forgotten it was he who had caused the death and starvation in the first place. He was not their savior, but their enslaver. Willow was one who would never forget.

"It may not be what it once was, but the view is still beautiful," said Athaliah.

Willow had not heard of Athaliah's whereabouts in quite some time. She was surprised to suddenly find her standing nearby overlooking the orchard. "How long have you been here, Athaliah?"

"Not long. One of Ankur's genetic mutations—he's calling them mastadonians—was able to lift me over the thorny barrier. It's not the most comfortable way in and out, but now that Ankur has allowed that old stubborn tree to have a living barrier surrounding the orchard, I have little choice."

"I thought you and the old tree were good friends."

Athaliah sat on the grassy knoll within arm's reach of Willow's outer branches. "Whoever told you that was a liar. I always thought you had reliable sources of information."

"No one told me anything. I assumed wrong. Believe it or not, you, Athaliah, are not a popular subject of conversation."

Athaliah responded wryly, "The great Willow, favored and beloved by all who know her—how could she ever be wrong?"

Willow no longer took on human-like silhouettes for Athaliah. Athaliah had visited many times, and there was no longer a need for illusions. They knew each other well.

"You look different, Athaliah."

"Really, how so?"

"You seem taller, larger, and your skin is odd—a bit translucent, if that were possible. It's as if you are being rewritten by the very choices you embrace."

"Maybe I've grown a bit taller. It's not unheard of. You've certainly spread out over time—taller as well."

"Is it true—the other changes of which I have heard?"

"Such as?" asked Athaliah.

"Have many of my brethren throughout the Realms lost their colorful crowns? Is there no more rustling from those that would replenish the lungs of the very slayers that seek their fall?"

"I don't know about everywhere. As far as I have been, I think so. The trees in the High Forest still stand, but not a leaf hangs from their branches."

"Okrad?"

"I'm sorry, my friend, but what few trees are left in Okrad will soon be felled for the betterment of Ankur's Realms. Ankur needs more wood to power his laboratories and, of course, to build. He never seems to stop building. The vast majority seem to love and fully support Ankur and his vision. I'm sure you know this. They feel that the joining of the Realms is a positive change for the future of all."

Athaliah paused, her eyes cold. "That wouldn't be too good for you, now would it?"

A few of Willow's branches retracted back away from Athaliah. A few others drooped down into a motionless despair. Willow remained silent for quite some time.

Athaliah, as hardened as she had become, still retained a glimmer of empathy. She could have continued with the details of Ankur's pillaging of Willow's kindred, but she said nothing more on the subject. Athaliah had only come to the Land of Indulgences, as it was now called, to see if Ankur's first was still producing offspring.

No one was allowed to eat the fruit of his special tree. Rather, the flesh of the fruit was allowed to rot—which it did quickly—so the seeds could be harvested and planted. There were some who had not yet eaten of the fruit, and Ankur was anxious to speed up production. Relying on the process of harvesting produce by natural means had always bothered him. Fortunately, the trees grew fast and bore fruit as early as their second cycle.

Athaliah finally broke the silence. "I'm surprised you didn't fight this harder."

"What could I have done? I'm just a tree. Our defenses are few against the likes of you and your kind. There's a verse in the Word: 'Make a tree good and its fruit will be good, or make a tree bad and its fruit will be bad, for a tree is recognized by its fruit.' One day, all in the Realms and beyond will recognize your fruit for what it is. I warned you long ago to take another path. You have chosen. Your heart is hardened."

"I suppose you're right," Athaliah replied. "Nothing you could have done would have stopped what is happening—or what will happen."

"What happens once you eat the fruit?" asked Willow.

"From what I've seen, it makes the living into lazy, wandering, useless fools. Unless they are given special orders, then they seem to act almost like drones, simply doing as they are told with no reservations whatsoever."

"But not you?" Willow asked. She peered closely at Athaliah, wondering if the girl was becoming something other than human—a vessel for Ankur's cold will.

"Don't be ridiculous. I will never eat of that abomination, as you call it."

"What if he finds out?"

"He must know. Although I play dumb like all of his other minions, I'm much more effective than any of them. He needs me now. He needs me to be who I am."

"Please, tell me what's happening to our world. Tell me what you've done. It's been so long since I've had a visitor from the outside."

"I guess it couldn't hurt. There's a large group that we call the Mara people..."

Athaliah spent the better part of the day talking with Willow. She, too, had little companionship these days. Although complicated, her relationship with Willow was a welcome respite from her usually mundane and often messy affairs.

Willow kept her promise in assuring that Athaliah's parents had water and food. They never saw their daughter, but they were told it was because of Athaliah that they were treated favorably in a world that was turning so dark. They asked no questions, but they mourned the loss of their only child.

Chapter 26

BENJAMIN AND THE GIANT

The blond child's blue eyes darted left and then to the right. When the path was clear, he ran behind the man passing out the fruit. There were several large wooden crates stacked high next to the supplier, who was barking orders. "Single file line, you bunch of lazy wretches!"

The gruff man was too busy to notice the small child, who was no more than seven turnings old, sticking his hands and feet between the crates' slats as he worked his way to the top. The nimble boy's eyes grew huge just before he reached up to grab one of the sweet-smelling glouscenshires. Even though hundreds were lined up to collect their cyclical supply of tainted fruit, no one but his own mother saw the wannabe thief.

Just as his small fingers caressed the coveted prize, she grabbed him and pulled him off the crates. She quickly carried him to a secluded area nearby. His mother sat him down on the hard, dusty ground and slapped his hand. The boy did not cry. It was not the first time he had attempted to steal from one of the regular suppliers.

She spoke in a harsh whisper, "If I've told you once, I've told you a thousand times to never eat that poisoned fruit."

"I know!" exclaimed the boy. He looked up into his mother's soft, loving eyes and wished he could behave better, if for no other reason than to make her happy. He was always getting into trouble. He just could not help himself. "I just wanted to touch one."

"I wish I could believe that. Beautiful things are tempting, I know. I won't always be around, Benjamin. I won't always be here to help you. You must learn quickly and you have to be strong—stronger than any child should have to be." She sat in the deserted alley next to her son. She wiped her brow as she slowly regained her composure.

Benjamin clenched his small hands into fists and struck the ground, pouting. "I'm tired of eating the same ol' boring bread!"

A tall, slender man interrupted the beginning of Benjamin's tantrum as he yelled from across the alley, "Lira! Is that you?"

Lira stood, brushing the dust from her dress. "Yes, Malcom. Benjamin and I were just about to line up for our scheduled ration." It was a lie, but a necessary one. It was safer for her and Benjamin if they appeared to have conformed to this new way of life.

The man's smile consumed his entire face. He twirled, seeming to dance, as he moved toward them. His arms moved up and down, undulating in slow motion. When he finally reached them, he touched Benjamin's nose with the tip of his long, skinny finger. "Boop," he said through giggles.

"I see you've already eaten from today's delivery," said Lira.

"I was one of the first in line. I was famished. Feeling so poorly, you know how it gets." He spun around in a complete circle, only stopping to stare up into the sky. "Isn't it beautiful?"

"What? What's beautiful? There's nothing up there but a boring ol' sky. You're just crazy. It's the poison fruit, isn't it, Mom?"

Lira gave her son's shoulder a hard squeeze and pulled him back toward her. Turning her head away from the man, she put her fingers to her lips. Benjamin knew the signal well and promptly clenched his teeth behind tight lips. Malcom laughed heartily. As he danced away from them, he mumbled. Lira doubted that he could understand his own self, let alone her son.

"Come, Benjamin, let's get home."

Benjamin was excited to be outside on delivery day. His mother had become more and more reclusive as he grew older. Benjamin held Lira's hand as they made their way through the crowds on the way to their canyon dwelling. There were lots of people and creatures dancing in the streets like the mumbling Malcom. Benjamin noticed that many of them seemed to have lost most of their clothing, or perhaps were too poor to afford it. Some were singing songs. He did not care for the voices, but he thought the idea was nice. He tried to imitate what he was hearing until his mom looked down at him with a strange look on her face. He stopped immediately.

When they made it to his favorite part of town, he noticed a new storefront. There were colorful masks and costumes in the window. They looked expensive. Although monetary currency still existed, most consumers traded goods and services since the Dry Death had destroyed their once thriving economic system.

Benjamin knew that his mom had coins; he had found them when snooping through her things. She had precious metals and jewels, but he never saw her use any of them for trade. Instead, she worked for a local wealthy family, cleaning and mending. His mom said she had to work because they were poor. He did not know what poor meant when he was younger. Now that he was older, he was starting to understand that poor meant "no."

No, he could not have this. No, he could not have that. He looked back at the masks one last time, the vibrant feathers mocking him with their high price, before his mother pulled him away. He did not like being poor.

Lira lifted Benjamin up by one arm into the air. He looked down just in time to see a man lying in the street whom he almost tripped over. The man was sick and emaciated, but probably just sleeping, or so his mom said. There were lots more like him, along the walkways and backstreets. Benjamin caught a whiff of the man, and his upper lip and nose instantly curled upward.

Before his feet had a chance to touch the ground, someone grabbed his other arm. He lost his grip on his mother's hand as he was lifted higher into the air—much higher—so high he could see over everyone's head.

It was a giant. A real giant had picked up the young boy and placed him on his broad shoulders. These titans were the most recent addition to Mara town. Benjamin was not sure where they came from, but he liked them. There were two types of these colossal figures. There was the oafish kind—that is what his mom called them—who were very strong and made funny grunts and other peculiar noises. They never seemed to hurt anyone, even while being so seemingly clumsy.

Then there was the kind that had nabbed Benjamin. They were the taller, more literate, and very cunning kind. They were fewer in number, but carried more political weight in Mara town.

"Put him down immediately!" screamed Lira at the top of her lungs.

It was too late. The giant's strides were much longer than hers, and the streets had become too noisy to hear a solitary voice raised in panic. Lira pushed through the crowd but could not keep up. There were tall giants, dwarf giants, and many normal-sized folks between her and her son. When a giant walked, crowds parted. For Lira, they barely moved.

She spotted a large water barrel under the eaves of a busy shop. She climbed on top for a better view but still could not see her son. She dropped her bag on the ground and quickly kicked off her sandals; they were no good for climbing. As it turned out, she could have left them on. As she was attempting to scale the rough stucco of the small building, a dwarf giant lent his hand. Lira nodded in gratitude as she stepped onto the large, chubby palm.

"S'no s'place for a s'woman to be s'climbin s'up to s'tops of shops, s'now is s'it?" said the gentle dwarf giant. Dwarf giants slurred almost all their words. At first, Lira had a hard time understanding them. Now that their numbers had grown amongst the Mara people, her ears had grown fond of the sound.

"Thank you, kind sir."

"'S'no s'problem at all," he beamed. Before he left, he even took the time to pick up her sandals and bag. Lira was amazed at how such big, puffy hands could manage such delicate tasks. Even though the dwarfs were only three-fourths as big as full-sized giants, their hands and feet were three-fourths larger.

Up high on the roof, above most of those in town, she scanned the horizon. She spotted her son on the shoulders of the giant. They were headed toward the tall caves, where the giants lived. It was quite a trek for a "smallie," as the shorter residents like the nearly six-foot Lira were called. She hastily made her way off the roof and set out toward the tall caves.

Benjamin had never ridden on a giant before. He could actually feel the wind in his hair from both being up so high and the speed at which the giant moved. He sat on the giant's right shoulder, holding tightly to his ear. At first, he wrapped his hand around a few coarse hairs poking out of the dark, cavernous ear, but his hand kept sliding off from the waxy coating. He wondered if that was where candle wax came from.

Benjamin shouted into the giant's ear, "What's your name?"

"Zorion," answered the giant.

"Where are we going?" the boy inquired, his voice strained by the rushing air.

"Somewhere. Anywhere. Enjoy the ride, little one. You're safe with me, Benjamin."

"How do you know my name?" Not waiting for an answer, Benjamin continued, "I'm afraid my mom is going to be very worried about me. Well, maybe angry even."

"She'll catch up soon enough."

The giant was huge, but not as big as a full-grown giant. It was said they took a hundred turnings or more to reach maturity. Zorion must have been an adolescent, thought

Benjamin. Still, he was able to step over entire buildings, as long as they were not too tall or too long. His gait was so smooth and steady that Benjamin could perhaps have let go of his ear entirely. Nonetheless, Benjamin chose not to chance it.

Benjamin could not have felt more secure. The giant was warm, and he even smelled good, like spices and smoke. His mom still had spices left over from when she lived in Okrad. She said there was no use for them here, but she would bring them down from the top of the cupboards and let Benjamin smell them every now and then. The spices, with their unusual aromas, always made her reminisce about old times and the old ways back in Okrad, before the evil Ankur. She used to make beautiful silk head wraps. She still had a few, but she never wore them here amongst the Mara people. She said that they should try to blend in and never stand out.

Benjamin wondered if he was standing out now. Could everyone below see him? Or was he too small and insignificant to be noticed sitting on the shoulder of a giant? Maybe if he stood up, they would notice him for sure. He did not have many friends in Mara, but if the neighborhood kids could only see him now. He let go of his tight grip on the giant's sticky ear, and with one knee down, he straightened his other leg. As soon as he felt steady enough, he straightened the other leg.

He was fully upright and standing. His head was almost even with the top of the giant's head. He smiled from ear to ear.

Zorion stopped to speak with a fellow giant. Benjamin took the opportunity to look into the crowd for any friends about. If they were down there, he would never have known. All he could see were the tops of heads. He looked back and could see all the way to where he and his mother lived. It was farther away than he had ever remembered being.

He noticed new buildings being constructed on one side of town. So many people and creatures were coming to the canyon. There was a large spring here, and the water was fresh and pure. His mom had told him that was why they had come, for the water, like everyone else—but he was starting to hear rumors. People said Okrad had lots of water for those allowed to live there, so that could not have been the only reason for their moving here.

The giant began walking again. Benjamin grabbed some of the giant's thick, wooly hair just in time to hold himself steady from the abrupt move. It would have been wise to take a seat, but he was having too much fun. The boy's mind became so distracted he forgot he was high on top of a giant. There were bugs with colorful wings buzzing around him. They were chattering among themselves, but up here, Benjamin was close enough to hear them.

"Who's the boy?" asked the baby-blue double-winged flier.

"Who cares! Just see if he has any nibbles," said the four-winged pinkish insect, eyeing Benjamin's soft hands as if they were the snack in question.

"He's too small, not worth it if he did," answered the double-winged one.

"I have nothing, no food to share. There's no food up here anywhere," said Benjamin.

Both creatures landed on the back of the giant and began picking up white flakes from the giant's clothing.

The four-winged pink one looked at Benjamin and asked, "If you're not up here for the nibbles, why are you up here?"

"I don't know, really," answered Benjamin.

"Not knowing—that's just so tiringly typical of you two-legged walkers."

"It's not my fault. The giant didn't tell me." Whether or not the giant heard them talking or just did not care was unknown to Benjamin.

The two insects kept gathering flakes and placing them in pouches on their bellies between their long, skinny legs. Benjamin could not make out everything they said, but he could tell it was about him, and it was not very nice. It was the way they kept looking at him, with their shifty eyes.

Finally, after filling their pouches with their favorite fare, the many-legged creatures hovered in front of Benjamin. In a taunting tone, while flapping its wings, the blue one said, "No one who goes into the giant's lair leaves alive. Little two-leggers like you taste great in giant stew."

Both of the bugs giggled with delight, their buzzing wings sounding like tiny, malicious saws.

Benjamin was not sure, but it sounded as though the two flake collectors were still laughing when they finally buzzed away. It did not matter; Benjamin did not believe what the bugs said. It was a mean joke, he was sure.

He hoped.

Chapter 27

THE JEALOUS ONE

The Five Realms of Here actually consisted of six. Or seven. It depended entirely on who was doing the counting—and it bothered no one but the cartographers.

The most well-known realms were called the Five Realms of Here: the Realm of Okrad, the Realm of Pixanese, the Realm of Restoration, the Empyrean Realm, and the Realm of Many. In addition, there were the Heavenly Realms, occupied by God and the angelic beings, and the more mysterious Earthly Realm. The Library of Truth belonged to no realm at all, existing independently of all others.

The Heavenly Realms were known only to the extent that they were revealed in the sacred Word of the New and Old Testaments. The Earthly Realm was known both through the sacred texts specific to the Five Realms of Here and the Biblical Testaments. The Earthly Realm was a mystery as great as any other, but the interpreters of the prophecies agreed that the fates of the Five Realms and the Earthly Realm were inseparable.

There were some who disliked this prophetic interpretation because they felt it elevated the Earthly Realm over their own. The "prophecy deniers," as they were called, referred to the interpreters of the prophecies by the derogatory term of "figments." The term implied that they were merely the stuff of dreams, having no basis in reality. Regardless of whether or not one believed the prophetic interpretations, all of the realms affected one another in some way. On that, everyone agreed.

The Empyrean Realm existed in the clouds and high above the clouds. It was often incorrectly called the Heavenly Realm by those who did not study the texts or were not taught the difference. The creatures who lived there rarely interacted with trespassers.

The Land of Mana and the Lake of Prosperity lay between the kingdom of Okrad and the Salt Lands. The entire area belonged to the Realm of Okrad. The realm was perhaps the most extreme in its contrasts: the driest, the wettest, the most abundant, the scarcest, the wildest, and the most cultivated.

The Realm of Restoration was a hilly, rugged land with no notable inhabitants. Other than the fact that it was hard to reach, no one knew why it was unpopulated. Some of the scriptures of the Five Realms seemed to suggest that it was a sacred land of miracles. A few philosophers thought that the Realm of Restoration would someday be the epicenter of the end of all realms. It was a pessimistic view, and not one entertained by many. Most gave the Realm of Restoration little thought or consideration. Only philosophers and prophets spent time contemplating such esoteric things.

The Realm of Many was the largest of all the realms. Its population was vast and spread far and wide over a diverse landscape, the highlight of which was a canyon so deep and wide that it brought all those fortunate enough to see it to their knees in awe. Most of its inhabitants, along with many from other realms, would eventually occupy the largest and deepest part of the canyon. The walls and caves provided shelter. The central spring supplied enough water for all who came to drink from it. The path in and out was straightforward and well-worn, making it easy, albeit lengthy, to travel to and fro.

The Realm of Pixanese was small, but it included the beautiful High Forest, which was filled with an abundance of interesting flora and humongous trees. A canopy of branches formed a dense covering over the forest floor, where the oldest and most mature trees were established. The kingdom of Pixanese resided in the canyon below the High Forest. Pixanese, with its rich culture and faithful inhabitants, had a strong influence on all of the other realms. Even though travel from one realm to another was rare, everyone knew that the opulence of Pixanese was beyond compare.

The prestige and position of Pixanese, lying near the center of all the Realms, were two reasons Ankur desired the cooperation of its citizens more than those of any other realm. He needed the Nectarions to trust him—at least for a time.

Using the sternest inflection of which she was capable, Beely addressed the dictator. "I demand that you restore water to the High Forest."

Beely stood in front of Ankur, who sat on what could only be called a throne with his loyal dog by his side. The throne was made of solid gold and embellished with large white pearl-like jewels set atop two rear finials. The throne was rendered even more ostentatious by the clear crystal pedestal upon which it sat. It was the most garish thing Beely had ever seen. She noticed that the dog's collar was adorned with smaller versions of the pearls.

Ankur waved his hand about dismissively until he abruptly motioned for Beely to come near. Beely, unsure whom he was motioning toward, looked to her right and then to her left. When she looked behind her, she was astounded to see that the line of citizens had gotten much longer since she had first arrived. When she looked back at Ankur, he was standing with his arm in the air and his elbow bent, as if to welcome her with an embrace.

After Ankur shoved his growling dog out of Beely's way, she had no choice but to oblige the awkward embrace. Ankur rested his arm on Beely's shoulders as he whispered in her ear, "I really wish you would refrain from being so demanding in front of the less desirable. I would not want to reprimand them if they thought behaving in the same manner was acceptable."

For a brief moment, the air felt thin again—too still, too enclosed—and Beely had to remind herself that she was no longer Ankur's prisoner. There had been a time—during those lightless three spans—when she had prayed only for silence, not rescue. The memory hardened her resolve now, and she reminded herself that this room had doors, and she was no longer counting days without light.

She finally responded, "Ankur—"

He placed two fingers on her lips before whispering, "Follow me to my personal chambers, and you can ask whatever you dare." He then looked around the reception hall until his gaze fell upon Athaliah. "Athaliah, would you please handle the remaining requests?"

Athaliah nodded as Ankur, followed by his smelly mastadonian, whisked Beely into a more private room.

The room was deceptively small considering the oversized entry doors. The furnishings were as garish as the throne from which Ankur had just stepped down. Beely counted eight ornately carved chairs around a long, polished, wooden table. This was obviously where Ankur intended to hold important meetings. The walls were flamboyantly swathed from floor to ceiling in red drapery that could only be described as bloody. A light fixture made from the horns of leering herd animals—now endangered—hung above the table, providing the only light in a room with no windows.

Ankur pulled out a chair for Beely. Once she sat, he walked to the opposite end of the room and seated himself in a smaller version of his ornate throne chair. His dog, however, remained with Beely, sniffing at every available orifice.

"I don't remember hearing that Okrad had precious metals," stated Beely, referring to the gold chair as she discreetly pushed the large, slobbering dog away from her satchel.

"Your memory serves you well. Okrad has never had any precious metals, or jewels, for that matter. Okrad has always been known for its fine silk. Could you imagine sitting on a chair made from nothing but silk?" Ankur laughed, but stopped abruptly when his guest failed to find the humor.

"But the curtains aren't made of silk." Beely looked for something to wipe the smell of dog from her hands, but other than the curtains themselves, there was nothing available.

"Such a good eye you have, Magistrate. They are made of aglorphia, the finest of materials from deep in the southern forests of Glycan, a small forest within the Realm of Many."

"Speaking of forests, that's why I came to see you today. The High Forest of Pixanese is suffering greatly. The trees need water. The few tributaries that had reserves have almost completely dried up." Beely was so distracted by Ankur's pet that her voice was not as confident as she had planned.

"I see. And what would you have me do about it?"

"Restore the upper springs."

"Restore the springs? But you are the magistrate of Pixanese. Is it not your job to take care of your own land?"

The normally calm and controlled Beely slammed her fist hard on the table. The dog was startled and backed away, eventually working its way back to its master. "Stop with the ridiculous games, Ankur. I agreed to your terms under one condition—that you spare Pixanese."

"And I have kept my end of the bargain. The kingdom of Pixanese and its inhabitants are all fine and well. Better than any other kingdom, as a matter of fact." He was, of course, not including his own kingdom of Okrad.

"The agreement, as you call it, was to provide for all of Pixanese, not just a portion."

"No. Our agreement was to allow a bit of water to continue flowing to the kingdom of Pixanese, not the entire realm. How in the Realms would you expect water for the entirety of Pixanese when so many others are hurting and doing without?"

"Are you quite serious? You are implying that we of Pixanese are the greedy ones?"

"I assure you, had your request been made public, word of your greed would have spread quickly. Rumors have already been spun concerning how the kingdom of Pixanese has somehow remained whole and prosperous while all others are in total chaos."

"And what are they saying about Okrad?"

"Okrad is supplying all of their most important needs, dear. Fruit from our orchards and water from our springs. Most of the enlightened creatures are grateful for Okrad."

"And in return for that lie, you have pillaged everything of worth from them."

Ankur stood up, placed his hands on the table, and leaned in toward Beely. "Watch your tongue, Magistrate. I have asked nothing of Pixanese other than its allegiance."

Beely stood at the other end of the table, copying Ankur in his aggressive stance. "You have our allegiance for one reason and one reason only: because of the agreement you made with me."

Ankur erupted in laughter. Beely could not discern if his reaction was caused by anger or simply a way of making her exceptionally uncomfortable. After his laughter subsided, he spoke in a whisper, "Do you think you are of any significance whatsoever?"

"I know that I made a mistake, Ankur."

Ankur relaxed as he slowly sat back down. "That's better, my dear Beely."

Beely walked around to the back of her chair and pushed it under the table before walking toward Ankur. She stopped one chair shy of his, where his dog sat growling. "You misunderstand me. My mistake was not about being here today, challenging your ongoing destruction of our way of life. My mistake was negotiating with you in the first place. My mistake was signing a contract with the devil!"

The dog growled again.

Ankur dug his fingernails into the soft silk covering of his golden chair. He took the back of his other hand and wiped his mouth. The motion served no purpose other than to give him time to think of an appropriate response. "You can let those in the High Forest know that since the trees are dying, they will soon be harvested to supply the other realms. Waste not, want not, I like to say."

The dog barked, seemingly in agreement.

Beely responded sternly, "Don't do this, Ankur."

"Or what?"

Seeing that he was unpersuadable and knowing that he was not good at controlling his impulses, Beely decided to do an about-face—both figuratively and literally. She knew this new leader of the Five Realms had obliterated entire kingdoms when they would not agree to his demands. She believed that she still held some influence over Ankur, or he would have already done away with her as well as Pixanese.

Beely refrained from speaking another word until she placed her hand on the door. She then turned her head and slowly uttered the last thing Ankur would ever hear from her: "If the High Forest dies, so will our agreement."

Before she could fully open the oversized door, Ankur responded, "You should have eaten the fruit. You fooled your husband and your mother, but I always knew. You have never really been under my influence, even though you betrayed your own people."

He paused just long enough to absorb how his words struck Beely's heart like a poisoned arrow. "But know this: I have gotten what I wanted from Pixanese. The secret spring is mine, and it will never be recovered by you or anyone else. You should join me and cease with your misguided devotion to Pixanese, or you will see everyone that you love die."

The door clicked shut behind her, but the threat trailed after her like a physical weight. *"You should join me... or you will see everyone that you love die."*

Beely leaned against the cold stone of the corridor, her breath coming in ragged hitches. For six turnings, she had lived a lie. She had told herself that the three spans she had spent in that lightless cell were the price she had to pay to save Pixanese from the Dry Death.

Now, as she walked out of the palace and into the dim light of the canyon, she saw exactly what her contract with Ankur had bought.

On her way back to the village of Pixanese, once the height of culture and industry, she felt as if she were headed toward a funeral for the living. No one looked up as she passed; their eyes were glazed and hollow, fixed on nothing. They were under the influence of the glouscenshire—Ankur's "gift" from the Land of Indulgences.

Her stomach turned. The "small culvert" Ankur had allowed them was barely enough to keep the people alive, but it was not enough to keep them whole. By revealing the spring, she had not saved Pixanese; she had only ensured it would die slowly, incapacitated by euphoria and a lack of ambition.

I am a traitor, she thought, the realization hitting her harder than any arrow. The survivors blamed her, and she could no longer find the words to defend herself. Her miscalculation had not just harmed her home—it had doomed every village beyond their borders that relied on that water. At the time, she had believed his threat to destroy Pixanese as he had all other major kingdoms. She had known he was not bluffing, but knowing that provided no comfort now.

The Word of God had been completely abolished. The shelves of the Library of Truth were sterile and empty. Beely finally faced the fact that her agreement with Ankur was a farce.

She began to pray. She prayed for the strength to atone for her silence. And then, with a trembling heart, she prayed for Ankur. She remembered how Christ had prayed for his enemies on the cross, and she knew that even if her people saw her as a "figment" or a traitor, she had to follow that example.

She did not know how to fix the world she had helped break, but she knew that the faith she had once hidden in the dark was the only light she had left to lead her.

THE CHILDREN

Maximilian looked around the store at the mostly empty shelves. The few things still available for sale were basic necessities: loaves of bread, preserves, dried legumes, milk, and eggs. There were no cuts of meats and very few fresh vegetables. He sifted through spices that were left over from before the conquering of the Realms—or "the joining" as it was sometimes called. After examining the spices more closely, he knew why they were still on the shelf: they were not from Pixanese, and no one knew how to use them.

Ankur had initially sold his plan to join the Realms as a way to encourage trade, but that promise did not last long. The only thing Ankur wanted to trade was his glouscenshire. Once his poisoned fruit infiltrated entire communities, most economic activity ceased, except for what was necessary to keep the basic needs of society functioning. There always seemed to be a few who were either not affected by the fruit or were smart enough to never consume it. These were the ones who profited most, taking the spoils of the addicted.

Max walked to the counter, kicking bits of trash aside to clear the way. There were no helpers to perform basic tasks, such as cleaning. The owner, minding the register, filled Max's canvas bag with nut flour, a few preserved vegetables, and the last box of star sugar. The owner said nothing, but words were not necessary to convey his thoughts or feelings. The look on the man's face said it all. Even though Pixanese was supposedly spared the worst of Ankur's "diplomacies," it still suffered greatly. While lower Pixanese had water, the inhabitants were still adversely impacted by the overall deterioration of living standards under Ankur's leadership.

Max wondered if the market owner, like Beely, refused to take the glouscenshire. Had he escaped Ankur's poison entirely, or—like Max—learned to keep its grip in check with small, deliberate doses?

Max left the market with his satchel filled with enough to make vegetable pies for at least a week. Walking through the town center, he saw very few residents. The streets, like the store, were cluttered with debris. The tree houses, hanging over the shops and storefronts, were dark and quiet. He wondered how Marybah was faring. He had not seen her since he reunited with Beely. He was tempted to walk by her picalo tree just to see if there was any activity. Rumor had it that she was receiving personal deliveries of the finest delicacies, which were usually only available in Okrad. Only Ankur could have been providing such opulence.

As Max walked on, he reminisced about the sounds of children playing in the streets. That was the thing he missed most: the laughter of the children. The only time the joyful banter of the young could be heard was during the delivery of the glouscenshires, and even then, it was not the same. The laughter came too sharply, too suddenly—like a reflex rather than joy. There was no innocence in the laughter derived from poison. The fruit provided a euphoric high when first ingested, but the body would crash soon thereafter. The euphoria did not last long. Furthermore, toward the end of the cycle, almost everyone had exhausted their allotted supply. The cycle was vicious, and Max felt its pull even now, like an itch beneath his skin that never fully disappeared.

Just before he turned the corner where his old schoolmaster, Beechum Salifars, lived, Max found an empachic on the side of the road. It was highly unusual to see a chic outside on its own.

"Are you okay, little fella?"

The light pink empachic almost appeared gray from the dust embedded in its fur. When Max spoke, it rose to its feet. It was hard to notice any movement, as an empachic's legs only averaged two inches in height. Nonetheless, Max could now see that its hair was matted in a clump of what looked like dried blood on its lower right side.

"Are you hurt, little one?" Max leaned over to pick up the chic, who did not protest. The creature trembled—not with fear alone, but with the dull resignation of something accustomed to pain. "You're not even able to purr, are you?" Max combed his fingers through the chic's fur and thought he felt a very faint vibration.

A young boy of perhaps twelve ran up to Max and yelled, "That's mine! Give it to me!"

The boy reached out with his dirty hands and long, unkempt fingernails in an attempt to grab the chic from Max's grasp. Max was too tall, confounding the boy's futile attempts to snatch the frightened animal. The chic retreated under his protector's arm, but only managed to get his head under Max's armpit. It let out a thin, broken squeak—sharp enough to make Max's chest tighten.

"Whoa! Hang on there, kid. What's your name?"

"None of your business. Give me back my ball!" yelled the boy.

"Ball" was a derogatory term for an empachic. The only ones who used that term for such a sensitive creature were either unscrupulous breeders or the superstitious. Since the joining and Ankur's prohibition of spiritual instruction, many had become suspicious of all miraculous things, especially the youth. Empachics were one such miraculous species, with the ability to calm and heal in a supernatural fashion.

Max addressed the boy. "Simmer down so we can talk. This little chic is injured. Allow me to take him home, and when he's better, I'll bring him back." It was a lie, but one that Max had no issue telling.

"You're a liar!" shouted the boy. "Liar! Liar! Liar!"

The boy kept chanting the word louder and louder until other townspeople started to ease out of the shadows. Only seconds ago, the streets had been almost completely empty, and now the hysterical boy was making enough of a ruckus to awaken his nearly catatonic neighbors. Max caught fragments of hollow stares and slack mouths—faces emptied by fruit and fear alike. He thought it wise to pick up his pace. The glouscenshire had undesirable and unpredictable effects on its victims. He walked briskly, with more purpose.

Since his bag was overstuffed, Max gently placed the empachic under his shirt. He began to take larger strides, which eventually turned into a slow run. The townspeople were obviously agitated, as some had even ventured off their porches onto the street.

He looked up as he passed his old schoolmaster's house to see Beechum Salifars sitting, motionless. He had no expression on his face whatsoever. The man, who never failed to greet Max with pleasant conversation before the joining, simply sat on his porch not even noticing his friend, who had a bulging, bouncing satchel on his back, an empachic sticking out of his shirt, and a boy of twelve screaming obscenities at him.

By the time he cleared the last house, Max realized the boy had given up his futile pursuit. Max took a moment to examine the injured chic as he walked the rest of the way back home. Max thought Reverie was light, at just under six pounds, but this dusty furball was even lighter—five pounds, tops.

He stopped for a moment, sitting down, to examine the chic's belly. He confirmed two things: it was a boy, and it was injured. There was a large red hematoma on his belly. The bleeding had long since stopped, explaining the matted fur. The injury was too uniform, too round, to have been an accident. The boy had not only referred to him as a ball, but was likely using him as one as well.

"You poor boy. Don't you worry, though. My wife will know just what to do with you. If you like our home, you're welcome to stay as long as you like." He gently rubbed the underside of the chic. The small chic let out a tiny squeak. A fragile sound—but one that carried just enough life to give Max hope.

A good squeak, thought Max. "I think that's what we'll call you, Tiny Squeak. Maybe Thai for short."

****

Beely was covered in mud up to her waist. Her hair, unbraided and disheveled, was only spared from becoming a ball of frizz because it, too, was matted with the crusty remnants of the day's labor. As her husband approached her in the field, with Thai safely tucked into his shirt, he heard Beely's wails from quite some distance away. As he got closer, he found his wife on her knees, hands clenched and mud dripping through the fingers of her tightly closed fists. She rocked slightly without realizing it, as if motion alone could keep the walls from closing in. It was the third day in a row that Beely had been in the field working on the sole remaining well that fed all of her beloved gardens.

"He's doing this to retaliate against me!" Beely announced between sobs. The words burst out of her, sharp and breathless, as though they had been trapped behind her ribs for too long.

Even though Maximilian had been under the influence of Ankur's drug for a while, he remained somewhat healthy. Beely encouraged him to eat other foods and exercise, and she insisted that he still work with his broraydings. He challenged her suggestions on a daily basis, but his respect and affection for her were unquestionable. The drug, as powerful as it was, could not completely extinguish the power of love. He eventually did what Beely asked of him. Even though he continued to consume the glouscenshires, he also ate other healthy, unadulterated foods. He walked to town with Beely often and continued working on their homestead. Somehow, despite his addiction, he still found enjoyment in training his beasts.

212

Although there were not many customers who could afford trained broraydings any longer, he practiced his craft with regularity.

He looked down at his wife and softly asked, "What can I do to help?"

She answered through her fading sniffles. "Nothing. I give up. None of this matters anymore." She paused for a moment as she looked around her beloved grounds. Her voice dropped, sounding hollow and distant. "What am I doing? What difference could any of this possibly make?"

Beely glanced at her garden and then at their house, which sat on the hill not far above them. Her gardens, and the land surrounding them, were only a shadow of their former glory. The gardens had grown unruly where water could reach and completely dead where it could not. The house needed its thatch roof repaired, and the stone pathways were drowning in overgrowth that had long since turned brown.

There was not enough help for the daily upkeep, with Max still somewhat under the influence of the drug. Her tears were not only for her gardens and her house. She felt lost. She knew she had failed Pixanese and perhaps the entire Five Realms of Here. She was fearful about the future. She was constantly overwhelmed with remorse.

"I know it doesn't look the way it once did, but life as we knew it will return someday," reassured Max.

She lifted her hands, examining the now hardening soil, feeling the grit bite into the cracks of her skin, and then looked up into her husband's eyes. "I'm not talking about this."

"Then what's bothering you?"

"You wouldn't understand."

He sat down next to his wife and grabbed her mud-encrusted hands in his. He stared deeply into her eyes and said, "I know I'm addicted to this stuff. Just like most everyone else seems to be, except you." Beely looked at him with surprise. "Yes, I know you haven't been eating the fruit. I may be high most of the time, but I'm not blind or stupid."

"I never said—"

"I know. I also know that you love me very much, or you wouldn't even be here now. I realize our marriage may have started under questionable pretenses, but my love for you is real. I could never love another. You are my beginning, and you are my end."

Beely wiped her eyes with the back of her hand, the only spot that was somewhat clean. For a moment, she let herself believe him fully—and the relief frightened her almost as much as the despair had. She sighed and said coyly, "Are you sure you haven't just taken the fruit today?" Just then, the malnourished and bruised empachic worked his way out of Max's shirt. "What do we have here?" asked Beely.

"I've named him Thai. I think one of the boys in town was abusing him. I thought we could look after him."

For the first time in days, Beely smiled. The sight of the injured chic stirred something protective and fierce within her—something Ankur had failed to grind out of her in the dark. She reached out her hands and said, "Aren't you beautiful. Come here, sweet one." The empachic sniffed Beely's hand in consideration but turned back into his rescuer's arms, burrowing under Max's coat. Beely looked surprised but also pleased. "That's a first!"

It was true; empachics adored Beely. She had never met a chic that did not immediately gravitate toward her. All of the chics living with them were friendly with Max, but it was Beely they preferred to smother with constant affection.

"Give it time. I'm sure he'll be wrapped around your little finger like all the others," said Max.

"No. I don't think so. This one has clearly bonded with you. It'll be nice having another one similar in size to Reverie. But I must warn you that the roofahs are no longer visiting. We must do our own administering of medicines and the like."

"I'm sorry, I hadn't even noticed. When did they stop coming?"

"Nothing, it seems, is as it was. The roofahs have taken refuge with the Mindalites. The Mindalites still have their own well water and the best hiding spots to remain safe from Ankur. I don't think they have been affected by the fruit."

"No one will admit it, but Ankur has been experimenting with many of the animals, especially those that can fly, such as the roofahs. If the broraydings were easily captured and trained, he would have undoubtedly wreaked havoc on their populations. Will things ever return to the way they were?"

The question was rhetorical, but Beely was tempted to answer it nonetheless. There was so much she wanted to share with her husband, but she was not sure he was ready to hear about her undercover activities. She did not fear her husband to any extent, but she was not sure of Ankur's ability to manipulate him into sharing information best kept secret. Contrary to what anyone in Pixanese might have been thinking, Beely had never ceased her efforts to undo Ankur's treachery.

As if Max were reading Beely's mind, he said, "It's been a week. I've tried to stop before, but this is as long as I have gone without eating the fruit."

"Well, you may not be oblivious to the things around you, but I obviously am. I didn't even notice you were trying to stop."

"You're so busy. Meeting with Ankur and his minions, trying to help the townspeople and the Twelve...I guess."

"You know about the Twelve? I must be getting sloppy with keeping my extracurricular activities secret."

"I've had moments of sanity over the last few spans. I'm seeing and understanding more of what's happening around us."

"You mustn't—"

"I would never tell Ankur anything ever again. I was wrong. Your mother was wrong."

"What changed your mind?"

"The children."

"The children?" she repeated.

"In town. There's no more laughter when I walk along the streets in the town center. No more innocence. It's so dark there—everywhere, I guess. It's one thing when adults make their own bad choices, but it's entirely another thing when we force those choices on the children. They don't deserve the wrath of our ignorance, complacency, and immorality."

Beely rose to her feet and looked around cautiously. "You mustn't let anyone know that you are no longer regularly eating the fruit, especially my mother."

Max responded thoughtfully as they slowly began walking toward the house. "I've been steering clear of your mother for many moons, in case you haven't noticed. Beely, I really thought that Ankur wanted to make life better for everyone. Even without the influence of the drug, I could never have imagined that this could have happened to our realms. It all happened so quickly."

"It's been six turnings. Actually, over six if you count the time Ankur had me unceremoniously locked away on his ever-expanding grounds."

"One day I will make it up to you, I promise," said Max.

"I don't blame you, love. It was exactly the way things needed to happen. It's not for you to know the details just yet, but all is going as planned. God is sovereign, and nothing happens that He does not allow to happen." She paused as if trying to remember something. "There's a verse in the Book. It says something to the effect of, 'Many are the plans in the mind of a man, but it is the purpose of the Lord that will remain.'"

"Planned or not, I was still complicit in how it all went down. I literally told Ankur when and where to find you. I tried with all of my persuasive ways to get you to ingest the glouscenshire."

Beely took his hand in hers, leaned over—careful not to press against the tiny empachic still hiding underneath his coat—and kissed her husband. "I forgive you. I absolve you of any wrongdoing. It's what you do now and from here on out that counts. The rest is behind us. It's not unlike the message of our Savior. You have repented, and you are embracing the truth. Now give it time, and all the rest will be revealed."

Max pulled her tightly into him and whispered in her ear, "I love you so very much, even if there is too little water to wash off all the dirt you have just gotten on my clothes." The little empachic squeaked from the pressure of their close embrace. Max chuckled as he let go of Beely and looked down at their new housemate. "I'm sorry, Thai. I forgot you were there. Let's go introduce you to the rest of our brood." He looked at the mud on his hands just shared by his wife and added, "After we get washed up, of course."

Chapter 29

TRANSFORMATIONS

Beely selected members of the Twelve based on their faith and unique gifts. Despite objections from Eudox, Beely added her husband to the list; however, she promised not to inform or involve Max until he was completely free of the glouscenshire's influence.

Beely knew Max possessed gifts no one else in the Twelve had: he was an expert tracker, a master at training almost anyone to fly, and above all, the kind of leader others would willingly follow to the ends of the Realms.

Beely made sure to choose at least one individual who knew how to interpret prophecy. If the Twelve stood any chance of defeating Ankur, they would need the wisdom prophecy provided. Yet Beely knew that while prophecy foretells events to come, it rarely reveals precise details of how or when they will unfold. This, Beely was soon to discover, was a blessing in disguise. Had any of the Twelve known the details of Ankur's recent transformations, they might have given up before ever getting started.

No one could have imagined the depths of depravity to which their self-appointed leader had succumbed. Ankur was wicked, and he would stop at nothing to conquer the Five Realms and beyond.

He wanted it all. By the sixth turning of his self-appointed reign, Ankur had monopolized every resource he desired—building materials, precious metals, exotic foods—and incapacitated his subjects with the spirit of pharmakeia more effectively than he had hoped. Resistance was virtually nonexistent once he seized control of the prominent kingdoms.

Yet, as was the case with most rulers, he wanted more. He desired to rule not only the physical realms but the spiritual realms as well. He wanted to be revered as the greatest and most powerful being to have ever lived.

Ankur became obsessed with conforming others to his image. In order to accomplish this profane goal, he was convinced that he would need to transform into something that could be replicated. Those closest to him, like Athaliah, chalked it up to psychosis, but none dared speak of his madness aloud.

The task of changing one's actual genetic structure was dangerous. Ankur was willing to risk his own life in the pursuit of becoming what he considered to be superior to all other life-forms. He wanted to become nothing less than the most formidable force ever to have existed in the Realms. Although he was willing to risk his life for success, he was not stupid. Before subjecting himself to any real bodily harm, however, he would first experiment on the weaker, the younger, and those most loyal to him. No one was safe.

"The time has come, my honorable and trustworthy followers."

Ankur stood in front of an assembly of several hundred men and women from Okrad. These were the followers who believed in him before the glouscenshire was introduced—the hardcore allegiants. They were all wearing dark komas on their heads. It was an eerie sight to see a room full of Okradians with their heads and faces completely obscured by the Okrad koma.

Traditional komas were rarely dark, never black, and they never completely covered the face. The dark koma hood had become a social phenomenon in Okrad. Those who wore the koma hoods were called mastadonians after the dogs kept by their sides. Even without the dogs, the title would have still suited them well. The two-legged mastadonians dressed completely in black, obeyed the commands of their leader without question, and threatened all outsiders.

Ankur motioned for Haberstitch, his lead scientist, to come stand by his side. "This brilliant young mind has created something very special for us. I have asked all of you to come today so you might be the first to experience the sublime shedding of all that holds you back from becoming the very best that you can be."

Haberstitch's eyes immediately darted from Ankur to those in the crowd. Lines formed on his forehead as panic began to grow. Was it possible that Ankur was talking about the genetic cross-enhancers he had been developing?

Haberstitch's heart began to race, and he found it hard to breathe, but he was careful not to show his confusion. He desperately searched the crowd for something or someone who could help. Surely Ankur was not about to do what he suspected. Surely Ankur was not so cruel as to inject all of these loyal followers with such an experimental and transformative chemical.

Ankur continued, "We of Okrad—your mothers and fathers, and all of you here now—have always been superior to those in the other realms. We are the rightful heirs to everything the Five Realms of Here have to offer. We are going to claim our reward, the honor that your parents and their parents worked so hard to attain."

Fair hands, contrasting against dark robes and hoods, parted komas to reveal hidden faces in the large crowd. There was much murmuring and whispering among the excited followers.

"Look at what has happened in the last few turnings of the moons. The Realms have fallen into despair. The inhabitants have gotten lazy, and the lands have suffered greatly. We of Okrad must lead the Five Realms into a new age. We must lead our weaker subjects into a time of enlightenment. Only with your help can our lands be healed of their afflictions." There was loud applause and cheering as the chatter amongst the crowd intensified.

While Ankur spoke, Haberstitch managed to find the only one in the crowd who might have had some influence in stopping Ankur. He spotted Athaliah alongside the farthest wall. Although she, too, was dressed in all black, her head was not covered like the rest. He slowly backed away from Ankur until he was hidden in the crowd, then quickly pushed and shoved his way to Athaliah.

He did not look up at her when he spoke, instead staring straight out in front of him. "The serum is not ready. It has not been fully tested. The results are cautionary at best."

Athaliah, also staring directly in front of her, asked, "Did it work on the lab rats?"

"Work? In what context? There is nothing to compare it to, and there has not been enough time to see the long-term effects."

"Follow me," she said.

Without waiting for a response, Athaliah took a few steps to her left and slid through a crack in an open door. Ankur was enjoying his moment with his followers. She knew his routine well. He would not be finished for a long while, and he was oblivious to anything other than the adulation of his devoted mastadonians.

Haberstitch was hesitant to follow Athaliah, but he had no other choice. He, too, knew Ankur well. He knew Ankur was planning to inject all of these people with the very concoction he himself had been formulating for the last five turnings. It could very well be a lethal injection, as far as Haberstitch knew.

It might not kill them immediately, but there were no studies on what might happen after long-term exposure. He wished he could have feigned concern for the mastadonians, but he knew that if the serum failed, he would most definitely be killed.

When Haberstitch entered the other room, he was shocked to find Athaliah disrobing. Her black cape and clothing lay on the floor. She was turned with her right side facing the door.

221

One arm covered her breasts, and her other arm was fully extended up toward the ceiling. It was night, and there was not much light, except for what crept in through the partially opened door.

"Don't be afraid. Come closer," she said.

Haberstitch walked slowly over, never taking his eyes off of Athaliah.

"Do you see it?" she asked.

"Astonishing. When did you get the injection, and who gave it to you?"

"The 'who' is not important, but I suppose the 'when' you will need to know. I received the injection three cycles ago."

Haberstitch, shy and reserved only moments before, walked up to the nude Athaliah and examined under her arm. "May I?"

"Of course," she answered.

He slowly ran his fingers over the delicate webbing along her ribcage all the way up to her wrist. He was mesmerized. He took his finger and gently poked at the thin membrane in between the veiny weblike structure. "Can you feel that?"

"If you only knew what I could feel." She dropped her winged arm and proceeded to dress. "I can feel the still air on my skin as if it were being blown by a strong wind. I can feel the blood coursing through my veins. It's like nothing I have ever experienced before."

"And?"

"I can hear…everything. Insects in the walls, rodents underground, birds high in the air; I can hear them all."

"Have you experienced any illness?"

"Of course I have. Do you think new appendages come without growing pains? When my wings first started coming in, I wanted to take a knife and cut them off down to the bone. The burning and itching were intolerable, and of course, I had no clue as to what was happening or what the end result would be. Still don't. I suppose they're still growing."

She peeked through the door. Ankur was still soaking up the adulation. She turned to Haberstitch and asked, "Do you think I'll be able to fly with these someday?"

"You have no idea what you've taken, do you? How much has Ankur told you about these experimental genetic enhancements?"

"Only that they would make us stronger."

Haberstitch shook his head in disbelief.

"What is it?"

"It's not for me to say."

Athaliah moved with pure instinct, faster than even she expected. Haberstitch found himself pinned against the wall, feet dangling, her hands clamped firmly around his throat. He gasped and clawed at her grip, struggling for air, but could not break free.

Athaliah hissed, "I want to know everything you know. What will I become?"

He found it hard to breathe, much less speak. Still, he mumbled the first thing that came to his mind, the first thing that might keep this woman from killing him. "I'll show you."

"What did you say?" she asked, practically crushing his esophagus. It suddenly occurred to her to loosen her grip so he could speak more clearly. He slid down the wall until his feet touched the ground.

He rubbed his throat before repeating, "I'll show you. Follow me."

As they walked toward the exit, leaving Ankur to finish his motivational ceremony, Haberstitch regretted his momentary panic causing him to involve the less-than-trustworthy Athaliah. He cursed himself out loud, resulting in a quizzical look from the woman who would surely end his life before the night was over.

The lab was not far. Ankur had created a whole complex in the middle of Okrad dedicated to his mission of becoming the supreme ruler. Just before they arrived at the lab's entrance, Haberstitch doubled over and relieved his stomach of its entire contents—and more, it seemed.

"There is no need to get so upset. I'm not going to hurt you," said Athaliah unconvincingly.

Haberstitch was amazed that he had conducted so many horrifying experiments and mutilations of living creatures, yet he had not once gotten ill from the sights or the smells. Now, faced with his own mortality, he could not contain his bodily functions. He hoped Athaliah had not noticed he wet himself long before he retched.

The two guards immediately recognized both Athaliah and Haberstitch, allowing them to enter the secure area that Ankur held most sacred. Ankur's highest-ranking underlings were never allowed to be under the influence of the Glouscenshire; they had to remain sharp at all times.

These most loyal mastadonians of Ankur's burgeoning army were richly rewarded with the finest foods and lived in opulent homes recently vacated by the once elite. Their reward came with a price, however. The slightest insubordination was met with mysterious consequences. Mysterious meaning deadly, by most accounts. Yet they believed in their master's vision for a unified realm and would follow him even unto their own peril.

Haberstitch led Athaliah to a part of the lab she did not know existed. He was moving fast and saying nothing. The Haberstitch she knew was rarely at a loss for words.

She knew Ankur was not telling her everything, but what could be worse than killing half the life in the Realms? What other wretched thing could Ankur possibly do? Whatever Haberstitch was about to show her was undoubtedly going to alter her perspective forever. She thought of Willow and wished she had considered the ancient tree's wise words more carefully. One thought kept invading her mind: was it too late?

Two more guards opened two heavy doors. The doors were so thick that Athaliah assumed they must be soundproof. Indeed, once inside, her assumption proved true. However, the massive doors were not to keep sound from entering; they were to keep the sound from exiting.

Athaliah recoiled as a cacophony of wet, rhythmic slapping—like heavy wings beating against thin metal sheets—mixed with high-pitched squealing that sounded as if it were being forced through constricted throats. Beneath it all were low, guttural sobs that penetrated her very chest.

Athaliah covered her ears just as Haberstitch leaned toward her and yelled, "You'll get accustomed to the noise soon enough."

They did not enter the room down the corridor where the cries were most deafening, but rather turned the corner, entering a dark, cold, quieter room. There was no guard at this door. Athaliah assumed there was no more need for security once so far inside of Ankur's mysterious shop of horrors.

They were in the place where Ankur's most secretive and delicate operations were performed, but there was nothing in this room but a cage partially draped with a thick black cloth. Haberstitch said nothing as he simply pulled on the drape and watched it slide to the floor.

Athaliah instinctively moved backward. Her eyes could not deny the terror that caused every cell of her body to excrete fear. She tripped over her own foot and fell back on her hands. She forced herself to raise her head.

On the cold floor, she stared into the eyes of the most ungodly monster she could imagine. She let out a scream of silent terror that no one could hear. The next scream tore from her throat, echoing down the halls. The creature recoiled into the far corner of its iron cage, emitting gurgling, wet, mucus-laden sounds in a desperate attempt to communicate. The sound was a distorted, bubbling rasp, as if the creature were trying to speak through lungs filled with liquid.

Haberstitch was shocked at Athaliah's reaction. The woman, who only a short time ago held him up against a wall with her bare hands, was now on the floor in total fear. He had expected a strong visceral reaction, but not the melted puddle now at his feet. She was totally incapacitated. He had nothing to help revive her—to bring her back to her senses. He said nothing while he watched Ankur's second-in-command realize the full extent of what she had gotten herself into.

The creature, along with Athaliah, began to compose itself. It was, of course, easier for the monster. The living experiment was quite used to others being repulsed. There it stood, if standing it was, in all its glory.

It had legs, but neither was straight nor equal in length. The creature tilted slightly to one side. Its arms, if they could be called such, were not as elegantly formed as its legs. The body was covered in patches of dark, coarse hair, just enough to let one know it was more animal than human.

The face, however, had a trace of recognition to it. The features looked both familiar and foreign, with soulish eyes. Whether the snout looked more like it belonged to a bovine or dog was unclear. The ears were long and floppy—of the mastadonian variety. There was no neck, only piles of flabby fat bunched up with what looked like many pus-filled tumors.

Athaliah, still not having said a word, embarrassed at her display of weakness, managed to eventually compose herself. She slowly made her way to the cage for a better look. Her nostrils filled with the smell of feces and urine. The pathetic creature did not advance toward her. It simply looked at its audience with curiosity, making Athaliah question who was really the one in a cage.

Athaliah knew, without a doubt, the thing before her was part human. How much of it was human, she was unsure, but it was once, at least partly, like her.

Haberstitch finally broke the silence. "She's seven turnings old. She was my first success."

"*Success?*" she asked, stunned.

"No one has ever merged two genotypes. The creature before you is an unparalleled breakthrough in genetic engineering. What is obviously a monstrosity to you is a work of art to me. She's really quite beautiful, in her own special way."

Athaliah could not immediately respond, but eventually managed to spit out her first complete sentence since laying eyes on the "success" story. "Was this once a person like you and me?"

Haberstitch's countenance changed from nervously worried to giddily confident. "More like you than me, since she was...is...female. Yes, technically she is still female. Though I doubt she could ever have children, even if there were a suitable candidate with which to breed her..."

He paused to look back at Athaliah to see how she was absorbing the information. Although she was standing in a fully upright position, her face was still paralyzed with shock, except for the twitch in her upper lip.

He brought his enthusiasm down a notch and continued. "If it's any consolation, she won't live much longer. The tumors have grown exponentially in the last two cycles."

Athaliah's confusion and shock were beginning to change to anger. "How is that a consolation, you stupid little sniblet!"

Haberstitch was short, but he was not nearly as diminutive as a Braewicker. It was perhaps the most derogatory thing Athaliah could have called him. It was to be expected.

"You would not have been injected with anything remotely as underdeveloped as what she received. Follow me." As Haberstitch led the way out of the room, the creature began to gurgle, perhaps in an attempt to speak. Athaliah turned for one last glance. The creature and Athaliah locked eyes. The soul within the dying flesh, trapped in the cage, was trying very hard to tell her something.

That was the moment Athaliah knew she had made a mistake. She had undeniably chosen the wrong path. Her heart broke for what was once a girl like she herself had been not so many moons ago. The time for reflection would have to come later. At this time, she desperately needed to ascertain what was happening to her own body. Would she become like the creature staring back at her?

When Athaliah turned the corner behind Haberstitch, she was met by several towering tanks of what appeared to be water. They loomed twice the height of a tall man and wide enough to hide a brorayding behind, glowing with a sickly, phosphorescent green hue that cast distorted shadows against the sterile walls. Thick, viscous bubbles blurred the fleshy forms floating within the sealed containers. The only sound was the rhythmic hum of the filtration system and the occasional soft thud of a limb drifting against the glass.

It was not until Haberstitch disconnected a tube and the bubbles faded that the bodies inside became clearly visible. "These three specimens are male, were male. Still are male . . ."

"I get it, Haberstitch. Are they alive?"

"Oh, no. Of course not. How could they be living in liquid? How would they breathe? Now that would be something, wouldn't it? If I could merge a terrestrial life form with one that lived in water . . ."

"Stop it! Why are you showing me these? What does it have to do with me?"

"Well, just look closely. They have fully formed legs and arms. They are quite functional."

"What's wrong with their heads?"

"Nothing. That would be expected." Haberstitch had a revelation, causing him to pause and look directly at Athaliah. "You have no idea what the variables are, do you?"

"Variables?"

"The species involved, for starters."

"I assume the constant genetic material is humanoid."

"Yes, yes, of course. That was always the primary core of the experiments. We tried quite a few variants with only one other constant."

"And that was?'

"Ankur made it clear that he wanted the best characteristics of the mastadonian. He's fixated on the breed, actually. I don't know why, but it was the one other constant genetic makeup, other than humanoid, I had to work with."

Athaliah walked within reach of the glass tank. She looked up and down at the creature floating inside. "I see, so the head on this one is mostly dog. The rest of the body . . ." She looked it up and down again. "The rest of the body is mostly human."

"Yes, exactly. Well, that would never work. We needed a more fluid integration of the two genetic maps. It would never do to have a sloppy mix of body parts."

"No, a *sloppy* mix, that would never do," she repeated angrily.

"These were a few moons ago."

"How did they die?"

"Oh, they didn't die. We killed them. Quite healthy, they were. They were too nimble for their little brains. They were also very loud, and Ankur couldn't stand it. We preserved them for reference and just in case we needed to extract any genetic material. We never did, or haven't needed to as of yet."

Athaliah frowned and her eyes narrowed. "Please tell me you have something more to show for your efforts."

"But of course. Do you think me a total barbarian, that I would stop at these less-than-ideal specimens? Not that I had a choice to stop. In all truthfulness, between you and me, I would have called it quits and gotten out of this realm in a heartbeat, but I know Ankur would find me and either bring me back or kill me on the spot."

Athaliah grew more impatient by the second. Her hands, although now with web-like skin between her fingers, still perspired profusely when she became anxious. She had never been more anxious than at that very moment. "What else do you have to show me?"

He led her down yet another hallway to one last door—a door that was more than an entrance to another room. To Athaliah, it was a door to her last hope. She knew whatever was in that room was related to what or who she would eventually turn into.

He opened the door. Athaliah thoughtfully stepped over the threshold. She was surprised to find a very tranquil room with gentle music playing. There were several women moving about. One was holding a clipboard and taking notes. Another was preparing food, or so it appeared.

The third woman was behind a glass wall on her knees. Athaliah could not immediately determine what she was doing, until the lady moved a few inches to her left. On the floor, playing with toys, was a small child.

Athaliah wasted no time with formalities. She opened the door and entered the room behind the glass. She positioned herself within a few feet of the child. She gasped. The woman tending to the child gave Athaliah a hard stare before being motioned out by Haberstitch.

Athaliah dropped to her knees, again in shock at the sight before her. "What's your name?" she asked the child, who appeared to be about four turnings old.

He stopped to look up at Athaliah and answered, "I'm Balom." He just as quickly returned to the game in front of him. This boy was accustomed to being watched and answering questions, but Athalia was a stranger to him. Even so, Athaliah moved in for a more thorough inspection.

She leaned over to pick him up. He recoiled, wrapping his web-winged arms tightly around himself. When Athaliah did not retreat, he hissed and flapped, lifting into the air a few inches before darting several feet away. It happened in a blur—she could hardly tell if he truly flew or simply used his legs to scramble backward.

Athaliah got the point: he was accustomed to being a lab rat, but he was not tolerant of strangers. She slowly backed out of the room, never taking her eyes off the child. She was not scared. She was mesmerized.

The arm-like wings were huge for his size, and he was strong and quick. His feet and hands looked perfectly human until he got apprehensive and flew, or jumped away from her, at which time pointed claws extended from where it seemed only normal fingers had been seconds earlier.

His eyes were large and round. His nose was large and flat. His ears were very similar to those of the first creature in the cage: they were floppy when relaxed but stood straight up when on alert. It was a human face with dog-like features. There was something else, perhaps a number of things, about him that Athaliah could not quite put her finger on. He was not hairy, yet there was a fine hair-like silk covering most of his body.

When she closed the door behind her, she turned to Haberstitch and asked, "Was he born this way?"

Haberstitch answered while the other three women continued with their routines. "Oh, no. He was a completely perfect human boy at the age of three."

"Where did he come from?"

"I have no idea. You would need to ask Ankur that. There were many children brought to the lab. Much experimentation. It has been the children who brought us the most success."

Athaliah spread her arm wide, slamming Haberstitch into the wall behind them. She took her hand, with its long claws, similar to the boy's, and wrapped it around the top of Haberstitch's head. She squeezed until a bit of blood trickled from where one of her nails penetrated his scalp. When he squealed, she released her grip.

She wanted to kill him. All of these children experimented on. All of their parents either killed or mourning the loss of their missing children. Yet she knew Haberstitch was not the mastermind. He was a mere puppet. A disgusting puppet. It was her cousin who needed to be killed. It was her cousin who was evil.

Haberstitch spoke meekly, "You seem surprised, yet it was you who gave the orders."

She hissed in response, "Are you a complete fool? What are you talking about?"

"Was it not you who gave orders to collect and ship the specimens?"

"Specimens? You mean dogs, the winged creatures, the fruit . . ."

"And the children. What are the children if not specimens?"

"I never ordered the kidnapping of young children," she insisted.

At this point all of the adults in the room were staring at Athaliah. When she noticed, she gave each a harsh look, and one by one, they went back to their assigned tasks.

Athaliah continued, "Why did you bring me here?"

"The last, most tested serum was injected into this child. There are others, at varying ages, but this one holds the most promise. You would have either been injected with the same as this child or something very close on the timeline."

"Timeline?"

"Let's just say, this specimen...child...is the closest sample...example...of what will happen to you. Keep in mind, we have not tested the latest combinations on adults, only children. There is no way of knowing if you will proceed similarly."

Athaliah was about to ask a question before she was distracted by a loud knock on the glass. She looked over at the enclosure, and the bat-like dog child was attempting to get her attention. Athaliah opened the door and entered, closely followed by Haberstitch.

The child looked up at Athaliah and lifted his arm. "Will you hold my hand?"

Athaliah was taken aback. She glanced at Haberstitch, who shrugged his shoulders as if to say, "Do whatever you like." Athaliah knelt down, grasping the child's hand. With his free hand, the child gently ran his small fingers under Athaliah's arm, tracing the largest veins in her webbing. After a moment, he leaned in and whispered, "Mommy?"

Chapter 30

TRUCE

A ray of light illuminated the small pool in the dark cave. The vaguely familiar creature stared at Athaliah from the reflective surface as if it were an apparition. A single wing, now a mangled stretch of leathery skin, twitched in the reflection, marring the symmetry of what she once was. It was not hard to imagine what the genetic mutation in Haberstitch's house of horrors would look like all grown up. There it was, beckoning Athaliah to join him under the quiet surrender of the glassy water.

Athaliah's nose still looked as though it belonged on a human face. She had not yet fully transitioned. She watched as a thin trail of blood ran down her chin after she followed the outline of her last recognizable feature with her razor-sharp claw.

She continued to stare at her reflection. It would be the last time she ever saw the bit of her mother that her father had adored so much. It would be the last time she would see the brows that her mother said were much too masculine, like her father's. It would be the last time she would ever see Athaliah.

233

As ripples from her tears spread, the hideous reflection of what she was becoming, what she had become—disappeared.

Beely stood at the entrance of the cave. She had heard Athaliah's subtle cries and hesitated before speaking. She was not even sure why she was there. Beely had received a message from a friend of Willow's to follow the dragonfly on that night and to tell no one.

It was a two-hour journey on foot from Pixanese, and though the terrain was easy, but still, her feet ached and her stomach growled. She wanted so badly to bring Maximilian. She needed him more than ever, but Willow had been clear: go alone and tell no one.

Someday soon she hoped she could tell Max everything so they could work together as a team, but for now, she would manage without him. Someday soon she would have the help of all the Twelve. Soon they would meet and work toward defeating Ankur, but for now she continued alone with few allies and even fewer resources.

Beely finally spoke, almost in a whisper. "'As water reflects the face, so one's life reflects the heart.' It's from a book called Proverbs."

She paused before continuing. "These caves were once filled with pools of water like the one you peer into now. It won't be long until even this one disappears. As a small girl, I used to speak with a creature from the cave pools. It was translucent; only its eyes were visible. They were sweet and innocent. They sang their words and always edified those they chose to speak to."

Athaliah did not look up. "I hear you are a good woman—honest and forthright."

"I'm sorry, but you have me at a disadvantage. I don't know who you are."

Athaliah laughed quietly as she wiped the tears from her cheeks. "Neither do I."

"Excuse me?"

"My name is Athaliah, but who I am is no longer important." Still bending over the small pool, she splashed the cool water on her face to wash away the blood and tears.

"Willow thinks you are important, or I wouldn't be here now. Why have you asked me to meet you?"

Finally standing, she turned toward Beely. "We are here because of your ineptitude. You were the one who was supposed to have stopped all of this. You are the one who has allowed the fall of the Realms!" hissed Athaliah. "Lira made sure you had the poisoned glouscenshire. She risked her life to make sure you had proof. Even now, Ankur pursues her because of that betrayal against him."

"I never told anyone who sent the glouscenshire. If Ankur found out, it was not my doing. You seem to have developed strong opinions of me. The least you could do is come out of the dark so I can see you better."

Athaliah rushed forward and pushed Beely, causing her to fall just outside of the cave opening. Beely hit the ground hard, knocking the breath from her lungs, but she never turned away from the one standing over her. The second moon was still high in the sky, and the light was sufficient. Athaliah stepped fully into the light, where the two moons caressed her hideous face.

Beely swallowed hard. The shock of the sight before her was greater than hitting the hard, unforgiving ground.

Athaliah peeled back a layer of crusty skin from her forehead. What lay underneath was raw in the glow of the moons. "My skin sheds continually. Someday, my sins will erase the entirety of my remaining humanity."

She looked solemnly at Beely. It was a frightening look, until Beely realized it came from remorse rather than hate. "I also spoke to cave-dwelling creatures. They were my only real friends in my youth. I was a normal girl who loved and lived as any other. I was once as beautiful as you—perhaps even more so."

"How is this possible?" Beely immediately regretted her response and quickly erased the expression of disgust from her face.

Athaliah laughed sardonically. She crept back into the darkness, behind the opening of the cave, where she could still be heard but not seen. "You have managed to lose everything. You have lost your sacred Word. You have lost the River of

Life. The High Forest is all but dead—the Dead Woods, as I now hear it called. Your great Pixanese is under the influence of Ankur's drug. There is no realm that isn't under the control of Mastad."

"Mastad?"

"The great Mastad, as he is now called. You know him as Ankur. He owns you, Beely Rembree. Was that not your father's name? He would be so ashamed of his daughter. You have failed at everything. You have lost it all." Athaliah's voice dripped with disdain and mockery.

"What is it you want? Why have you summoned me here?"

"To give you one last chance."

Beely rose to her feet. "Explain."

"You knew, and you did nothing."

"I tried—"

"You doubted yourself. You doubted the prophecies. You even doubted your father."

"It's not over."

"You so-called believers amaze me. You profess with your mouths that you believe, but your feet are slow to follow. It was so easy for Mastad to take over the Five Realms. He had no opposition whatsoever."

Beely responded angrily, "Why didn't *you* stop him?"

"Had I attempted to, I would not be here to help you now. Make me one of your Twelve. I know one has been lost," said Athaliah.

Beely was not surprised that Athaliah knew about the Twelve, specifically that one of the members had chosen to cut off all ties out of fear of repercussions from Ankur. Beely suddenly considered that Athaliah might have threatened this individual.

Beely tried not to match the seething tone of her adversary. "I could never trust you."

"You have no choice. Make me one of your Twelve, and together we will defeat Mastad. I am Athaliah, his cousin and the one he trusts most. I will be the thorn in his side."

"You're related to that monster! How could we ever align ourselves with you?"

"I will tell you where the Word still exists in our world. You must figure out how to retrieve it, but I will give you a way. If my cousin ever found out I helped you, he would see to it that my last breath was filled with anything but air. I will need to trust you as much as you will need to trust me."

"Why are you offering to help me?"

Athaliah laughed again. "It has nothing to do with you. Let's just say I have plans of my own."

"First, answer me this: is Lira safe?"

"For now. The giants are helping her. Best to concentrate on us right now. The followers of prophecy say that the Five Realms of Here will never be free without the Word. It must be returned."

Beely approached the cave and stepped into the darkness side by side with Athaliah. "If you can tell me where to find the scriptures, we have a way to keep them hidden from Ankur."

Athaliah took Beely's face in her hand. She gripped it tightly and moved it slightly until it was illuminated by the moons. "There is something about your face. Something hidden yet familiar."

Beely, no longer willing to remain submissive, knocked Athaliah's hand away from her face. There was no reaction or retaliation from Athaliah. Beely was strong, tall, and formidable, but she was no match for Athaliah, and they both knew it. Athaliah had all the power in this meeting, and it was always going to begin and end on her terms.

Beely responded, "You have been told the truth. Without the Word, we will all be lost. If you tell me how to find the scriptures, and if you can convince Ankur to let the waters flow in the High Forest, I will consider making you one of the Twelve. Ankur made a promise to me that he has not kept regarding the water for Pixanese."

"You're in no position to negotiate."

"Am I not? You're the one who arranged this meeting, not me. You won't reveal to me your motives. You have obviously been genetically altered, and by the looks of your current state, your metamorphosis is ongoing. Only God knows what you will eventually turn into."

The words stung Athaliah. How could Beely, supposedly so righteous, be so cruel? Yet the woman with wings knew Beely was right. No one knew how much Athaliah's genetic modifications would change her. She was not sure if she could even trust herself.

Athaliah was growing more isolated and lonelier with each passing season. She would not even meet Ankur in the light of day. She did not want anyone to see her face, not even the one who had created her.

"He did this to me. He is a thief and a liar. While I may never have been perfect, at least I was human. I once had a soul. He will pay for what he has done to me."

"Motives built out of revenge never serve their bearer well," said Beely with a hint of compassion.

"Revenge is all I have left. I don't pretend to be innocent. I played my role. It's ironic, really. As my body continues to change, so do my plans. My ending is not yet written. There are more choices to make."

Athaliah held out her hand with its long, claw-like fingers and gave a high-pitched squeak followed by an incomprehensible chattering noise. Immediately, a chiropter came swooping down from the cave ceiling and landed on her finger.

It all happened so fast.

Beely could only watch as the chiropter looked at Athaliah and chattered briefly before quickly darting into the air toward Beely. Before Beely could even move, the bat took hold of the dragonfly that had guided Beely to the cave.

Beely raised her arms in objection, but it was too late. The bat carried the dragonfly into the darkest recesses of the cave. Beely knew the terrible fate of the dragonfly was sealed, but still, she felt compelled to plead her case.

"If you say you have choices, why must you continue making such bad ones? Command your bat to return my guide immediately!" Beely demanded.

"Sometimes hard choices must be made. We can't risk Ankur ever knowing we have become allies. He must never know, or both of our lives will end worse than the dragonfly's."

"You honestly believe I would become allies with you after you demonstrated such depravity against an innocent?"

"You and I both know that dragonflies have no capacity to keep secrets. They chatter indiscriminately. Nothing can be done to change that, it's in their nature. Sometimes the means justify the end," said Athaliah.

"So you would have me strike a deal with the devil?"

"Oh, no. You've already done that. Now I'm asking you to strike a deal with his second-in-command. Look, Beely, I'm the only one who can help you get back what you let slip through your fingers. The Realms are being held captive. Join with me, and we will set them free."

"Assuming for a moment that I might choose to trust you, where can I secure a copy of the Bible?"

"Now you're starting to think like a commander instead of a simple politician."

Athalia moved ever so slightly so that a fraction of her face was illuminated by the remaining light still filtering through the cave opening. "In the earthly realm, there is a screaming bird of silver with large, stiff wings that will enter our realms. A book will remain on that metal bird. You must retrieve the book."

Beely raised her arms in frustration. "You're speaking complete gibberish!"

"I know it sounds extraordinary, but you have no choice but to believe me. There is a painting in our realm that will lead you to the Bible. It is a most special painting with miraculous powers to take you to the past, or in this case, the future."

"Assuming I understand a modicum of what you're talking about, if the Bible comes to our world in the future, why not let it remain in the future? It's safer there than here, is it not?"

"The Word will never be safe in this world unless it's protected from the evil one. You must get it before Ankur becomes aware of it, and you must protect it for when the others come."

"Others?"

"You really need to brush up on prophecy. I haven't the time to explain it all now. First, find the painting and save the last remaining Bible in the Five Realms."

"You don't know where this miraculous painting is, do you?"

"Unfortunately, I acted in haste and was unable to make that discovery. I trust you will be able to succeed where I have failed. You will find the painting. You *must* find the painting."

"And then what?" she asked incredulously.

"Follow the rainbow."

"What in the realms does that mean?"

"Look, Madam Magistrate, I don't know every jot and tittle. You're going to have to do some of the work yourself. I have consulted with the prophets—both the ones that remain and the ones that have disappeared. The information I have given you may not be complete, but it is accurate."

Beely looked behind her, away from the cave. The first moon was setting behind the canyon, and the second was not far behind.

"I must go before it gets light. I have one last question. What did you mean when you said there was something familiar about my face?"

"You are not ready to hear the answer to that, and it will not help in what you need to do. Find the painting and follow the rainbow. See if the others will allow me to be one of the Twelve, and I will see what I can do to help with releasing water into the High Forest."

"I can't promise anything, but I will tell them what you have done here today," said a skeptical Beely.

"I will leave one of my chiropters near you at all times. If you need to send me a message, when the night is darkest, call out, and it will come. Heed my warning; if Ankur—Mastad— ever discovers our alliance, he will stop at nothing to end us. Then there would be no one left to defeat him. The Five Realms of Here would be lost forever."

"The book that I follow teaches, 'For we wrestle not against flesh and blood, but against principalities, against powers, against the rulers of the darkness of this world, against spiritual wickedness in high places.' Your cousin thinks he is the one we battle. I know he is merely an instrument of evil. I know with whom my victory lies, and that is why we will win."

"We shall see," said Athaliah as she crept farther back into the cave.

"May I give you a bit of advice?" asked Beely.

"You may."

"When the Word returns—and it will—read it. It's never too late to repent and put your faith in the One. He is faithful to forgive."

"First things first, Magistrate. Find the painting." Athaliah's voice trailed off, barely audible as the shadows claimed her once again.

Beely lingered at the mouth of the cave, the cool air brushing her face. She did not step into the darkness. Some transformations, she knew, were not meant to be watched—but resisted.

Afterword

Thank you for joining me on this journey through the Five Realms. While this particular chapter has closed, the saga is only beginning.

If you are eager to see what happens next in this prequel trilogy, turn the page for an exclusive first look at Book Two: **The Quenching Fire**.

If you found *Cruelty of Thirst* enjoyable, it would be a huge help to prospective readers if you would post a review on Amazon and Goodreads, or share your thoughts on social media. Your support helps other travelers find their way into the Realms.

The Journey Continues...

Cruelty of Thirst is the first of three prequels designed to reveal the ancient secrets of the Five Realms. If you are ready to see how these legends culminate in the great struggle for the Word, the original **Messengers and Thieves** trilogy is available now:

- **Where the Garden Begins** (Book 1)
- **A Leaf of Faith** (Book 2)
- **Roots and Branches: The Battle for Here** (Book 3)

All titles are available on Amazon and other online retailers.

Plays by J. Suthern Hicks

Turtle Tears: A Play in Two Acts, *Home, Hearth, and Oreos:* A One-Act Play

Children's Books by J. Suthern Hicks

Charlie and Chocolate's Purrfect Prayer and *Charlie and Chocolate's Furry Forgiveness*

Music by J. Suthern Hicks

Time to Change: An eleven-song album performed by Seven Years

To get alerts on new releases, please follow:
Facebook.com/jsuthernhicks
Instagram.com/jsuthernhicks

Contact the publisher directly:
Humbleentertainment@yahoo.com

A Glimpse into the Future

The alliance in the cave was only the beginning. While the Five Realms stand on the precipice of darkness, the roots of the struggle reach back much further than Beely Rembree ever imagined.

Behind every prophecy, every political shift, and every "accidental" meeting, there are secrets kept in the shadows—and mothers who will do anything to ensure their children survive the coming storm.

Get ready for the next chapter of the saga:
The Quenching Fire
Sneak Peek: Book Two of Springs of Eternal Life

Chapter 1: Marybah (The Wedding)

Her face was covered with a large, dark scarf—just in case her daughter, the bride, happened to see her lurking amongst the invited guests. Although she had paid for the wedding, she had not been invited to attend.

Marybah thought it doubtful her daughter would have recognized her, even without the disguise. It had been many turnings since they had seen one another, and her physical transformation was profound. When no one was looking, Marybah reached into her bag for a treat. What she really craved was a hit from her pipe, but that would have drawn unwanted attention.

Time had not been kind to Marybah. Once, she had been one of the loveliest citizens of Pixanese. Now, the lines on her face revealed a lifetime of anguish; she had few friends and lived a lonely, solitary life. Yet despite the rift between them, one thing remained: she still cared deeply for her daughter. After all, if not for Marybah, this grand wedding might never have taken place.

Her money had been well spent. Unbeknownst to Beely, her estranged mother had ensured the venue was affordable. Marybah had used the many secrets she kept against her enemies and friends alike to facilitate the grandest wedding the kingdom of Pixanese had ever seen—or would likely see for generations.

Beely—like Marybah's own mother—had always loved anything that grew from seed or spread from roots. For such a botanical enthusiast, there was no better place in all the Five Realms to hold the wedding of one's dreams than beneath the great falls of Pixanese.

Marybah walked as close to the majestic waterfall as she dared, careful not to let the cool mist ruin her hair or favorite scarf. She inhaled the sweet, fresh air as she gazed up at the tallest waterfall in all of the Five Realms as the water poured down from the heights of the High Forest.

Feeling the weight of the day's journey, she leaned against a tree fern, staying upwind of the roaring cascade. Partially hidden by a large frond, she could still see all the pre-wedding activity. She had originally planned to be long gone before the ceremony began; a veiled guest lurking behind a fern throughout the nuptials might draw unwanted attention.

She had scouted around the waterfall in the past, but never noticed just how beautiful the area truly was. On either side of the falls grew the famous carrier vines. They were ancient and thick, bearing flowers of deep red, dark purple, and bright yellow. She had once tried to get the vines to carry her to the top, but either it was a myth—or they felt her unworthy.

Marybah took another treat from her bag, lamenting that she had never witnessed the feat herself. The vines were very particular about whom they interacted with—and even more selective about whom, or what, they would carry.

She still had not seen Beely and suspected she would not see her anytime soon. She successfully fought the urge to have another treat as she watched the groom mingle with his guests. As it stood, she might never meet her son-in-law in person—but from afar, Maximilian was strikingly handsome.

The ceremonial wardrobe hugged his youthful, muscular frame commandingly. His shoulder-length, unbridled hair was free of any headdress. Marybah had not seen such a thick mane in many moons. Judging by the cluster of female guests around him, her daughter was clearly the envy of every eligible woman in Pixanese. There was no finer catch than Maximilian Wren.

Beauty and brawn, however, were not on any list Marybah might have had for suitable suitors. Mr. Wren came from one of—if not the—most respected families in all of Pixanese. Marybah suspected that, behind closed doors, they had protested their son's engagement. It had not been their plan for their only son to marry the daughter of a well-known Plotist—one who had divorced his wife, no less.

Beely's father had belonged to a small minority that most considered conspiracy theorists—unwelcome, especially in Pixanese. Marybah chuckled to herself, imagining how the groom's parents must have wondered how their son had ended up proposing to someone like Beely Rembree. The fact that Maximilian was his own man ranked high on her list of admirable qualities in a suitor.

The meeting between the Plotist's daughter and the son of Pixanese's most influential family had been no accident. Marybah would never have left such an encounter up to chance.

Marybah's mind drifted back to the day she met with Propo—her ex-husband's best friend and most loyal protégé. Propo had never been good at hiding the fact that he disliked his best friend's wife. He would never have agreed to meet her of his own accord—but even a genius like Propo needed work.

After Marybah's husband had died, Propo had found securing employment difficult. No one wanted to hire a rumored Plotist—someone who believed in "outlandish" theories and interpreted prophecy in ways unappreciated by the masses. Propo had become desperate, and Marybah knew it. The look on Propo's face when he walked in and saw Marybah behind a desk resembled someone coming face-to-face with a soiled diaper.

"Marybah?"

"Hi, Propo. It's been too long, hasn't it?"

"What are you doing here?"

Marybah rose and walked over to him. "What? No pleasantries before getting down to business?" Propo froze as she leaned in to kiss him on the cheek. His confused expression matched his disheveled appearance. He looked older than his age, with gray, thinning hair—an oddity in the Realms, where health and vitality were as common as air. He stroked his short beard with one hand and used the other to adjust the leather belt underneath his tunic.

"When has anything ever been pleasant with you, Marybah?"

"Touché, my friend, touché." She returned to the desk and sat. "Please, for the sake of old times—good or bad—sit and hear what I have to say."

"And why should I do that?"

"Propo, my dear, have a curly and sit." She pushed the plate of curlies—one of her favorite treats—toward him. When it was obvious he was not receptive, she added, "Look, we may not like one another—"

"Like one another?" He shook his head and grunted. "There is only one person in the Realms I truly despise—and now I know she still lives both in sight and sound!"

"'Hatred is a root that never dies until it bores through the host, splitting it in two...' My mother told me that."

"Well, she knew you well, didn't she?"

246

"I understand our past," she said, brushing off the jab. "But I want to discuss the future—something I hear you're well-versed in."

"What could you possibly have to say that I would want to hear?"

"It concerns our Beely. I know you love her—possibly as much as I do."

At the mention of Beely, Propo softened. "What about Beely? Is she in trouble?"

"Not yet. But if we don't act, she could be in serious trouble—soon."

Slowly, and somewhat begrudgingly, he pulled back the only free chair and sat down. "I'm listening."

"I couldn't care less about prophecy or the Plotist agenda," she said flatly.

"Just get to the point—quickly," he demanded.

"The job you came to interview for is yours—if you want it."

He threw up a hand. "What does this have to do with Beely?"

"I knew the Realms would eventually face challenges. Change is inevitable, and things have been stagnant for centuries. For reasons that may differ from your own, I too believe even more difficult times are coming—perhaps even apocalyptic ones, if the Plotists are right."

He pressed her further. "And…?"

"Beely needs protection—something neither of us can give her. I can't, because she wants nothing to do with me. And you…because you have no means."

She noticed Propo becoming increasingly impatient with her assessment of his current state. As far as Marybah was concerned, she was simply expressing necessary facts. She paused, reconsidered, then got straight to the point. "Beely needs to marry into a family with influence."

"And you went to all this trouble just to get me here—why?" he asked.

"There is no other that Beely listens to and respects more than you—since her father passed, of course."

"I'm beginning to understand. Go on."

"There is a young man named Maximilian Wren."

"The Wren family, yes. I know none of them in a friendly way, and I'm the last person they would ever associate with."

"I don't need you to interact or influence them. I need you to make sure that when Beely meets their son, she does not let the opportunity pass her by."

Propo leaned over, examining the plate of treats, and picked a few of the finer offerings. He was not too proud to accept a handout in this precarious time of his life. "What opportunity?"

"An opportunity to marry up, to progress toward something greater in life, to be someone important."

One by one, Propo placed three curlies into his mouth and chewed. He took his time before finally swallowing. "Beely needs no other person, man or otherwise, to advance her position in life. She is well liked in the community, even with her late father's much-maligned image. She is a woman of great character and talents, and most everyone in Pixanese knows this."

"All the more reason to make sure she secures her rightful place in Pixanese society."

Propo selected three more curlies and repeated his questionable consumption habit, further annoying Marybah in the process. He relished the look of disdain from his audience. "Marybah, what is all of this about?"

"Do you trust that I would put my daughter's best interests above even my own?"

"I would need to know to which interests you are referring."

"Must you be so hurtful?"

"Continue," he said dryly.

"In terms that you will understand—to make things as simple as possible—the Plotists' conjectures may not manifest as they predict, but the results will be the same," she said, finally gaining his full attention.

"Explain."

"Hell is coming to the Five Realms of Here, and if my daughter doesn't secure a position of authority, she will succumb to the whims of a dictator. She may not even survive. Most won't."

He sat back in his chair. "Interesting thoughts from someone who has fought the Plotists from the very beginning. You sound more like a believer than even Mikalo."

"My ex-husband was a dreamer. He was a philosopher. There wasn't a practical bone in his body. What I'm talking about is quite practical. There will be a power struggle, and Pixanese is the only realm equipped to bargain for its survival."

Propo took a small wooden pipe from his robe pocket. He watched Marybah's face as he lit the dry leaves and took his first drag. He knew she abhorred the smell of dead nettle leaf. He had given up smoking many moons ago and had only recently taken it up again. It was the only small luxury he could afford. It was even more luxurious to see the wealthy and pretentious Ms. Rembree squirm beneath the smell of dead nettle smoke floating all about her face.

"Tell me, is this about saving Pixanese or your daughter?"

She waved the smoke away. "Can't it be both?" After he rolled his eyes, she confessed. "My daughter, of course. Pixanese may just benefit because of her and our wise choices."

"You are as slick as an oarsman!" He thought for a moment before adding, "What would you have me do?"

"If she comes to you for advice—even if she doesn't—you need to encourage her about how great this man is. She trusts you. She loves you like a father or a brother; I've never been able to quite discern which. Be a father to her. Tell her the things that will save her life—that will help her flourish. If she marries Maximilian Wren, she will not only save her own life, but his, yours, and perhaps all of Pixanese as well."

"And you. Don't forget your life."

"Will you do it?" She was almost pleading.

"I will consider what you have proposed. If I agree, and I'm not saying I do, Beely must never find out about this conversation. If she ever finds out, you will not be happy with the result—I promise you that."

Propo took one more long drag from his pipe, exhaling in Marybah's direction, before he stood up to leave.

"The job is real, and it's yours if you want it," she said sincerely.

"No thanks. If you want to monitor me, you'll have to try much harder. How did you track me down, anyway?" he asked.

"If you want to stay hidden, *you'll* have to try much harder," she answered. Propo shrugged and left without looking back.

A harried wedding organizer placed a hand on Marybah's shoulder, startling her. "I'm sorry, we need to ask all guests to remain behind the pillars."

She pointed toward the large crowd. Marybah's reminiscing had caused her to lose all track of time. It was too late to leave the impending nuptials without being noticed.

Marybah lowered her head, further hiding her face. "I apologize." She walked briskly to her far right, avoiding as many guests as possible. She found a perfect spot inconspicuously located amidst several large ferns and a boulder. If she stood on the far side, no one would notice her interloping. She leaned her weary body against the large rock that was nearly twice her size.

All the guests she could see, without exposing herself, were beautifully adorned in their finest clothing and jewels. There were lots of red dresses and richly colored robes. Had there been enough light filtering through the trees, all the precious jewelry would have sparkled like stars. True to Marybah's prediction, there were too many guests to count. The union was a popular one in Pixanese. Everyone wanted to celebrate the adored young couple. Maximilian and Beely were practically royalty in a realm where such a concept had never before existed.

Marybah had to step away from the voluminous boulder to see the main attraction. Fortunately, everyone was looking in the other direction—toward the bride. She might have been imagining it, being so far away, but her daughter looked much like her maternal grandmother.

Beely was tall, graceful, and walked down to the front of the waterfall as if gliding on air. Her long, flowing hair was free of the usual braids. The little bit of light left from the day rebounded off the canyon wall, highlighting the bride's dark tresses like a halo.

Marybah hoped Max had learned that her daughter was more than just a pretty face. Ever since she was a small child, Beely had been strong, stubborn, and always breaking the rules. Beely would need a man who could match or even exceed her drive and ambition. Yet, on this special day, she was the perfect bride—calm, graceful, and exuding joy.

The early evening breeze blew away from Marybah. She could not hear all the words spoken, only the faint sound of water hitting rocks before heading downstream through the village.

She did not need to hear everything. She knew all too well the meaning of marriage in the Five Realms—if for no other reason than her own marriage, which had failed miserably and all too publicly. Ironically, the one line she heard the officiant clearly recite, as if he knew she were there, was, "The union of a man and a woman is a covenant before God, never to be broken." There were very few divorces in the Realms, but times were changing. Fortunately, thought Marybah, her daughter's marriage only needed to last long enough for her to become the magistrate of Pixanese. It was the nearest thing to a political leader that a society with no need for leaders would accept.

Now that the union was almost complete, Marybah just wanted to get home and smoke her pipe.

Then it happened.

The most incredible sight witnessed by the residents of Pixanese in a century. The carrier vines, adorned with the most extravagant and vibrant blooms, began to move. Right after the vows and a most passionate kiss, as if on cue, the thick, ancient vines gently wrapped around the bride and groom as a mother might caress her newborn child.

The woody fibers slowly lifted the newlyweds up until they disappeared behind the waterfall. The crowd gasped in unison. There was even a shriek. Marybah heard later that a woman fainted when the newlyweds vanished. It was a most spectacular sight, to be sure.

That's when she knew. Her daughter would be the first and only magistrate in all of the Five Realms of Here. Pixanese would survive what was coming. She, too, would survive.

******

This was a preview of **The Quenching Fire**, *Book Two of the* **Springs of Eternal Life** *prequel trilogy.*

The Journey Continues:
Springs of Eternal Life (The Prequel Trilogy) *Cruelty of Thirst* (Book 1) — Available Now *The Quenching Fire* (Book 2) — Available Now *Breath of Embers* (Book 3) — Coming Soon
Messengers and Thieves (The Original Completed Trilogy) *Where the Garden Begins* (Book 1) *A Leaf of Faith* (Book 2) *Roots and Branches: The Battle for Here* (Book 3)

www.ingramcontent.com/pod-product-compliance
Lightning Source LLC
Chambersburg PA
CBHW031714170626
46808CB00005B/1744